D0475366

# A DEADLY INJUSTICE

# A DEADLY INJUSTICE

A Nick Zuliani Mystery

## Ian Morson

This first world edition published 2011
in Great Britain and in the USA by
SEVERN HOUSE PUBLISHERS LTD of
9–15 High Street, Sutton, Surrey, England, SM1 1DF.
Trade paperback edition first published
in Great Britain and the USA 2011 by
SEVERN HOUSE PUBLISHERS LTD.

British Library Cataloguing in Publication Data

Morson, Ian.
  A deadly injustice.
  1. Mongols – Fiction. 2. China – History – Song dynasty,
  960–1279 – Fiction. 3. Murder – Investigation – Fiction.
  4. Detective and mystery stories.
  I. Title
  823.9'2-dc22

ISBN-13: 978-0-7278-8062-8  (cased)
ISBN-13: 978-1-84751-364-9  (trade paper)

*All Severn House titles are printed on acid-free paper.*

Severn House Publishers support The Forest Stewardship Council [FSC],
the leading international forest certification organisation. All our titles that
are printed on Greenpeace-approved FSC-certified paper carry the FSC logo.

Typeset by Palimpsest Book Production Ltd.,
Falkirk, Stirlingshire, Scotland.
Printed and bound in Great Britain by
MPG Books Ltd., Bodmin, Cornwall.

# PREFACE

The extraordinary life of Niccolò Zuliani (1232?–1320?) is only just coming to the notice of scholars as various documents begin to emerge from China. That he preceded Marco Polo to the heart of Kubilai Khan's Mongol Empire is now undisputed. The details of his life there are a matter for scholarly argument and debate. Much of what we know to date is based on the account known as *The Life and Travels of Messer Niccolò Zuliani* written by the Chinese scholar Xian Lin in the early 1300s. He claims to have copied down his account 'from the lips of Messer Zuliani in the last years of his long and varied life.' However, it now appears that by 1310 Zuliani was no longer in China, but back in Venice, where he lived for at least another ten years. But if Lin's words about Zuliani's 'last years' are not taken literally, and perhaps as meaning his last years in Cathay, then there is no conflict in these facts.

How Zuliani arrived in Kubilai's summer capital, Shang-tu – more dramatically called Xanadu by some – has already been told in the first volume of his travels (*City of the Dead*, Severn House, 2008). This second volume centres on an investigation undertaken by Zuliani deeper inside Cathay, and is intriguing for scholars for a particular reason. He watches, for the first time, a Chinese play in the genre *kung-an*, or crime case, and he meets a playwright called Guan Han-Ching. A person called Kuan or Guan Hanqing is now deemed to be one of the most accomplished of the playwrights from Yuan times in China. His best known play is *The Injustice to Dou-E* or *Snow in Midsummer*, concerning the unjust execution of a young woman. She is exonerated, and calls down curses on the people who executed her, including a fall of snow in midsummer. If the playwright that Zuliani met was indeed the same person – and the case Zuliani is investigating has some vague resemblance to the story of Guan's play – then this is a very intriguing insight into a period when the Mongols were patrons of the theatre. Was the playwright we know the one in the chronicles? If so, then Guan emerges as a person concerned with justice and the conflict between Chin and Mongol ways. This is especially intriguing as Zuliani's chronicler, Xian Lin, claims of his text that 'every word is accurate.' After studying it for a year, I have no reason to believe otherwise.

Dr Brian Luckham
Manchester Trafford University, 2011

# PROLOGUE

The old man spooned the last of the nutritious soup into his toothless mouth, and lay back feeling satisfied. Things were working out beautifully. The girl seemed more amenable now he had beaten her. She obviously could not have learned from her previous husband about the Three Duties of a woman. They were obedience to your father before marriage, obedience to your husband after marriage, and obedience to your son after your husband's death. Always obedience, and always to the male line. He guessed that perhaps her first husband had not lasted long enough to instil the concept of her duties into her properly with a stick as he should have done. It was said that he was a sickly boy, who had grown up into a sickly man not suited to marriage. His mother had arranged for the girl to marry him, probably against her will. At twenty, soon after she got married, she had been made a widow. This naturally made her a tarnished woman, as she had belonged to another. Though he surmised that, being weak and ill, the husband may not have even carried out his obligations as a husband. She could still be a virgin, but he didn't know. He supposed she might make a fuss if he tried to test her with an egg as many did in rural areas. He thought he would insist on it all the same. But be that as it may, the old man knew he could not be choosy when it came to finding a wife for his stupid son. It had taken him a while, with several rejections and much compromising, before the girl had come to his attention. Yes, this one would do. Especially as she came with a mother-in-law, who would suit his needs. A double wedding could be arranged. And if it didn't work out for him concerning the old lady, he could have the young girl for himself.

His stomach rumbled, and he felt some discomfort bubble up. When he tried to ease around on his bed in order to find a more comfortable spot, he found he couldn't. He realized that his legs seemed to be numb, and he had some difficulty turning over. He cursed his old age, and coughed harshly. His chest felt tighter than usual, and he found it difficult to draw in a deep breath. Once again his bowels bubbled, and he clenched his buttocks against an uneasy feeling of looseness. He felt a wave of nausea suddenly rising, and didn't know if he would vomit or shit first. He began to panic and tried to rise from his bed but his limbs were useless, not responding to his increasingly sluggish brain. He felt very ill, and tried to call out for help. But the only sound he could make was a sort of rattle in his throat. His vision began to dim, and his head spun. Finally his guts gave up the struggle and gurgled horrendously. His last act before dying was to besmirch himself from both ends at once.

# ONE

*Better a diamond with a flaw than a pebble without one.*

I needed to get away fast. I was being pursued by a mad dog in the shape of a Keshikten Guard. And as you know, the Keshikten are not to be messed with. I mean, anyone whose job it is to be bodyguard to the Great Khan of All the Mongols in the Year of Our Lord 1268 is a fearsome opponent. There are twelve thousand of them reputedly, under the control of four captains, each with three thousand men. Their duty roster lasts for three days and three nights and it keeps them in the Khan's palace alert, sleepless and on duty all that time. So when they are finally off duty, they are inclined to indulge their personal fancies to an extreme degree. Mongotai's predilections were drinking and gambling. I came across him in one of the low taverns that thronged the streets of Old Khan-balik.

The avenues were narrow, and filled with the babble of a mixture of races from all over the world. They were all out to find some brief pleasure in their hard lives. Work hard, play hard was an appropriate creed for those who struggled to survive at the margins of the Great Khan's empire. Not that anyone in Khan-balik was at the geographical edge of the Mongol Empire, you understand. Far from it. A site to the north of the teeming old city that some Chinee called Yenking and others Tatu had been partially cleared by the Khan. His new winter capital and palace was being built there. So the rest of Old Yenking to the south of the new ramparts now found itself on the doorstep of the hub of the Mongol Empire. But many of those who lived and worked there fed off the scraps of the Khan's opulence. That's what I mean by living in the margins. And I should know. I am one of the scavengers.

My name is Niccolò Zuliani – plain Nick to my friends – once of Venice and more lately Shang-tu, the summer home of Kubilai Khan, the Great Khan of All the Mongols. Shang-tu is better known in the West as the fabled city of wealth and opulence, the mystical Xanadu. What drew me there was what would draw any Venetian worth his salt. Wealth, trade, and a chance to con some fool out of his hard-earned cash. But as soon as I had arrived in Xanadu, I had been sidetracked into solving a gruesome murder that had taken place there. A death that tarnished its reputation somewhat, and had brought me to within a whisker of being killed myself. But I survived, and earned the gratitude of Kubilai Khan himself. Now the same enticing possibilities that had taken me to Xanadu caused me to follow the Great Khan to his new winter palace at Tatu, or Khan-balik, or old Yenking. Its name depended on whether you were a Mongol, a Turk or a lowly Chinee. I used them all depending on whose company I was in. Most recently, it had been Tatu, as I foxed Mongotai with the old pot game swindle.

The backstreet tavern where I was drinking didn't have a name. It didn't need one, because the brew it served up was so rough that even if a name existed, you wouldn't recall it after a few bowls of the harsh rice wine. I had been drinking for some time, hunched in the corner of the low-ceilinged hut well away from the other sullen habitués of the place. The other drinkers didn't like me because I was a barbarian, and therefore, in their eyes, capable of a lack of good manners, or even a mindless act of madness. I was an unknown quantity to them. But at first they tolerated my presence, only occasionally casting worried glances my way. Then gradually, as the night wore on, the room began to clear. Whether it was my foreign presence, or the call of more important pursuits, such as servicing a mistress before returning home to the wife, or cutting open a full purse and robbing someone better off, I know not. Suffice it to say that eventually the only customers of the drinking den were Nick Zuliani and a big bear of a Mongol dressed in the dark red silk shirt and fur-trimmed jacket of a Keshikten guard. Where he had been sitting had made his presence invisible to me when the tavern was full. But as the other drinkers left, I could see him, and he could see me. I should have been warned off as soon as I saw what he was, but the fact he was well in his cups, and therefore incapable of making sense of what was about to happen, drove me on.

I pushed myself up from the low stool I had inhabited for the last hour or so and, swaying a little unsteadily on my feet to pretend a greater drunkenness than was true, made my way over to where the Mongol had planted himself. He was on a similar stool to mine, and stuck behind a small table. In the way of all inveterate drinkers embarking on a long session, he had managed to wedge himself in place with the furniture. He would not fall over, even when totally incapable of rational thought. Being well down the road to that state, I thought he was ripe for the picking. Bleary-eyed, he looked up as I approached.

What he saw was a tall, red-haired man, thickly bearded in that manly way that the Chinee consider shockingly animalistic and foreign. He would have guessed I was in my thirties, despite the fine tracery of lines at the corners of my eyes and mouth that made me look older. My cheekbones are high and deeply tanned in the way of seafarers. My green eyes, too, had the faraway look of a sailor. Though some said they could also see in them the distant stare of a man with deep pains buried in his soul. The truth of that I will tell you about later. At this very moment I smiled the smile of a fellow drinker, and flopped down next to him. He seemed to tolerate my barbarian presence, not even suggesting by a wrinkling of the nose that he had smelled something off. The less polite Chinee were prone to do that to foreigners, the Mongols less so. I called for some more rotgut and gestured to my new friend that he could take his share. In the way of a Westerner I stuck out my hand, and offered him my name.

'Tomasso.'

I wasn't about to give him my real name, now, was I? The beefy Mongol grunted, took my hand and squeezed hard.

'Mongotai.'

I gasped and retrieved my mangled fingers from his grasp. He grinned, exposing broken and blackened teeth. I decided to keep well away from his exhalations as even the rotgut wouldn't be enough to mask the stink from a mouthful of teeth that bad. I poured him a drink from the white porcelain jug, and began my spiel. I had been in this part of the world long enough to have a good grasp of the Mongol tongue, you see. Now was my chance to test it to the limit.

'I've had some luck today. I sold a blade that I bought for next to nothing, and made a tidy profit. I'm flush with money, and willing to test my luck further. How about you? Do you feel lucky?'

Mongotai grunted and threw the brew in his bowl down his throat.

'You speak funny.'

I thought, well, that's OK, your breath smells funny. But he was a mark, so I kept my thoughts about his oral hygiene to myself. Besides, I had washed as recently as three weeks ago, and smelled as sweet as a khan's concubine. In fact, I had been scrubbed by a woman who had almost become one of the Great Khan's concubines. Her name is Gurbesu, and she had been part of an annual batch of Kungurat girls sent to Kubilai Khan as tribute. And that would have been her fate, except for a chance encounter en-route with an adventurer called Nick Zuliani. I stole her virginity before she got to Kubilai's summer palace at Xanadu, rendering her useless for his purposes. Once her state was known, she had been smuggled out of the Inner Palace by her chaperone before she embarrassed everyone in front of the Khan. But that's another story, which you may have heard me tell before. Gurbesu was dark-skinned and with a thick mane of hair so black that when it was oiled it was darker than the darkest night in the Desert of Lop. But I digress. I will return to my complicated love life later, if you like. It makes for exciting reading. For now, I must content you with explaining how I fleeced the smelly Mongol. And ended up with him hounding me out of Khan-balik.

He had said I spoke funny. I suppose I did to his ears. I poured more rice wine into his bowl.

'Maybe this will help you understand me.'

He grunted, and swilled it down in one gulp. I leaned closer, as though I had a great secret to impart to my new-found friend.

'Have you heard of the pot game?'

He looked puzzled, and my hopes were raised. If he had heard of it, I would not be able to play the con on him. I drank down my rice wine, and wiped the bowl clean with my sleeve. I then placed the bowl on the table between us.

'This is the pot. We each put an equal amount of money in it, say fifty yuan, and then bid on the pot.'

The Mongol's beady eyes gleamed at the idea of gaming with a red-haired foreigner. Mongols love gambling, and can't resist an opportunity to indulge. Their innate sense of superiority makes them overconfident, particularly with foreigners. He was cocksure he could take me, drunk or not. He pulled out a pouch from his fur-trimmed coat and threw the requisite coins in the bowl. I did the same, matching his money with my own.

'Now, there is a hundred yuan in the bowl. We each bid in turn, and whoever bids the highest gets the pot.'

Mongotai could not take his eyes off the pile of shiny coins in the bowl, so I offered to start the bidding.

'With a hundred in there, I reckon it must be worth offering forty as my starting bid.'

Mongotai snorted in derision.

'I bid fifty.'

I grimaced, as though going any higher would cause me a pain in my purse.

'OK. I'm going to bid really high to get this hundred. I bid seventy.'

I fiddled nervously with the little pile of coins in my fist, as if I was short of funds. I could see the rice wine befuddled brain working hard behind the screwed-up buttons of eyes in the centre of Mongotai's face. He grinned, reckoning he had me on the run. He laughed a short barking laugh.

'Eighty!'

I threw up my hands in defeat.

'That's too rich! You are too good for me. You win. Give me eighty yuan and you can have the pot.'

Eagerly, the poor fool paid over his eighty, and gathered in the hundred in the stained rice wine bowl. I got up, shook his hand and left the gloomy tavern.

The first rule of the quick con is to get away as soon as you have fleeced the mark in case he spots how it was done. Did you see how it worked? Half of the pot was his money already, so he gave me eighty to buy back his fifty along with my fifty. That left me thirty up on the deal. Unfortunately, it was in the street that I made my big mistake. I stopped to count my coins before I was well clear of the tavern. Suddenly I heard a roar like the sound of a gale ripping at the sturdy sails of a trading vessel bound for Venice, tearing them to shreds. And bringing down the mast in the process.

Mongotai must have been brighter than I thought. He had just worked out the scam. He came out of the tavern so fast that the flimsy walls trembled as though an earthquake was ravaging the city. I took to my heels and ran before he could catch me.

'Where've you been, Nick? Chu-Tsai is looking for you. He says it's urgent. And why are you out of breath?'

Gurbesu's shapely figure was a pleasant sight after the hairy demon that was Mongotai. But her face was distorted into a mask of disapproval. She must have smelled the stink of cheap rice wine on me when I tried to plant a kiss on her full, red lips. She pushed me away, and not for the first time I thought of my lost love in Venice. Caterina Dolfin was fair where Gurbesu was dark, and slim and boyish compared to the Kungurat girl's rounded voluptuousness. But I had not seen fair Cat in a number of years, and she was a thousand miles and a lifetime away. So I put Cat out of my mind, and grabbed at Gurbesu's accommodating hips, pulling her to me. This time she didn't protest so much. That was the attractive thing about her – she could not resist my charms for long.

'So many questions. I am out of breath because I thought of you and ran all the way home. As for Chu-Tsai, he can wait. I have some business far more urgent with you, my dear.'

The silken surfaces of our Chinee clothes slid enticingly over one another as we embraced. Gurbesu sighed deeply, and gave in to my blandishments.

Lin Chu-Tsai was becoming impatient. He had asked Gurbesu to find Zhong Kui and bring him to the palace. Zhong Kui was his pet name for the foreigner Nick Zuliani. Nick had won it both by being as tenacious as the legendary demon of that name, and by the bushy beard he wore which resembled the demon's own. The original Zhong Kui was said to have been a man who committed suicide after failing his palace examinations. Reborn as a demon, he had vowed to rid the world of other mischievous lesser demons. And whereas Lin Chu-Tsai could not conceive of the self-confident Zuliani killing himself over a failed test, he nevertheless thought of him as someone who had become a harrier of bad men. Nick had proved his worth as a hunter of murderers to the Great Khan – Kubilai – and thereby won a place as official Investigator of Crimes. But now Lin Chu-Tsai, Clerk to the Minister of Justice of the Mongol Empire, had need of him himself.

'Where are you, Zhong Kui? We must be on our way today, or suffer the consequences.'

He looked again at the document he had been handed by Ko's servant that very morning. It purported to be a command from Kubilai himself to look into a criminal matter in the town of Pianfu. A murder, indeed. But the fact that it came through Ko Su-Tsung – Lin's arch-enemy in the Khan's palace – made him deeply suspicious. What was Ko doing referring a case of murder to him? The cadaverous, cold-hearted man was now effectively the head of the Censorate, a terrifying government department that kept an eye on all other government depart-ments and officials. Ostensibly, its role was to eradicate all forms of corruption. But that very grave duty afforded the Censorate, and Ko Su-Tsung, the ultimate corrupting evil. He wielded power over the fate of every single person working for the Great Khan with no one in a position to challenge him. There was no one to watch the watcher, meaning that proof of misdeeds were hardly ever required by Ko – mere suspicion was enough to ruin a man for ever. Lin Chu-Tsai lived by an opposite code that demanded evidence of wrongdoing. Ko needed none.

Lin put the paper down on his desk, and pushed it away from him. It was as if he were trying to deny its existence. He was sure it was a trap to ensnare him and Zhong Kui both. But he knew he would have to comply with its demands, or fall into the other trap of dereliction of duty. Sighing, he picked up the offending document again, and perused its contents carefully. If he was to avoid the trap, he needed another brain urgently.

'Where are you, Nick Zuliani?'

# TWO

*A good fortune may forebode a bad luck, which may in turn disguise a good fortune*

While Lin was fretting, I was hurrying through the vast building site that was Kubilai's new capital, with Gurbesu in tow. Her pleasure at our dalliance was tempered now by her recollection of Lin Chu-Tsai's sense of urgency. In fact she was getting more and more angry with me for the delay, for which she felt she would be blamed. In fact our current lack of speed was her fault. I would have gone faster, but her tight Chinee robe didn't allow for rapid progress. Her wooden pattens also slowed her down as they fitted so loosely. Even so, our speed meant they clattered an irate tattoo on the stone cobbles of the streets in the old town.

Once we were out of Old Yenking and over the Yun-Ho river bridge we were grateful for the stout footwear. We were approaching a building site of massive proportions. This was Kubilai Khan's latest and grandest project after the Great Enterprise, as Xanadu had been called. But where Xanadu had been a reflection of Kubilai's Mongol ancestry, this new capital was Kubilai looking forward. It would be all Chinee, and was the first step to the Great Khan establishing a new dynasty. I had heard tell that the architect who was creating this most Chinee of capitals, however, was an Arab by the name of Ikhtiyar al-Din. Lin had told me that he had seen detailed plans drawn up by the Arab for passes and gates, audience halls, roads and residential quarters, reception rooms and administration offices, shrines, guard houses, stores and quarters for officers on duty in the imperial household. In addition to all that practical and domestic architecture there would be pools, ponds, gardens, parks and places of dalliance. The grand astrologer had selected a propitious date and work had begun. A multitude of artisans had already descended on the site, measurements were taken, and the necessary materials assembled. The new city and palace were to be in the form of a series of ramparts nesting pleasantly one within the other like the layers of an onion. At the moment though, it was simply chaotic.

Thousands of workers scurried like ants across the huge area that was to be the personal palace and administrative centre of Kubilai's vast empire. They were still building the ramparts that meandered over hills and along three winding rivers. And these ramparts were made of mud beaten down between wooden shuttering until it was solid. The end result of all this feverish activity was that clinging, wet earth filled the whole site. It began to stick to our shoes until they weighed like lead. Finally, Gurbesu's feet became embedded in a particularly cloying patch. She halted, and cried out.

'You'll have to pull me out, Nick. I can't move.'

I yanked hard with little success and a bunch of curious Chinee workmen began to gather to observe the fun. They grinned at Gurbesu's predicament making all sorts of suggestions in a language I barely knew. But it was clear from their gestures which part of her anatomy they thought I should grab in order to effect her release. They gawped even more when Gurbesu's silken robe came open at the top. The buttoned-up bodice beneath barely contained her large breasts, as Chinee undergarments were not designed for such voluptuousness. Her face turning red – with embarrassment or anger I couldn't tell – she yelled at me to pull harder.

'Get me out of this mess.'

I pulled. With a deep sucking noise, her feet came free leaving her wooden pattens stuck in the mud. She groaned, but regained her composure and control of her undergarments. Ignoring the gawping workmen, she trotted ahead of me, her white socks quickly turning black with more clinging mud. I hurried after her as we made for the lake that bordered the western edge of the site. This was where Kubilai had his temporary headquarters while the new Tatu was being built.

When we had arrived some months earlier, the lake was still choked with silt and plants, its margins dotted with the remains of previously rich Chinees' summer houses. These were by now slowly decaying all around the edges of the lake. Kubilai had quickly had the area cleared, and had selected Jade Island, set in the southern end of the lake, as his temporary home. It was said there was a palace within a palace on the island, and in this second palace Kubilai's corpulent frame lounged on a vast bed inlaid with jade and gold. From there, he watched as great quantities of wine were dispensed from a huge jade urn. I hoped for a summons to his palace one day, as I wanted to partake of that bounty.

But Jade Island was not our destination today. So we ploughed through the filth of a city in the making towards one of a scattering of the old summer houses that had been left standing. They were positioned close to the new bridge that now linked the southern end of Jade Island with the surrounding land. The summer houses were convenient, if temporary, locations for those who ran the vast and overworked bureaucracy that was needed for Kubilai's ever burgeoning empire. Inside one of them my boss, Lin Chu-Tsai, was no doubt fretting over my late arrival. I did not want him to know what had caused our delay, and tried to hold Gurbesu back. But before I could get my story straight with her, she was stomping angrily up the wooden steps and into Lin's summer house; a move that was no mean feat in muddy white socks and no shoes. I strode after her, my boots leaving large black footprints on the steps and tiled floors.

Inside, everything reflected a picture of calm, except for Lin Chu-Tsai's face. This was most unusual, as my friend was normally the most even-tempered of men, with a serene mood that he ensured was mirrored in his surroundings. Despite the dilapidated nature of the exterior of the summer house, Lin had quickly created a subtle interior with items he had brought from his residence in Xanadu. Lattice-work wooden screens, deep mahogany in colour, hid the worst of the cracks in the walls, and a fine vase stood where the light from the window of his office lit up its translucent blue porcelain. A low table in the centre of the large room that was Lin's office and living space was surrounded by deep silken cushions. Each cushion was richly embroidered with a different Chinee pattern ranging from rampant dragons to strangely shaped unicorns. The table top was usually stacked with neat piles of papers on which Lin was working in his capacity as Clerk to the Minister of Justice. For in reality, Lin was the embodiment of justice in Kubilai's empire, and he did all the work attributed to his master, a Turk by the name of Alawi Kayyal. The Minister held his post because of the quaint and repressive system of hierarchies in the Mongol Empire.

At the top of the heap sat the small number of people who could call themselves Mongols. I made the mistake of referring to them as Tartars when I first arrived in Xanadu, because this was the name the western world used. Perhaps as a reminder that they were once thought of as the Hounds of Hell – or Tartarus. I was soon told that the actual Tartar tribe was one that Kubilai's grandfather, Chinghis, had slaughtered for the treacherous murder of his own father. So I quickly learned that it was not Tartars, but Mongols who rule the world in these parts. They were not many in number, but they were the princes and the overlords of everyone else in the empire. Below them, and trusted to run things for their masters, were the *Se-mu Jen* – non-Chinee foreigners many of whom were Turks and other Easterners. Coming third in the heap were the *Han Jen* like Lin, who were Chinees from the conquered North of that vast land of Cathay. Finally, beyond all contempt at the bottom were the *Nan Jen* – Chinees from the as-yet unconquered South. Lin's fate was to be the clerk to a drunken Turk who found it difficult even to put his mark on the bottom of the documents Lin wrote for him without smudging it. So the truth was Lin Chu-Tsai was *de facto* the embodiment of justice in the Mongol Empire. And now I was his right-hand man. It's a strange world, isn't it?

When we entered the summer house, Lin was not seated at his table with its usual stacks of papers, but was standing looking out the window at Jade Island. When we entered, he turned round abruptly. Chu-Tsai was a man of average build with a chubby face that nevertheless was quite pallid due to the necessity of his indoor existence. His jet black hair was pulled back tightly from his face, and hung in a plaited queue down his back. This was still shorter than usual, due to a fire some time earlier that had robbed him of most of his hair. His small hands and slender fingers, normally so graceful, were now clasped tightly round a paper scroll. His tendency to overweight was probably due to the fact that as a child his parents had had him castrated. The hope had been that, as a eunuch, he would stand a greater chance of progressing at the emperor's court to a position of power. The irony was that the Mongol overlords who grabbed the throne of China in his youth cared little for such Chinee niceties. In the end Lin had made his way by use of his intellect and his not inconsiderable sharp wits, and not because he had no balls. In fact, I would say he had balls a-plenty. Just not between his legs any more. He was a man of decisiveness and a bold one too. Today, he looked nervous and unsure of himself.

'Master Nick. At last.'

I began to explain what had taken us so long. That is, I lied about what had taken so long, not wishing him to know I had preferred to romp with Gurbesu rather than answer his call immediately. But, as I formed my excuses, he held his slender hand up.

'That is of no importance now. This is.'

He waved aloft the paper that he held in his other hand. Behind me, Gurbesu sighed and slumped down on to one of the cushions that were arranged around the low table. I glanced down, and watched as she peeled the dirty socks off her feet. Lin looked on disapprovingly at the sight of her bare feet, then took my arm and guided me to the other side of the room. We looked out over the lake towards Jade Island, as he explained the bind he was in. That we were both in. On the surface, it appeared to be a straightforward investigation of a murder case. But for Lin it had darker undertones.

'You see, Master Nick, Ko has no formal reason to be acting for the Great Khan in a simple case of murder. He suggests it is a delicate case concerning a local official who may be corrupt, and that is why he has intervened. He further goes on to say that it requires my attention in particular. That the Great Khan specifically asked for me to go to P'ing-Yang-Fu –' he gave the town its formal name – 'and that you should come with me.'

I shrugged my shoulders, not seeing what the problem was.

I was more concerned about the mountain about to land on me that was Mongotai, actually. If we had a reason to leave Khan-balik, I was more than happy to comply.

'Then let's go.'

Lin looked at me as though I were a little child who did not understand the world. He could be very obtuse and irritating at times, but I had learned to listen to him. He had been brought up in the convoluted world that made up Cathay, and could see currents under the muddy waters that were invisible to me.

'What's the problem?'

A look of distress crossed Lin's face. He didn't like openly pointing out my failings, as it offended his sense of politeness. And to have to explain would show up my ignorance. So he carefully phrased his reply.

'The request – which in essence is a command that has its origin with Kubilai – has come through the agency of Ko Su-Tsung. So it is really Ko who has caused the request to land on my doorstep. The apparent purpose is to investigate the ruling of a death sentence made by a prefect on a Chinee woman, who is now languishing in gaol under threat of execution. The prefect acts for his Mongol overlord in P'ing-Yang-Fu, which by the way is a journey of at least two weeks from here, so we have little time. The problem is that we will be in effect arbitrating between a lowly Han Jen woman and a Mongol governor of high status.'

'If she's guilty, what's the problem? We can confirm the verdict and get on our way.'

I could see Lin was distressed by my cavalier approach. He pressed on with his insight into Chinee politics, and the serpentine coils of the civil service that ran Kubilai's affairs.

'If she were guilty, there would be no point in us being there. Therefore I assume she must be innocent, or Ko would not want us to go. Oh, it will suit him that we are in some forsaken backwater of the Khan's empire, leaving him free to plot his way back into favour at our expense. But if it were only that, I would not be worried too much. No, I am certain we are being set up to be in an impossible position. We will find her innocent, and have either to suppress the truth, which

Ko will use against us, or judge in her favour and embarrass a highly placed Mongol official. We can't win, Master Nick. Ko has us in a stranglehold.'

I grimaced, my mind racing.

'You said at the beginning that whether the command originated directly from Kubilai or not, we would have to go, yes?'

'Yes. Ko must have persuaded him of the importance of the matter.'

'Then we do not have an option. We must go, so let's get on. There will be time a-plenty to plan our strategy on the journey there, if it takes as long as you say.'

Lin appeared almost relieved by my apparent fatalism. He gave a short nod of his head that I took as approval.

'As ever, you cut through my indecision like a sword through a watermelon, Nick. We will make ready.'

I didn't point out to him that my decision sounded, even to me, more like avoidance than decisiveness, and had been driven by my desire not to have Mongotai's sword slice through my cheating brain as through the previously mentioned melon. But twas the decision made, so I grabbed the sulky Gurbesu's arm and pulled her to her feet. Throughout my discussion with Lin, I had failed to consult her, and I knew she would now resent being dragged off to pack for a long journey that she had not agreed to. But I knew she fancied the chance to see more of Cathay, and wouldn't object for long. I grinned and looked down at her bare feet.

'Come on, Gurbesu. Be good, and I might even buy you some new shoes.'

I know how to win the heart of a girl, don't you think?

# THREE

*If you wish to know the mind of a man, listen to his words.*

Gurbesu and I hurried back to Old Yenking in the south of Khan-balik in order to tell the others our new plans. The buildings there still clung to the old grid of streets laid out before Kubilai's grandfather, Chinghis, had laid waste to the Chinee city. Ironically, this act had assisted Kubilai. Fifty years later, he had fewer buildings to clear away in order to build his new winter capital. Many had already been obliterated. Most still remained to the south, and that is where we were living. Like most of the foreigners in the Great Khan's empire.

My little entourage was made up of Gurbesu – the Kungurat Tartar girl from the North, Tadeusz Pyka – a Silesian Pole from Breslau, and Friar Giovanni Alberoni – a Venetian like myself. He and I had come together in strange circumstances, each drawn to the pole star that was Kubilai Khan. Friar Alberoni had picked me up out of the gutter in Sudak in an area some call Crimea. I had been going through a bad patch in my life, forced out of Venice through little fault of my own. Missing my lover, Caterina Dolfin, I had for once made a mess of my business dealings, and had resorted to the consolation of the bottle. Though I would not admit it to him, Alberoni saved me from myself, and offered me a job as bodyguard for his trip to the furthest edge of the world that was the Mongol Empire. The friar was an odd cove who had set his heart on chasing a myth, though he didn't see it that way. You see, things had seemed to be going from bad to worse in the Middle East. Saracens were grabbing chunks of the Holy Lands back from Crusader knights, who had taken their eyes off the prize, and set themselves up as mercenary kings and counts of various tracts of God's country. The successes of previous crusades were therefore crumbling away.

Suddenly, there was a tale circulating of a great Christian king in the East, who would save Christendom in its hour of need. He went by the name of Presbyter, or Prester, John. Alberoni wanted to do something about it by seeking him out and pleading for his help. I thought he was wasting his time, as to me it was all a scam relying on people's yearnings for a saviour, who would descend from the heavens at the final moment. Such miracles did not occur in my world. But the trip to Xanadu drew me, and I agreed to help him. Predictably, our initial search failed dismally. But then, just as we were about to give up, we had come across stories of Nestorian Christians in Kubilai's empire. And in Xanadu, we had encountered an old man, a prisoner who had been long incarcerated by Kubilai's family. He could have been the man Alberoni was looking for. The trouble was he had disappeared as mysteriously as he had appeared to us. One moment, there he was in his cell, the next moment he had slipped into the shadows like a will o' the wisp. Alberoni's search had thus come to an end. But it was what had brought him and me to Xanadu in the first place. And led me to be Kubilai's hunter of murderers.

Gurbesu, we had met on the way to Xanadu. As I told you, she was with a bunch of young girls intended to be Kubilai's virgin brides – part of an annual tribute from their tribe. Unfortunately for Kubilai, Gurbesu had been wilful enough to respond to my seductive manner. She had also been wild enough to escape from the harem, and take up with me. Her black, oiled hair, and shapely curves were in complete contrast to the willowy figure of the blonde-haired Cat, who I had left behind in Venice. But I didn't know if I would ever see my Venetian lover again. So who could blame me for taking up with Gurbesu? I certainly didn't feel guilty, especially when Gurbesu's dark-skinned arms were wrapped around me.

The final member of our group was Tadeusz Pyka. He had experienced a more turbulent means of reaching Kubilai's court. More than twenty-five years earlier, in 1241, the Tartar hordes had swept across Europe. They had seemed like a terrifying army of the Devil, killing all Christians in its way. And indeed, Tadeusz had been lucky to survive the devastation of his home town of Breslau. What had saved him was that he was a silversmith. The Mongols were beginning to see the value of skilled men, and he had been brought back to Xanadu in chains to ply his trade for the benefit of the Great Khan. Twenty years on, he had no longer any wish to return to a home where he would find no one he knew. Kubilai's court was now his home, and, when we met, his local knowledge had assisted me in my quest to find a murderer at that court. Besides knowing his way around, he had other skills – his nimble fingers could pick almost any lock in Christendom and beyond. He was therefore invaluable to me.

It was Tadeusz who was at the door of our lodgings in Khanbalik when Gurbesu and I returned with our news. He is a small, wiry man with a stubbly beard that doesn't grow on one side of his face where he was once badly burned. That deformity is the legacy of the Tartar invasion of his country. Now, the burned side of his face glowed bright red, and I knew he was worked up about something.

'Nick. I am so glad you are back.'

'Why, Tadeusz? What on earth is the problem?'

He grabbed my arm and dragged me into the large room that we all shared. It was in a state of chaos. Well, to be honest, it was usually in a mess. With four independently-minded individuals occupying the same lodgings, it was not to be expected that everything would be neatly stowed. I did try and make an effort at tidying myself. I mean to say, I had often told Gurbesu to tidy the room, but this had been met with a stony stare that reminded me of Cat in many ways. I don't know why I seemed to be burdened with incompliant women in my life. But I suppose I would have it no other way. Arguing with your woman had its compensations when it came to making up afterwards. Suffice it to say, our quarters in Old Yenking were rarely tidied up.

Now however, the room was in even more of a mess than it normally was. I looked around, immediately noticing that two large saddlebags lay in the centre of the chaos. They were already stuffed with clothes and papers that stuck out haphazardly. I could see that the clothes were those belonging to Friar Alberoni. I groaned.

'What is the friar up to now?'

'He says he is leaving. His quest is at an end, and he has no further purpose here in the land of idolaters.'

I threw up my hands in despair. If I was honest, I would have to admit that Alberoni was superfluous most of the time. But he did have his uses sometimes. It's not that I revel in idolatry myself, but I just seem to have little need of God. But when I do need Him, then I usually find I have to call on His services at short notice, and having a priest at hand is useful. Besides, Alberoni was still my only connection with Venice in Kubilai's vast empire. Even though he comes from the long low strip of an island beyond Venice called Malamocco, and so isn't a true-bred Venetian. Still, we could talk to each other about La Serenissima when I was low, and dream of returning there. It seemed that Alberoni was now planning his return more precipitately than I could hope for.

'What on earth can I do to persuade him to stay, do you think?'

Alberoni's voice gave me my answer.

'There is nothing you can do, Niccolò. I am determined to go.'

The tall, angular figure of Friar Giovanni Alberoni appeared in the street doorway. His long black robe was shabby and patched in numerous places, but he always gave the impression of neatness, and that somehow translated into a sense of closeness to God. His eyes glittered with resolve, and he scrubbed at his smoothly shaved chin. Not for him the rough unruly beard that I adopted in my role as the demon Zhong Kui. No, he was habitually scraping at his chin every three of four days, just like the Chinee. Mind you, our hosts had little to scrape off their chins. Even the Mongols had a sparse thatch compared to my glorious red bush, which admittedly was beginning to show some grey hairs. I tried my last card, knowing the friar hated being on horseback.

'Your only means of getting back will be to ride, and it is a long, long way home. Also it will be dangerous for you to be on your own. Which you will be, for you know I can't come with you until I am released from my duties by the Great Khan.'

Alberoni's resolve melted for a moment as he contemplated sitting on the back of a horse for weeks on end. But then I saw the stubbornness return to his eyes.

'I have determined to go, and go I shall.'

I sighed, seeing that I would not be able to stop him making the long trek home. Leaving him to his packing of the already crammed saddlebags, I turned instead to Tadeusz, and told him of our plans.

'We have a new commission. I am to investigate the murder of an old merchant in a town some days south of here. It seems that his prospective daughter-in-law has poisoned him, and she has been condemned to death. But Kubilai has been petitioned to re-examine the case, as some believe her innocent. It will be a mess, and Lin Chu-Tsai will have to arbitrate between the Chinee girl and her supporters, and the local Mongol lord.'

Tadeusz grimaced.

'That puts us in a hopeless situation.'

'Yes. Lin thinks he has been set up by his old adversary, Ko, and I believe him. We can't win either way, unless we can come up with something extraordinary.'

'Where is the girl to be found?'

I pulled out the document Lin had given me, flattening it on the low table with the palm of my hand, and scrutinized the script. It was in Turkish, so I could understand it – written Chinee was still just a confusion of lines and dots to me.

'She is held imprisoned in a town called –' I ran my finger along the word, rehearsing it in my head – 'called P'ing-Yang-Fu. It is some twenty days journey south-west and is close to the Kara-Moran river.'

I heard a gasp behind me, and Alberoni suddenly piped up.

'Kara-Moran. That means Black River in Turkish, doesn't it?'

I frowned, not knowing where this was leading.

'I believe so.'

Now Alberoni was at my elbow, staring at the paper I held in my hand.

'And in Chinee, that is Hwang-Ho?'

It was Tadeusz, with his superior knowledge of that tongue who answered Alberoni.

'Yes, that is correct. The Hwang-Ho is a very large river, a mile wide in places, leading out to the ocean on the edge of the world.'

A seafarer by birth, I shuddered at the thought of sailing to the edge of the ocean and tipping off. At least the seas beyond the lagoon of Venice were bounded by land. Beyond Kubilai's empire to the east there was a big island called Cipangu, and then, nothing. But Alberoni wasn't interested in where the river flowed out to, apparently, but the very opposite as it turned out. He abruptly interrupted Tadeusz's geography lesson.

'Yes, yes. That is the place.'

He grasped my shoulder, and looked into my eyes.

'Niccolò . . .' Where others called me by my familiar name, Alberoni always used the formal version. He had been the Zuliani family priest for years. 'Niccolò, I have been a little precipitate. I now see I should not abandon you at this juncture. Especially if you will be in some danger if you make the wrong decision. I should be there to advise you. I will come too. After all, my bags are packed.'

I narrowed my eyes and stared suspiciously at the priest, not sure what had changed his mind. But I had to admit his companionship would please me, and his presence could be useful.

'Very well. We must all hurry to prepare, though. Lin has sent for ponies for us all – including you, Friar, as he assumed you were coming with us.' I grinned evilly as I mentioned Alberoni's hated transport. He had insisted on using a cart to make the long journey from west to east six years ago. The trip had been interminable, and I recall almost being seasick in the lurching, swaying vehicle. Me – a Venetian practically living on water – being seasick. It didn't bear thinking about. But since our time in the Mongol Empire I had become almost as at home on the back of the hardy little ponies the Mongols used, as on board ship. Gurbesu could ride like the wind. She had been practically brought up on the back of a horse. Such a life as the one she led would not have suited the Chinee because they placed great store by verifiable virginity in a bride. Sitting astride a horse would not have been conducive to retaining that state. As well as proof by virginal blood, it is said that one of the ways of ensuring the virginity of a bride was by using a pigeon's egg. If it did not break on insertion – if you take my meaning – then the girl could not be a virgin. Gurbesu would have failed gloriously. Tadeusz could ride reasonably well too, by the way. Which left Alberoni and Lin Chu-Tsai.

Our Chinee friend hated travelling, and like Alberoni abhorred the back of a horse. So I knew he would arrive in a carriage of some sort. But he would not wish to share it with the friar. In his opinion, we Westerners sweated fearsomely, and did not wash often enough. For my part, I thought the Chinee elite washed far too often, immersing themselves as they did almost every day. I preferred to change my clothes regularly, and keep myself sweet-smelling that way. I say I preferred it. To be honest, it was Gurbesu who had got me into the habit of changing clothes, swearing she would not lie with me if I wore the same clothes more than three days together. I therefore packed my saddlebags with lots of silk shirts and loose trousers in the Chinee style, together with a couple of short jackets and an informal long robe decorated with dragons called a *bei-zi*. I was quite the dandy in my Chinee clothes. Gurbesu too had her own version of the *bei-zi*, which was cut to fit snugly round her curves. The thought of how the clothes fitted her so well had me on the verge of suggesting to her that we adjourn to our bedchamber. But just as I was about to do so, we heard the sound of horses' hooves on the broken cobbles of the old city street where we lived. We were ready to go.

Lin was not with the horses, but had given the ostler a message that we were to set off and he would meet us soon enough. I pushed and prodded Alberoni on to the back of his pony, which we chose for him as the one looking the most docile, and the rest of us mounted more easily. The friar jiggled the reins, but could not make his steed start, so I moved my pony alongside his and gave it a kick. With a yell of horror from Alberoni, and a look of annoyance from his mount, the two of them moved away in more or less the right direction. The rest of us followed in his wake, keeping up the encouragement that Alberoni was unable to supply.

# FOUR

*A journey of a thousand miles begins with a single step.*

Our strange and erratic procession finally came together ten miles west of Khan-balik at the great marble bridge over the river called by some Pulisanghin. It was a big bridge with twenty-four arches and twenty-four piers because the river – that Lin called Hun-Ho – was a very big river that ran all the way to the ocean. The bridge was made of grey marble and ten horsemen could have ridden abreast across it. Our little entourage did not make such demands on it. While Gurbesu and I had ridden fast ahead of the others for the pure joy of it – and in my case to make sure I was well out of the reach of Mongotai – Tadeusz and Alberoni were plodding along at a more sedate pace. We had all arranged to meet up at the bridge, as Lin was to be coming from another direction in his carriage, according to the message sent by the ostler. Gurbesu and I knew we would have a long wait for the others to catch up, so we dismounted and sat in the shade of one of a row of columns along the bridge. Each one was set on the back of a marble turtle and topped by a lion. We sat fondling each other, watching the brown waters surge under the river.

Eventually, we could see the rest of our party arriving and rearranged our clothes. Lin must have encountered the slower riders some miles back, for they were all together now. Lin's carriage was beautifully upholstered with fine-spoked wheels only marred by the mud they must have picked up from the building site that was Kubilai's new citadel. Alberoni, uneasy on his docile pony, stared enviously at the ornate carriage. Lin, ignoring the friar's stare, waved enthusiastically at me as he came closer. Gurbesu and I stood up and walked over to the carriage, leading our ponies by their reins.

Up front sat the driver of Lin's carriage and his new servant,

Po Ku. He was a tall, wiry young lad, whom Lin had personally selected from his own family's province. Lin's previous servant – Yao Lei – had been a two-faced traitor who had reported on his master's activities to his real master, Ko Su-Tsung. Po Ku still had the scent of the farm about him, and was inclined to be clumsy. He had already driven Lin to distraction by breaking a fine bone-china plate that Lin treasured. But Lin bore the burden with stoicism in order to have a servant who, by virtue of his coming from Lin's home region, he hoped had not infiltrated his household on the orders of his long-time enemy. Lin looked glad to see me again.

'I have all the paperwork on the case right here.'

He patted at an ominously large heap of documents, some fastened with silk cords that lay on the seat next to him. My heart sank at the size of the pile.

With us all assembled together, Gurbesu and I remounted and, at the pace of Lin's carriage, we began our long journey south-westward. Though I was all for pressing on, Lin insisted our first stop be a mere thirty miles beyond the bridge at Cho-Chau, where several fine hostelries were available. I think he was feeling the jolting of the carriage and wished to rest his back. Once we had settled in our accommodation, he and I decided to tackle the mountain of paperwork and plan our strategy.

Leaning back on a silk cushion to ease his backache, and picking diffidently at his rice-bowl, Lin began to tell me what he knew.

'The accused is a girl of twenty, named Jianxu. Her mother-in-law, Madam Gao . . .'

I quickly interrupted.

'Mother-in-law? Then this girl is married. Where is her husband?'

'Dead. He died soon after their marriage apparently, leaving his mother and wife destitute. This was the beginning of their problems. In order to survive, the old lady agreed to marry a trader by the name of Geng Biao. He had a son – Geng Wenbo – who took a shine to the younger girl.'

'The one found guilty of murder?'

Lin nodded patiently at this next interruption. I knew he

liked to lay out the facts neatly and in chronological order, and I was for always irritating him by trying to cut to the chase. I raised both hands by way of an apology and let him continue. We had two weeks of travelling in which to examine the facts. There was no hurry. Though we also had to make a plan to extricate ourselves from the trap that Ko had driven us into. If we were to avoid putting ourselves between a rock and hard place, I would need to devise a strategy and soon.

'I'm sorry. Go on.'

Lin smiled in that gentle but telling way of his, and continued his narrative. I could see that he was pleased at, once again, schooling the barbarian in the calmer ways of the Chinee. Outside, the sun was setting and the humidity of the day was falling away. A cooling breeze blew in through the open window. Lin carried on in that droning voice of his.

'Jianxu, apparently, was reluctant to marry again. Maybe she was still mourning her first husband, maybe Wenbo was not much of a catch. The two ladies' fortunes would, after all, be secured by the marriage of the older lady, her mother-in-law, to Old Geng Biao. There was no need for Jianxu to marry Geng Wenbo also.'

I was about to query Lin on his use of the expression 'old' in relation to Geng, but his raised eyebrow indicated to me that he would explain everything in time, and I needn't interrupt again. I slumped back on to my own cushion and picked a pear off the low table at my side. Biting into it, I sucked up the juice noisily.

'Old Geng is how he is called in Pianfu – P'ing-Yang-Fu – by his neighbours it seems. It is not a term of endearment, but accurate nevertheless. He is in his seventieth year. Or should I say he was, for he is our victim and therefore dead. Jianxu's victim, if we are to believe the paperwork.'

He patted the pile of documents on the table then passed me a linen napkin.

'Wipe your chin, Nick. I know a demon like Zhong Kui need have no manners, but I am determined to teach you some so you can carry them back to the barbarian West when you go.'

I laughed ironically.

'If I go back. It seems I am not my own master any more, but the slave of Kubilai Khan. It is he who will decide if and when I can return to Venice.' I was angered by the thought, but I wiped my chin as bidden. 'But then his and my wishes coincide at the moment. I have no desire to return as yet. I am having too much fun.'

What I said was not entirely true. I yearned every day to return to La Serenissima, and Caterina Dolfin. But I had left under the cloud of an accusation of murder, and my safety, if I did return, was uncertain. I finished the pear, and wiped my lips with the back of my hand. Lin winced at the crudeness of my action, and continued.

'Anyway, the question of Jianxu's marriage to Wenbo became irrelevant a few days after the proposal was made. The old man suddenly upped and died. The details are unsavoury, so I shall not go into them now – you can read them for yourself.' He waved at the pile of documents to indicate that the full gruesomeness of Old Geng's death was recorded in detail somewhere in the heap. Lin did not like dwelling on the nastier aspects of death.

'Suffice it to say that poisoning was the clear cause, and on her being examined, Jianxu confessed.'

I started up from my cushion.

'Confessed? You did not say that before. Then why are we even going to P'ing-Yang-Fu? And who petitioned the Khan for a re-examination of the case, if she admitted she did it?'

'Calm down, my little demon. Confession is part of the legal process in Cathay. Criminal law has a moral purpose in ensuring the guilty not only are caught, but that they repent and see the error of their ways. A person cannot be convicted unless he – or she – confesses.' Lin pulled a face, turning slightly away from me. 'Sometimes extreme measures are required to extract a confession.'

I stared at him in disbelief.

'You mean torture? So Jianxu will have been tortured in order to get her to confess to the crime that she may not have been guilty of committing?'

Lin calmly turned his face back to me.

'Do not you have the same procedures in your world?

I have met priests such as Friar Alberoni who tell me that
torture is a normal procedure for Westerners too.'

It was my turn to look away, embarrassed by his retort. Of
course he was right. The Church was prone to use torture on
heretics to induce repentance. And in cases of treason, a man
might be tortured to extract names of accomplices. But to
torture a young woman merely to obtain evidence? I thought
that was plain wrong, and I tried to make my point.

'Yes, but in most cases in the West, what is called half-proof
is needed before proceeding. That means there must be some
initial evidence of guilt before torture is applied. Where was
the proof that this girl may have murdered the old man?'

Lin pointed to the papers on the table again.

'Read these, and tell me what you think.'

'You know I cannot read Chinee or Mongol script, only
Turkish. And that rather poorly.'

'Then trust me. I have read them all. There was reason to
examine Jianxu strongly. But of course you are right in another
way. A confession obtained in such a situation is a flawed
piece of evidence. That is why I need you to do what you do
best, and uncover the truth.'

Lin knew he could always win me over with such flattery.
And, predictably, I gave in to it.

'Very well. But tell me one thing. You didn't answer my
question concerning who petitioned the court of Kubilai in
support of this girl, Jianxu.'

Lin smiled his little enigmatic smile again, and patted my
knee.

'Ah, just a bunch of vagabonds, one of whom you will meet
in ten days time when we get to T'ai-Yuan-Fu.'

He liked a good secret, did Lin Chu-Tsai, and refused to
say any more to me about the matter. I could not imagine how
a bunch of vagabonds and ne'er-do-well Chinee could exert
any influence with Kubilai. But then they didn't have to. It
was the sneaky Ko Su-Tsung who had lifted the case out of
obscurity and convinced the Khan to consider it. A hopeless
case, supported by a ragtag of lowly Chinee, was a perfect
trap in which Lin and I could be ensnared. I still didn't know
how we were going to save ourselves, and it was not until we

reached T'ai-Yuan-Fu that I had an inkling of what truly awaited us.

The following morning, we reassembled and continued on our journey. A mile beyond Cho-Chau the road forked, one branch going westward still in Cathay, and the other south-east towards Manzi and the southern lands not yet conquered by Kubilai. Our direction was westward, and we passed on the way salt works where men laboured by pouring water over salt-laden earth then boiling the brine in big iron cauldrons. Lin told me they exported the pure, white salt to many countries, bringing in a great deal of wealth for Kubilai's coffers. I have to say, I lost interest in his explanation of the industries that we passed. That was until I spotted some well-tilled fields and land dotted with low growing bushes that were very familiar to me. Lin saw where my gaze was turning, and nodded.

'Yes, they are vineyards, Nick.'

Things were beginning to look up.

The girl sat and shivered in the cold mud hut that was her cell. Her thin green cotton robe did little to keep her warm as the night approached. She could almost feel the chill of autumn creeping across the barren land she could see outside the little window set in the door to her cell. There would soon be frosts turning the broken earth white and hard. But she would not see that. She would be dead by the executioner's hand. Another shiver ran up her spine, this time caused by the fear that ran through her every fibre. She did not like the fact that the road to where she was being kept was also visible from the window. It was unlucky to have a door facing a road.

She huddled up on the little pallet which was the only furniture allowed in her cell, picking at the scabs on her feet. Her luck had been bad recently, particularly since the death of her husband. But she had turned twenty a month ago, and she was convinced that her big luck cycle was returning. She needed the luck – *yun* – or she would not survive to see the winter. She had begged the boy to help her, to petition the Khan if necessary. He was not the brightest person to have your fate dependent on, and had looked at her with horror when she had suggested going over the prefect's head. But she had smiled at him through the bars on the cell window, and reached through to stroke his hairless chin, suggesting who else he might rally to her cause. She knew she had aroused him, and that should be enough to get him to do as she wished. He had left with a scared look on his face, but lust in his eyes. Pulling her knees to her chest, she felt a little warmer. Yes, the *yun* was flowing in her direction again. She could feel it.

# FIVE

*Those who have free seats at a play hiss first.*

The weather was changing, and we could see the dark clouds sweeping across the broad plain to our left. We hurried on as fast as we could, but a flurry of rain hit us just as we reached the outskirts of the town of T'ai-Yuan-Fu. It was a large and prosperous city, and I was pleased to discover from Lin that its chief industry was winemaking. We rode – a rather damp cavalcade – in towards the centre of the city through narrow streets thronging with people despite the wet weather. They were nearly all Chinee, and each person's status was shown by the clothes he wore. The crowds of common workers were garbed in simple cotton clothes dyed brown or green with patterns stencilled on them. On their feet they wore cheap leather shoes, as apparently tradesmen and farmers were forbidden to wear boots. Such footwear was reserved for the wealthier officials and merchants. You could identify them by their more opulent robes. Most of the better-off men we saw in the streets wore informal dress – a *bei-zi* – tied up at the front and adorned with embroidered dragons or flowers. Only those on official business wore the full gown, or *pao*, the sleeves of which were long and covered the hands to show the person did no physical labour. The colour of the robe further designated a man's importance. Though Lin Chu-Tsai did not choose to flaunt his power, he had that morning changed into the red robe of a high official for our entrance into the city. His sleeves were the requisite three chi' wide. He also wore on his head the *fu-tou* of his rank – a rounded hard cap with two stiff wings on the back projecting sideways. Many people turned to look at us, but this could have been the sight of me as much as Lin's formal robes. Few people here would have seen a Westerner, let alone one with red hair and a bushy beard. I had let my hair grow on the journey, as this was my way of impressing the locals.

We wound through the streets, avoiding puddles where we could, eventually reaching a large square. In it stood a most peculiar construction. It was a large platform set high on bamboo stilts, and it was open on three sides. To the rear was a tented structure with a canopy that stuck out covering the whole platform. Large flags flew on the front corners. As our little cavalcade stopped before it, I was aware of a flurry of activity to one side of the platform. A shape flew towards me, and I instinctively reached for my dagger. Lin, who was by now standing up in his carriage to get a better view, leaned over and restrained me from making a grave error.

I saw that the figure was someone in female garb who had sprung on to the platform by performing a long, acrobatic somersault. As her feet slapped down on the front of the staging only feet away from me, I had to restrain my pony from rearing and throwing me. Her painted face stared dejectedly at me, and her long sleeves hung down to the ground. Then she began staggering uncertainly round the platform, and I thought her drunk. Out of the corner of my eye, I saw Lin was enraptured. He was staring at the woman with a look of awe on his face. Her gait changed from her drunken lurch, and she suddenly resembled a lion pacing round a cage too small for it. Her breath quickened and her shoulders jerked. Finally she fell exhausted on to the floor.

Behind me, I heard the sound of clapping hands. It was Lin expressing his approval of the acrobat. I was puzzled. The leap of the saltatrice had been spectacular, but what had all the other mugging been about?

'What did that all mean, Lin?'

He looked at me, his eyes wide in astonishment.

'Do you not know?' He then raised his hand in acknowledgement of my expression of ignorance. 'Silly of me, why should you? That was as perfect an enactment of the passion of Empress Tu as I have ever seen. We call it *tso-yi* – a stylized way of expressing feelings and thoughts through actions.'

I looked back at the woman, who was now grinning

impudently at me, and then bowing to Lin. She was a slender-waisted woman with a rounded but pleasing face that shone through the make-up. As I stared at her, she turned and slinked offstage, gyrating her hips in a way quite as pleasing as Gurbesu's own gait. Thinking of her, and then of my admiration of the acrobatic saltatrice, I glanced across. Gurbesu was dismounting from her steed, and it shielded her from me. She hadn't seen my keen interest in the young woman. I leaned down towards Lin, a sly thought in my mind.

'I should like to meet this Empress Tu. She is clearly very . . . supple.'

Lin looked a little surprised at my salacious comment, but then winked, and grinned broadly.

'I will arrange an assignation for you, Nick.'

I patted his shoulder in a man-to-man sort of complicity. Even though he had no balls, Lin knew what I liked. I whispered in his ear.

'Gurbesu doesn't need to learn of it, of course.'

'Of course not. Leave it all to me.'

I, too, then dismounted, along with the weary Alberoni and Tadeusz Pyka, both of whom had lagged far behind on the last leg of the journey. Following Lin's carriage on foot, we led our horses to where we would stay for the night. It was just off the square, and was as comfortable a hostelry as we had experienced on our long journey. Thinking of the little empress, I left Gurbesu to her own devices, and walked across the inner courtyard of the hostelry to Lin's rooms. As ever, he had already surrounded himself with tranquillity and calm. Po Ku was a quick learner in how to please his master, and busied himself in the shadows arranging his master's travelling posses-sions. Lin was seated on a low bench with a silk cushion on it. I noticed the unicorn shape embroidered on the cushion that protruded from under his buttocks. It was the emblem of the Censorate, the government department of his deadly enemy – and mine too – Ko Su-Tsung. He grinned when he saw where I was looking.

'Forgive me my little petty triumph. I like the idea of sitting on Ko, and arranged for his emblem to be sewn into the fabric of this cushion. He saw it soon after I obtained it, and I think it puzzled and pleased him at the same time. He does not know how I employ the cushion.'

I laughed.

'You can fart on it for all I care, Chu-Tsai.'

Lin grimaced at my Western coarseness, and motioned for me to sit opposite him. I dropped inelegantly down on to the other bench. I still could not get used to the lowness of all the furniture in Cathay. Benches and tables had legs no taller than the little dwarf dogs they were fond of breeding here. I yearned for a good, long-legged hunting hound, and a similarly shaped Venetian chair to lounge in. Grovelling on the floor was not conducive to action, if a swift exit or an attack was required. Lin reached across the table and picked up the stack of documents that had accompanied him in the carriage.

'We must go on looking for a way of extricating ourselves from our dilemma. I have studied the paperwork associated with the case of Jianxu time and time again, but I cannot see where the chink in the armour is located.'

I held up a finger to emphasize what I was about to say, and he looked at me expectantly.

'Then we must turn our examination away from the case, and towards the magistrate and his Mongol overlord.'

'In what way?'

'They have to be corruptible in some way or other. All officials are.' I was suddenly aware of a red flush covering Lin's face, and hastened to correct my error. 'Except for you, old friend. You are the exception that proves the rule. And it is why you are lucky to have me.'

'Why is that, my little demon?'

'Because I am as corruptible as any official, so I can guess what their actions might be before they have even thought of them themselves.'

It came to mind that the last time I pulled a fast one on a Mongol – Mongotai – in the bar in Khan-balik, I had needed to flee pretty quickly afterwards. I decided I would not like to try and outwit the Mongol governor who ran the district in which we were travelling. I might not live to tell the tale. But the prefect was another matter. I decided the Chinee magistrate was the best bet for leaning on.

'Do we know anything about him? The judge in this case?'

Lin rifled through the papers, extracting a paper roll. He unfurled it.

'He is called Li Wen-Tao. And I do have some information on him.' He read in silence for a few moments. 'This is interesting. He is a man of middle years, who should by now be in a higher position, I would say.'

'Good. Then he has got a secret vice that holds him back, and even if he hasn't, we can seduce him into one. Then turn it round against him.'

I rubbed my hands together, eager for the challenge.

'I am beginning to like this case already.'

'Good. And tonight by way of relaxation you will enjoy a play onstage in the square.'

I grimaced, thinking of the simple miracle plays with their religious and moralizing themes I had seen in Venice. They did not appeal at all. Lin, on the other hand, seemed quite excited by the prospect.

'You will enjoy it, Nick. The theatre is very popular in Cathay, and the plays tell all sorts of stirring tales, including what we call strip and fight thrillers. Sword against sword, or mace against mace. But tonight it is a different sort, and an appropriate play for us – *kung-an*.'

'*Kung-an*?'

He winked knowingly.

'It means a crime case tale. How appropriate is that? But I have business in mind too, as one of the men who framed the petition to Kubilai is here.'

'Our case?'

'Yes. He is a writer of plays too – a young man beginning to make a name for himself. Though it may not help him that he has a young man's thirst to see justice done for his race.' Lin's face had a solemn look about it. 'Arguing the case of a Chin woman against the decision of a Mongol governor is not how to become famous. Notorious, perhaps.'

Lin looked down at his boots and sighed at the injustice of the world. But when he looked up again, there was a brightness in his eyes.

'Never mind that. We will speak with him briefly and

afterwards you can meet the person who played Empress Tu for you this afternoon.'

I felt a tingling in my loins. But I refrained from scratching my itchy balls, knowing how it hurt Lin's feelings. Still, I grinned wickedly, imagining the supple girl gyrating just for me.

'A secret assignation after good entertainment and plenty to drink. Perfect.'

I crossed back over the courtyard, and, watched by a curious Gurbesu, began to dress in my finest.

Later, the square was crowded with people, most of whom had richly embroidered robes on. They strolled around, bowing to their superiors and taking acknowledgements from their inferiors. Rows of benches had been set up facing the stage, which was now lit with flaming torches, and most spaces were rapidly being occupied by the elite. In the very front row lounged a small group of Mongols dressed in clothes quite different from the rest of the crowd. They wore short tunics in blue or red and trimmed in fur with grey trousers. One or two of this small elite had embroidered silk tunics but their mien was nevertheless militaristic. The man at the centre of attention had a full coat of boiled leather strips that marked him out as a cavalryman. Lin pressed my arm and hissed in my ear.

'See the one dressed like a soldier? That is Taitemir, the governor. His remit covers this city and the one we are journeying to. He is Li Wen-Tao's boss.'

As he spoke, the man to whom he was referring turned to scan the crowd behind him. His cold gaze took us in too, stopping on my fine features for a chilling moment. Taitemir's face was hard and composed, his stony eyes outlined by crows' feet that radiated from their corners like the sun's rays. He was used to peering into the far distance at an enemy and scaring them with his look. I was glad I had decided not to get involved with him. He would have seen through me in an instant. Even now, I would have kept well clear of him, but Lin was bolder. He squared his slim shoulders and strode towards the Mongol overlord of the region. I reluctantly followed, with Gurbesu, Alberoni and Tadeusz close on my heels.

The crowd, impressed by Lin's red robe, parted, and we all sliced through the throng with ease. As Lin approached Taitemir, the Mongol deigned to give him a perfunctory look. Lin bowed low, and Taitemir's gaze focused on me. He screwed his eyes up as if assessing an enemy, though it may just have been in curiosity at the barbarian he observed before him. Then Lin's head bobbed back up, and I was spared being stripped to the bone by Taitemir's gaze. We made our way to a space on the second row and settled down to watch this phenomenon so new to us Westerners called a play. Lin spoke to a neighbouring member of the audience then turned to me.

'It is a new crime case play called the *Mo-Ho-Lo Doll*. Mo-Ho-Lo is an Indian demigod – a snake-headed demon – whom we Chin have made into a handsome youth with a serpent's head cap. Dolls of him are used on the festival held on the seventh day of the seventh month.'

Suddenly an acrobat sprang on stage and the tale began. Occasionally, Lin gave us a whispered running commentary at the expense of hisses from our neighbours. The story that began to unfold was one of a wicked apothecary who lusted after this man's wife. My pretty empress from earlier in the day played the part of the wife. The apothecary poisons her husband, and then when she refuses to marry him he denounces her to the court as the murderer. By now, I wasn't paying any attention to Lin's commentary as I was riveted by the pretty acrobat I had encountered earlier. She was willowy and alluring, and even I could follow the plot relating to her being accused of murdering her husband. I could see that the man who lusted after her had done the deed of course. And that he would accuse the woman when she refused his advances. Lin leaned closer to whisper in my ear and avoid Gurbesu hearing. He needn't have worried – she was entranced by the whole play and giving it her full attention.

'The person you wish to see is called Tien-jan Hsiu. It means Natural Elegance. Be at my rooms after the play finishes.'

I nodded my head, eager for the play to run its course. By

the end, the object of my lust had been exonerated and rewarded for her purity. I hoped the actress – I think that is the word I should use for these performers – was not quite as pure as the woman she portrayed on stage. With the play finished and the actors vigorously applauded, the crowd began to disperse. As we got up, I looked back to the stage to catch a sight of Natural Elegance, but all I could see as the burning torches dimmed was disappointing. The striking view to the rear of a Chinese mountain was now just a flat and pallid painted back-cloth with creases in it. I marvelled that I had been so taken in by it all. One of the male actors walked across the stage, his painted face now bare, and I could see his acne scars. He, who had a short time ago been an evil giant of a man, was no more than a skinny youth. I shrugged my shoulders and sighed. Gurbesu was at my side, so I took the opportunity to make my excuses.

'Darling, I must go and talk with Lin again.'

She stroked my cheek and pouted.

'But it's so late, Nick.'

For a moment I almost relented. But it was only a moment. Natural Elegance's suppleness came to mind again, and I tried out a miserable look on my face. I hoped it was as convincing as the actors' mugging had been.

'We will be on our way again tomorrow, and we have little time left to plan. One of the petitioners in our case is here, and we must speak with him. It is a shame, but duty calls.'

She gave me a funny look, and I thought I had overcooked it. But then she sighed and squeezed my hand.

'I will stay awake for your return. Just in case.'

I gave her a brave but sad smile, and we went our separate ways through the milling crowd.

# SIX

*One should be as careful in choosing one's pleasures as in avoiding calamities.*

Lin's rooms were lit by a few small lamps, creating pools of light and shade. Mainly shade. His servant, Po Ku, was nowhere in evidence, and peering into the gloom I could just make out the familiar figure of my friend reclining on a low bench. He had already divested himself of his formal robe and relaxed in his white silk shirt with a red sash around his waist. He raised a hand and beckoned me in.

'Zhong Kui, you look very demonic tonight. Did you like the play?'

I slumped on the bench opposite, loosening my own fur-trimmed Mongol jacket.

'What I could understand, yes. It was an interesting story of a murder that was not too far from our own case. A woman suspected of murdering her own husband, and incriminated by the real murderer. Is that what you expect to find when we get to P'ing-Yang-Fu?'

Lin gave a little high-pitched laugh. The brutal castration as a boy had left him with a light voice that he often masked by whispering. It gave him an air of mystery and self-control which was actually quite in keeping with his actions. When he spoke out loud, however, he piped rather childishly.

'I wondered if you would see the parallels. Maybe we have both learned something from this trifle of an entertainment.'

'Ah, yes. We should be looking for the spurned lover.' I paused and licked my lips. 'Talking of lovers . . .'

Lin smiled a strange enigmatic smile.

'Yes. It is all arranged. But first we must see Guan Han-Ching. He is the petitioner I told you about.'

'The scribbler of plays?'

A clear voice rang out from behind me, speaking in the Mongol tongue for my benefit.

'I may be a second-class citizen in Kubilai's empire, occupied in the lowliest of trades. But I would like to believe that I am the best at what I do, sir, and more than a scribbler.'

I turned round to look at the interloper. In the doorway stood a tall, well-built young man, probably in his twenties. He was clean shaven, and his hair was cut short, unlike Lin's and those of his class who wore a long queue hanging down their back. He affected the clothes of a peasant, wearing brown homespun with a green pattern to it. But I could see that the motif was woven in the cloth, not stencilled as a common man's would be. Under the coarse outer garment the edge of a silk shirt poked out. He also wore the leather boots of a scholar. He noticed the direction of my gaze, and shuffled his feet.

'I am a mere clerk in the Office of the Grand Physician. And, it seems, a scribbler of plays in my spare time.'

He may have thought to embarrass me by throwing my words describing him back at me. But it took more than that to cause me to blush. I smiled blandly and relaxed back on my cushions. There was an awkward pause until Lin waved his arm, indicating that Guan should come in. But the youth stood resolutely at the door.

'I will not disturb your august personages more than is necessary. I merely came as you bid me to announce myself and my intentions. I acted as scribe and fellow petitioner to Geng Wenbo.' A sardonic grin flitted across his lips. 'His own skills at writing and composing a suitably grovelling letter to Kubilai were limited. I was in the town when the case came before the prefect, and I saw the great injustice that was taking place. I could not stand back and let it happen.'

Lin broke into what was obviously a carefully considered speech.

'And you no doubt saw the situation would enhance your reputation, and would make an excellent *kung-an* play.'

Guan, to his credit, was not put off by Lin's deliberately rude interruption. A quiet smile played across his face.

'Indeed, Master Lin. You have me there. A great play for sure, that will stand as a beacon for the cause of justice for years to come.' He looked me in the eye. 'You believe in justice, do you not?'

I surprised myself with a reply that sounded deeply philosophical.

'Truth and justice are ephemeral creatures that can have different skins at different times, like the chameleon lizard I have seen sailors bring back from lands beyond the sea.'

Guan was nonplussed by my reply, and his prepared presentation was broken. He recovered himself enough to say that he would see us again in P'ing-Yang-Fu, and then bowed out in to the night. Lin laughed breathily, and patted me on the back.

'That was a very thoughtful retort of yours. And the simile was excellent. I have seen such a lizard, and the changing of their skin colour is remarkable.'

I blushed at the compliment and confessed the truth.

'I borrowed the idea from you, Chu-Tsai, as well you know. Though I confess the imagery was my own. I have been saving it up for just such a moment.'

Just as I finished speaking, I was conscious of another figure standing in the doorway. The well-built Guan had not returned, however, because framed by the moonlight, I could tell this was Natural Elegance. Her hips were slightly tilted and her shape curvy. My mouth went dry. Then she stepped into the room, and the light from one of the lamps fell on the figure's face. I gasped in shock. The luscious Empress Tu, the sweet Yu-Niang from the play, the lubricious Natural Elegance was a youth. A pretty, willowy youth, but a youth nevertheless. I turned to Lin and scowled.

'You knew.'

Lin had a big grin plastered on his face.

'Forgive me for deceiving you. It was so amusing seeing how you lusted for Tien-jan, when I knew all along that she was a he.' Suddenly his tone became severe. 'Besides, you should not have forsaken Gurbesu for a passing . . . amusement.'

For once I had to agree with him. Gurbesu's charms were

suddenly all the more attractive, when compared to those of young Tien-jan. I silently thanked the God that I was not sure I truly believed in for saving me from a grievous error, and beat a retreat from Lin's rooms.

Gurbesu was surprised but pleased when I burst into our room a few moments later.

'You are earlier than I thought, sweetheart.' She gave me a piercing look that I feared meant she had seen right through my subterfuge. 'I imagined you would be hours with Lin and his visitor, and then looking over all the documents in that case.'

I brazened it out and shrugged nonchalantly, as though we had solved the problem easily.

'It was not such a difficult matter, after all. And our interview with the playwright Guan, who drafted the petition, was brief. It would seem he is more interested in making a name for himself than chasing justice for Jianxu. Though like many young men he burns with the idea he sees injustice everywhere. He hails from that part of Cathay where fifty years ago the leaders went quickly over to the Mongol side to save their skins. They were called the Black Army according to Lin, and escaped relatively unscathed from the invasion. Maybe Guan feels guilty about his ancestry. Who knows?'

I unfastened my Mongol jacket and eased down on the low bed, reaching out to Gurbesu's hips.

'So now we have the whole evening to ourselves.'

As I felt the warmth of Gurbesu's thigh, I shuddered at the thought of touching Natural Elegance, and finding a male member between 'her' legs. I wiped the image from my mind, but as I grabbed her, Gurbesu's face fell.

'Oh I am sorry, dear. I thought, when you said that you would be hours that I would invite Tadeusz and the friar to our room. We are going to have a little supper. You are welcome to join us, naturally.'

Before I could protest, the door suddenly opened, and the aforesaid pair poked their heads in. Alberoni smiled broadly.

'Ah, Niccolò, you are here. I wanted to ask you about something before we got to our destination.'

I think I must have replied a little sulkily, because Alberoni gave me a strange look, and shook his head. Gurbesu, noticing the awkwardness, started bustling around, producing smoked meat and fresh fruit from somewhere. And a stone flagon of Chinee rice wine. Tadeusz was already laying on the table some dried fruit he had brought with him. He cast a glance at me too, before asking me about the details of the case.

'Will it be resolved easily, do you think?'

I shrugged. It seemed to be the only communication I was capable of at the moment. As we settled down together at the table, I looked out of the window and across the courtyard. In Lin's rooms I saw a shadowy figure embracing Lin tightly. Before the lamp in the room was extinguished, I felt sure the figure looked willowy and elegant. I returned my attention to the others in my room, but not before Tadeusz also had seen what I was looking at. I tried to concentrate on the matter in hand.

'Let's see what we do know.'

Tadeusz had placed an oil lamp in the centre of the table, and its flame cast a circle of light in which we all sat. To my right sat Gurbesu, who was biting into a peach. I watched as the juice ran down her chin. She smiled and wiped it away with delicate fingers. She then waved them in the air.

'Don't look at me for enlightenment. You have told me nothing so far. I feel that I am just along for the ride.'

I brushed aside her self-deprecating words. I knew how useful she would be when it came to talking to the main suspect – and presumed perpetrator – Jianxu. She could use her wiles on a man to get him to talk, but more importantly was able to extract the innermost thoughts from another woman. And truths often emerged from such a meeting of minds that would have been held back from me or the other men. I reckoned even Alberoni would benefit from her powers of truth-finding in his confessional. The friar was the next round the table, and I raised a questioning eyebrow towards him. He clasped his hands together.

'I did manage to talk to Lin on our way here. I understand that the poor girl confessed to the crime. What more is there to say?'

I gave a harsh and braying laugh.

'Do you know how they obtain a confession here? They use a bastinado, beating the soles of the person's feet until they cannot stand the pain any more. Then they confess.'

'Are you saying there is no place for torture in extracting the truth?'

I thought of all the ways a suspected person would be abused in the West – the rack, the head crusher, or thumbscrews – and shook my head.

'Not if you are a seeker of the truth. A confession is easily obtained – the truth needs winkling out. Taduesz, do you have any observations to make before we reach P'ing-Yang-Fu?'

The little man leaned away from the circle of light and stroked his beard. When he spoke from the darkness, it was with a quaver in his voice.

'Do you not think, Nick, that the girl has been deliberately placed in the picture to allow the real killer to escape free and clear? Are not Chinee girls very obedient sorts, who would go out of their way to please? How could she possibly be the killer?'

I nodded, agreeing with him as far as it went.

'You are right. There is something that stinks in this whole case. Not least the involvement of Ko Su-Tsung in its being brought to our attention. We will tread cautiously, but we will find out the truth.'

I marvelled at how, under Lin's tutelage, I had become so enamoured of the truth. Maybe such an obsession came with being in your thirties and no longer a youth. Before being appointed Investigator of Crimes by Kubilai Khan, I was more concerned with what gave me the most profit; whether it was within the law or not. In fact I much preferred sailing close to the wind, and then on beyond the boundaries of legality. It made for greater excitement and a lot more pleasure when the enterprise came off. I looked at Tadeusz, who had once more leaned forward into the lamplight. The side of his face burned in the fire set by marauding Mongols was red and shiny, but his eyes were cool and impassive. I slapped his back.

'Now pass me the wine before I start crying like a baby at my own softness.'

\*     \*     \*

The girl wiped a tear from her eye, and looked through the bars at the boy who stood outside.

'Thank you, Wenbo. You have saved my life. I owe you everything, and I will show you my gratitude when I am released.'

She accompanied the final sentence of her outpouring with a modest, but meaningful look. After all, it did not harm to promise, when the chances of having to repay that promise were so slim. Still, she had taken the first step, and the flow of *yun* was moving in the right direction. The boy had come with the news that very morning that an investigator had been appointed in Tatu, which some called Khan-balik, and that he was on his way. The executioner's sword had been stayed, and that was what mattered. It was no good to her if she were exonerated after her death. Some may think her soul would be saved, and her reputation restored. But what good was that to her if she was dead and buried?

The spotty face of Wenbo swam before her eyes, and she once again wiped away the tears of joy. She fixed a smile on her face, and glanced modestly down at the ground.

'I thank you, Geng Wenbo.'

The boy seemed transfixed, unclear as to what he should do next. He was already beginning to irritate the girl, and, without raising her eyes, she hinted that she would like to be alone now.

'My fate is still uncertain, and I wish to compose myself should the wheel of fortune not turn in my favour in the end.'

The boy stammered an apology for intruding on her contemplations and slouched away. She waited a moment and gave a cautious look up. He was walking down the unlucky road that led to her cell. When he was far enough away, she breathed a sigh of relief, and hugged herself. She hoped the next person she would see coming towards her cell along the road would be the investigator. In her mind, she began to marshal her thoughts. If he was as clever as she imagined, it would not do to get her story all mixed up. Let the others be tripped up by him, she would play her part well.

\*　　\*　　\*

'That play we saw made me think.'

As the light from the lamp got lower, we had moved closer to each other to stay in its beam. Alberoni rubbed his smooth jaw and yawned.

'I didn't follow all of it, as I couldn't hear Lin's explanation. What was it about the play that got you thinking?'

Gurbesu stared into my eyes with those big brown orbs of hers.

'Was it the wife, Yu-Niang, confessing under torture? Just like this case of ours?'

I shook my head.

'No. I liked that chief clerk, Chang Ting, best. He reminded me of myself.'

Tadeusz threw his head back and laughed. I wanted to know what he found so funny in what I said.

'I understand some Chinee, you know, and followed a few of the lines. The clerk said he hated those who – how did he put it? – who "fiddled the law."' He put a solemn look on his ruined face. 'How could he then have been like you?'

I took it that Tadeusz was teasing me about my fondness for skirting round the borders of legality, and wasn't seriously taking me to task. In fact, I was glad he seemed to be more relaxed, more like his normal self. He was usually such a quiet and uncritical man, but he had been more than a little edgy during our journey. I put it down to the strains of the long trip.

'I may flirt with what is unlawful, that is true. But no, it wasn't that I was thinking of. Chang Ting cracked the case of the Mo-Ho-Lo Doll by filling in the missing facts. Facts that had been ignored before. No one checked on the unidentified man who brought Yu-Niang news of her husband's illness. It was only when she remembered the doll that she could trace the doll-maker and he provided crucial information about the real murderer. Another witness was bribed to say Yu-Niang planned the murder with her lover. But when Chang Ting investigated, it turned out there was no lover. But, most importantly of all, no one had checked the source of the poison that killed Yu-Niang's husband.'

There was silence as everyone pondered my great exposition. I looked around expecting admiration, but all I saw were puzzled expressions.

'Damn it, don't you see? It's the same with this case. No one has followed up the mystery of the origins of the poison.' I turned to the little silversmith.

'Tadeusz, I want you to make that your job when we get there. You have some of the Chinee tongue as you have just reminded us, and can talk to the locals. But if you get stuck, you can always talk to Lin.'

He nodded, and looked down at the floor, embarrassed by everyone's attention suddenly being on him.

'What about the Mongol overlord – Taitemir?' This was Gurbesu's question. 'He looked a fierce fellow at the theatre, surrounded by all his cronies.'

A shiver ran down my spine.

'I would rather not get entangled with him, if I can help it.' Gurbesu would not leave it, however.

'But if some wrong has been done, he could be at the centre of it. You will have to talk to him along with the Chin prefect.'

I sighed, knowing that Gurbesu had a point, and that she would not give up, if she felt she was in the right. So I diverted her from her purpose by giving her a task I knew she would relish.

'You are right. Lin and I will have to deal with him, I suppose. And I want you to talk to the girl. Find out the truth from her.'

I stroked her hair, which, as she leaned into the light, hung like a curtain over her round, olive-skinned face. The others must have noticed my tender gesture towards Gurbesu, because both Tadeusz and Alberoni rose, and wished us goodnight. I recalled that when they had arrived, Alberoni had said he wanted to ask me something.

'What was it you wanted to know, Friar?'

There was a distant look in his eyes, and he shook his head.

'Oh, it will keep for another day, Niccolò.'

The two men discreetly left the room. The lamp flickered, went dim, and died. In the darkness, I felt Gurbesu squeeze my arm.

'Are you so very tired, Nick?'

I grinned, though I didn't imagine she could see me doing so.

'Not yet, my darling one. But I think I will be soon.'

# SEVEN

*One never needs their humour as much as when they argue with a fool.*

We completed the journey to P'ing-Yang-Fu in six more arduous days of travelling. Gurbesu and I could have got there in five, but the other riders, and Lin in his carriage, held us back. Alberoni complained of a persistent back ache, though I think he meant some spot lower than that. He certainly was a pain in the arse himself. The closer we got to our destination the more whining he got about it. The daily conversation went something like this.

'Will we be there soon?'

'I have told you. It is six/five/four more days yet . . .'

Taduesz was unusually silent, and just sat uncomplaining on his pony as it jogged along. Lin was his serene self, his nighttime encounter with Natural Elegance in T'ai-Yuan-Fu – if such it was – not being mentioned by me. But finally we crested a rise in the fertile meadowlands we had been passing through, and the city came into view. Beyond it rose the grey outline of far distant mountains, but Pianfu, as Lin called it, lay on a flat plain. From where we stood, I could see the grid-like pattern of streets and thoroughfares. The weather was cold but still dry, so a cloud of dust hung over the city. The curve of red-tiled roofs, like waves in a sea of ochre stretched for many *li*. The Chinee measure of distance was always unclear to me, but I reckoned on three *li* to make a league or a mile roughly. Let's just say that as I looked over the plain, I could barely see the other side of Pianfu.

We descended the hill and rode into the outskirts. Soon we were on a main thoroughfare, which must have been forty paces wide and ran through the heart of the city. Every half mile or so this broad road opened out into a square, around which stood large stone buildings. To my eye they looked like warehouses, and indeed most of the squares we passed through had a market of some sort. One sold game, and I could see stalls plentifully supplied with stags, harts, hares, and rabbits, and all sorts of fowl such as pheasants, francolins, quails and ducks and geese. Another square had all sorts of vegetables and fruits, strange to my eye, though I did recognize pears and peaches, and bags of raisins. The third square had stately buildings on all sides, but was quieter than the others. I thought it unusual, and trotted beside Lin's carriage to ask why. He gave me a dark look.

'If you come here after dark, you will see more activity.'

Stupidly, I still didn't know what the business of the square could have been.

'After dark?'

'These apartments you see are the residences of women of the town. In the evening you will see them parading attired in great magnificence, and attended by many handmaidens. It is said they are highly accomplished in the use of endearments and caresses to suit every sort of person. I am told some foreigners call it the Square of Heaven.'

I grinned, and cast a look around to see if any of the 'women of the town' as Lin euphemistically referred to them had risen from their beds. All windows were shuttered, however. Lin took the opportunity to remind me of our purpose here.

'You, of course, will be too busy to find your way here again.'

As we passed through the centre of this vast city, curious eyes turned our way just as in T'ai-Yuan-Fu. My beard was quite luxuriant now, and I could not have looked more like the images of the demon Zhong Kui. A few of the people in the garb of labourer or peasant made a sign with their fingers, probably to ward off the evil emanating from my presence. The more prosperous, and so less superstitious, reserved their discreet glances for Lin Chu-Tsai. They could see our little procession heralded the arrival of an important official. Once again he was in his official court robes, and it was obvious he was a man of consequence. As if to further emphasize his importance, Lin clicked his fingers at a passing man. His fine embroidered robe suggested he was a prosperous merchant, but he still hurried over to Lin's carriage and bowed low.

'What does your honour wish to know?'

'Tell me where the house of the prefect is located. This little town stinks, and I would prefer not to dally in it too long.'

I stared with astonishment at Lin. His peremptory tone and denigrating words were quite unlike the man; especially as the city was so startling in all its aspects. But he ignored my querulous look, and fixed the other Chinee with his cool gaze. The man blushed.

'I am sorry our hamlet displeases you, your honour. You are correct though; the place smells of unwashed bodies and old meat. But what can poor people like us do? I am sure the prefect will ensure your stay is as pleasant and as brief as possible.'

He raised an arm, covered down to the fingertips in a silken sleeve, and pointed in the direction we were already travelling.

'The prefect's house is on the southern edge of town, close to the river. It is a fine house with a red tiled and prettily gabled roof. You cannot miss it.'

Lin waved a desultory hand, also hidden in his opulent sleeve, and the humiliated merchant scurried away. Po Ku urged the carriage horse on, and we proceeded along the wide but bustling avenue. I rode my horse close up beside Lin's carriage again, and glanced his way.

'I have never heard you be so authoritarian, Chu-Tsai. It was quite a revelation.'

I could see a blush forming on Lin's neck, and he sighed.

'You have only seen me in either the summer or winter capital until now. There is no need to assert my authority where I am already known. If I was not respected for my very position at the court of Kubilai, I would not be able to do my job. This may be a big city, but it is still in the provinces – the back of beyond as far as such high officials as we are concerned. And if I do not make myself known immediately as someone who will not stand any nonsense, I might as well sneak back north. Or kill myself.'

He nodded back down the avenue to where the merchant was already in a huddle with several other well-dressed individuals. They were staring in our direction.

'The story is already spreading that someone of importance is in town, and that he is not impressed by the show of wealth that is so evident to the locals. I will be well respected, and many will try to find out about me and my entourage. It should help our enquiries, don't you think?'

I laughed at Lin's ingenuity, and pulled a ferocious face.

'Especially if the rumour includes the fact that Zhong Kui is on their tail.'

We made our way through the suburbs of Pianfu, and in the final square we passed on the way a large building with a familiar smell to it. I spurred my horse towards a set of large doors that stood partially open. Inside I could see stacks of wooden barrels, and at the back of the shed large copper urns. The smell was unmistakeably that of a winery. I licked my lips, and urged the horse back level with Lin's carriage.

'Perhaps you can arrange for the winery we just passed to provide some of its produce to the great and important official from Tatu.'

Lin gave me a hard look.

'You should not risk getting drunk before you have solved this case. We require our wits about us. Besides, you do your-self a disservice to imagine only I can command the respect of the local dignitaries. Me a mere human and all. You are the great and mysterious demon appointed by Kubilai as his Investigator of Crimes. They will hold you in awe and fear. Your *paizah* will be enough to see you drowned in free wine.'

He was referring to the small gold tablet that both he and I held as a badge of authority from the Great Khan. I touched the front of my jacket, and felt the tablet nestling inside it. It was about fifteen inches long and five fingers wide, with a hole at the top end. Mine and Lin's had a lion's head stamped on it, which made us more important than a commander of the Mongol army, but less so than one of Kubilai's great barons. Their *paizah* had a gerfalcon on it. All tablets were printed with an inscription which read as follows – '*By the strength of the great God, and of the great grace which He hath accorded to our Emperor, may the name of the Khan be blessed; and let all such as will not obey him be slain and be destroyed.*' It was a very useful weapon in an empire ruled by bureaucracy.

I turned the head of my horse back towards the winery, and told Lin I would find the prefect's house on my own.

When I did find the house, I could see why Li Wen-Tao chose to live where he did. The noise and bustle of the city – the cries of the pedlars and shopkeepers, the curses of the draymen and porters as they barged their way past fortune-tellers, scholars and monks blocking their way, and the warning call of the men bearing ladies in sedan chairs – all was but a distant hum. A stand of trees masked the grand-looking house from the stare of the common crowd, and the river behind it lent an air of tranquillity. I jumped from my horse and handed the reins to a fearful servant, who cowered at the sight of my whiskery face. I gave him a snarl for good measure, and stomped towards the elegant main doors. The prefect had indulged himself by having imperial dragons carved on the doors. He would have been severely punished for such presumption in the capital. Here, out in the sticks, he could get away with it. I slid the doors back and barged in, keeping to my role of demon and personal investigator to the Khan.

In the main room of the house, a fat, middle-aged man sat like a Buddha at a table in the centre of the room. By his side sat Lin Chu-Tsai, whereas Friar Alberoni and Tadeusz Pyka had to content themselves with sitting at some distance in the furthest corner of the room. Of Gurbesu there was no evidence. The fat man gazed at me, a look of indignation forming on his face. He was pulling his embroidered robe around him, and I could see that each side of the skirt had a *bai*, or panel, sewn in it to add to the bulk and his importance. He didn't really need it as he was as broad as a horse's backside anyway. The robe was blue to signify his rank. I was pleased to let him see that my Mongol jacket was red, as was Lin's official robe. We outranked him and he knew it. I marched over to the table and slumped to the ground in a deliberately inelegant manner. I saw the flush of contained anger in Li's face, as I rudely reached for the porcelain jar of rice wine that stood on the table between us. Politeness and etiquette dictated that I should have waited to be offered a drink. But I was past caring about this fat prefect, and I wanted to get him flustered before

I interrogated him about Jianxu. Lin, I could see out of the corner of my eyes, had a knowing smile on his face. He patted the ruffled prefect's arm.

'Forgive the Investigator of Crimes, he is a barbarian. We are trying to train him, but he will use his own . . .' He paused tellingly. '. . . brutal ways to find out the truth.'

The disconcerted prefect's fat, jowly face fell, and his red flush turned white with fear. He managed to gasp out a few words from his now dry mouth.

'I am sure you will see that everything here is in order. And I will cooperate fully with you.'

I smiled coldly, knowing I might have his attention now, but that he would soon recover his composure. Then he would try to find ways of wheedling his way back into Lin's favour. I would need other ways of dealing with him then. For now, I would enjoy his rice wine. I gulped the fiery fluid down, and dreamed of the wine I had commanded to be sent to our quarters. Even though I didn't yet know where we were to be staying, I could lay a bet that the owner of the winery did. And the whole of the rest of Pianfu too.

The harassed servant scurried across the courtyard in the old quarter of Yenking. He was nearly bowled over by a group of eight court officials kicking a ball. This solemn pastime was called 'Eight Immortals Crossing the Sea', and involved skilful passing and ball control rather than tackling and scoring. It was often impossible for the outsider to understand who was winning therefore. The servant cared only that he was not knocked down or delayed from delivering what he held in his hand. His master – Ko Su-Tsung – was waiting anxiously for the message. As Head of the Censorate, Ko could have chosen to be in the building site that was Kubilai's new inner sanctum. But he was a fastidious man, and could not bear the thought of his robes and shoes being muddied. It was enough that he was borne into the Great Khan's presence every day in a sedan chair that at least spared his clothing. Besides, his spies could come and go in the old city without being observed. Kubilai's government was made up of three large bureaux – the Secretariat was responsible for all civil matters, the Privy

Council for all military matters, but the Censorate was responsible for ritual, and spied on *all* government officials alike.

The servant, who had just negotiated the elegantly robed men playing football, lived in fear of his master. It was said Ko Su-Tsung had a file on everyone, no matter how lowly, and that therefore he could twist everyone to his own ends. The humble servant didn't know if that was the truth, and he didn't want to find out the hard way. He reached the inner room where Ko habitually spent his days like a spider in the centre of a web, and coughed discreetly to announce his presence. His master's sharp, impatient voice called him into the room. The servant silently glided in, holding out the paper he had taken from the sweating horseman moments earlier. He briefly raised his eyes to glance at his master. Ko was tall and cadaverous. If he was a spider in his web, he didn't seem to gain much sustenance from the titbits that regularly came his way. His face was a skull with dry parchment-like skin pulled over it. His eyes were deep-set, and black as coals, though they still somehow burned with the ferocity of that marvellous stone. The servant dropped his gaze from Ko's piercing stare. He had long ago conceived the thought that his master had long ago actually died, but that Ko was so frightening that no one, not even the Devil himself, had had the nerve to tell him so. He was therefore more than happy to be summarily dismissed from Ko's presence.

Ko Su-Tsung opened the message and began to read. It told him that Lin Chu-Tsai and his entourage had left T'ai-Yuan-Fu and were almost at their destination. In his mind he calculated the time taken for the letter to arrive. The Mongol postal system – the Yam – was remarkably efficient with horse-riders changing their mount every twenty-five miles. They were thus able to cover one hundred and twenty-five miles in a day. So Lin would even now be in P'ing-Yang-Fu. He returned to the message contained in the letter. Aside from some dull factual information, it also told him of a possible sexual liaison between Lin and a young male actor. Ko licked his lips at the morsel. The suggestion of forbidden lascivious behaviour on the part of his old adversary would be a strong bargaining tool in the future. It might even serve to bring Lin down. Ko's spy was doing well. And though Lin and that barbarian assistant of his had not yet become embroiled in the vexing case of the Chin girl, his lines of communication were opened.

He lifted his writing instrument and began to compose a reply to the letter. His instructions included a command to make use of the sexual misconduct outlined by the spy in a way that would smear Lin's reputation. In two or three days Ko knew his instructions would be in the hands of the spy, and Lin's mission would be all the more impossible. And it had been an undertaking that was fraught with dangers in the first place. The girl's execution, confirmed by the regional Mongol governor, had been delayed by the apparent interference of Lin Chu-Tsai. Whatever the outcome, Lin's standing would be undermined. Ko finished the letter and called for his servant. He was so pleased with himself that, for once, his thin, cadaverous face split into what passed for him as a smile. To his petrified servant it was the death-grin of a skull.

# EIGHT

*Govern a family as you would cook a small fish – very gently.*

The girl was unaware that she was, albeit obliquely, in the thoughts of someone so highly positioned at the court of Kubilai Khan, so many *li* away. It was enough that she now knew the Investigator of Crimes was in Pianfu. Wenbo had come scurrying along the unlucky road that very morning. He bore the news that a delegation had arrived the previous afternoon, led by a most important official dressed in a red *pao* robe. He was accompanied by foreigners – a small monkey of a man with a burned face, a tall, black-garbed, ugly man who must be a Western priest, and a woman who looked as though she came from the Kungurat. Then the boy looked at Jianxu with a mixture of fear and awe on his face.

'And the official had his own personal demon with him.'

Jianxu could barely restrain her laughter. She didn't believe in ghouls and demons – not completely anyway. Wenbo saw her look of scorn, and frowned.

'It's true. He had hair and a beard made of fire, and a big nose just like Zhong Kui.'

Even Jianxu shivered a little at the mention of the demon hunter of lesser demons. But then, what did she have to fear from Zhong Kui? He would find her innocent of any crime, wouldn't he? She had sent the boy away, and huddled all day in the corner of her little cell puzzling over the meaning of what Wenbo had told her. With the onset of the cold of the night, she slept fitfully.

But in the cold light of day, on a frosty morning that heralded an early beginning of winter, she felt more confident. There were no such things as demons, and that stupid boy was just teasing. Stretching her stiff limbs, she scooped up the cold rice the gaoler had left on the shelf inside the cell door, and forced herself to

eat. Her stomach rebelled, and she had a griping feeling of
anxiety at the impending arrival of the investigator. But she
swallowed and kept the meagre allowance of food down.
She would face the investigator with confidence and convince
him of her innocence. Moving to stand at the grille set in her
cell door, she began her vigil.

I must say that I rose at a leisurely pace that morning. A
pace dictated by the cold outside the house we occupied, and
the warmth of the bed I shared with Gurbesu. I had awoken
to her coiled around me, her bare breasts pressed into my
naked back. She was asleep, and snored lightly in a most
pleasant way, her hot breath coming at regular intervals to
warm my spine. I stretched an arm out of the coverings
to reach for the cup of wine I had left by the bed the night
before. But in the night it must have been knocked over, for
it was on its side and its remaining contents were spilled on
the tiled floor. I cursed quietly and began to ease my body
out of Gurbesu's clutches.

When we had been brought to the house where we were to
stay last night, prominently stacked in the courtyard at the
centre of the large and well-appointed building were several
barrels. I could see that I had been right. The winery where I
had waved my badge of office and demanded their wares knew
exactly where we were staying. The barrels of wine had been
delivered while we were still in conference with the prefect,
and Gurbesu had supervised their storage. The reason she had
not been at the prefect's house, apparently, was that Li
had protested at a woman being present at the interview. Before
Lin could object on her behalf, she had stormed out, and
demanded to be shown where we were staying. When we
finally turned up, she muttered darkly about the place of a
woman and how she had tidied up in preparation for the arrival
of her betters. I knew better than to try and placate her in this
sort of mood, only feeling sorry for Li, who had made an
implacable enemy.

With nothing else to do that evening, it was not long before
I had cracked open one of the wine barrels and tested the
contents. The wine was a little delicate for my palate, it being

more used to the robust, raw power of a good Rhenish. But I decided it would most definitely do. We had little to do other than settle in, and I had soon retired to one of the inner rooms with Gurbesu. I had already been the worse for wear, but not so much that I could not play my part in the bedchamber. The trouble was that suddenly I couldn't get Cat out of my mind.

I had left Caterina Dolfin behind six years ago when I got into that trouble in Venice, and only later gathered that she must have been pregnant with my child at the time. It had been Gurbesu who had read the signs when I described how strange Cat had been before I fled the Signori de Notte – the strong-arm men of the Doge. Of course, I had no way of knowing if it was true that she had been pregnant, but over the last few months I had begun to build an image of a sturdy little red-headed boy. He was perhaps five years old now, and was walking and talking. And probably already charming the girls like his father could. The thoughts drove me mad, as I wasn't going to be there to see him grow up. I had only my imagination to depend on. On the other hand, I have to admit I would probably be a terrible father, indulging the boy and turning him into an unholy terror. Just like I had been as a child, except my relationship with my father hadn't been one of doting parent and indulged child. Far from it – Agostino Zuliani had been a bastard.

Still sitting on the side of the low pallet that was our bed in the Pianfu house, I turned to pick up my discarded clothes. I knocked over the silver cup I had just righted, and it made a clattering sound on the tiles. Gurbesu stirred, and reached out for me. I wasn't there, because I was hopping on one leg already, trying to pull on my Mongol-style breeches. I cursed again, and Gurbesu opened her big, brown eyes, casting a lazy look in my direction.

'What's got you all riled, Nick?'

'The ghost of my damn father, breathing down my neck again. And these breeches. I always seem to get both legs in the same side.'

After a struggle, I finally got both my legs into separate legs of the breeches, and not both into one. Last night's wine consumption had clearly left my brain somewhat fuddled.

I hoped my undershirt would not be as recalcitrant. I could not bear it if Gurbesu laughed at me in my present agitated state. I did get entangled in a sleeve that was inside out, but to give her her due, Gurbesu simply tilted her head up cupping her chin on her palms. Her supporting arms barely hid the heavy downward pull of her full breasts. She sighed, reaching up to pull the sleeve the right way out, freeing my captive arm.

'This must mean you are thinking about your own child again. And Kat-Erina.'

She had a funny way of saying my lost love's name that always got me going.

'No I am not. What makes you think that?'

'Because you only think of your father when you are thinking of being a father. And why are you so angry at your father, anyway?'

'Because he was a bastard. He hated me and my mother. But he got his comeuppance in the end.'

'What happened to him?'

'My mother killed him.'


Jianxu's vigil eventually paid off. Long after the sun was high in the sky and had thawed the earth, she saw two people walking down the unlucky road towards her cell. Their outlines were unfamiliar to her, even though she couldn't quite make them out at first. She knew the gait of her gaoler, an old man with bandy legs, and the scurrying lope of Wenbo. No one else came to her cell. These two people were upright, and strode boldly along. She could see that one wore red, and assumed that was the Investigator of Crimes, who had come all the way from Tatu. But as they got nearer, she realized that the one in red was a woman. She was dressed in a close-fitting jacket with a skirt that trailed on the ground lifting the dust. The taller figure was that of a man, and he was dressed like a Mongol overlord in a gaudy long jacket trimmed with fur. From beneath it poked out blue breeches, and his feet were clad in thick leather boots. But it was his face that was most astonishing.

It seemed Wenbo had been right. Despite his clothing, the man was clearly not a Mongol for his skin was of a different colour, being pale under the tan of someone who led an outdoor life. And his long, sharp nose was bigger than a Chin's nose. But it was his hair that defined him. His ginger beard covered the lower half of his face, and, as the wind picked up, the hair on his head flew around him like flames. Truly, the demon-queller lived, and was coming to Jianxu's door. She backed away slightly, unsure what to expect, at the same time disappointed that the investigator had not come himself, but had sent only his tame demon.

I had agreed that morning with Lin that I would speak to the girl and that he would talk further with Li Wen-Tao, the prefect. He had found out from the papers that Jianxu was educated and spoke passable Mongol. If her knowledge of the language was no worse than mine, we would get along fine. Lin suggested I take Gurbesu with me, as Jianxu may feel more at ease with another woman present. I said I had intended to do that anyway.

'Gurbesu can wheedle information out of women in private that I couldn't get out of them with torture.'

Lin smiled in that funny way of his.

'I thought you didn't approve of torture.'

'I don't, that's why I use Gurbesu. Or sometimes the good friar. It's amazing what people will say to a priest thinking he will not divulge their secrets. Though I can't think of any use for Alberoni at the moment. Which is just as well, as he seems to be preoccupied with thoughts of his own. He wanted to speak to me the other day, but then shied away from telling me what it was he wanted. Oh well, I suppose he will tell me eventually. Anyway, Tadeusz does have his orders. He has suggested that he goes round the workshops and talks to the traders – other silversmiths and the like – and sees what is known about the murder case. We have official documents coming out of our ar—' I held back on the coarse expression, knowing how it pained Lin. Instead I indicated the pile of papers at his elbow. 'Out of our ears. But we don't know the gossip. Gossip will tell us far more than all these reams of court paperwork put together.'

Lin nodded, and stood up, straightening his long sleeves so they hung once more over his fingers.

'Let's get on, then. The sooner we know everything the better equipped we will be to extricate ourselves from this mess.'

I was puzzled for a moment as to what Lin meant, until I realized that he was referring to having been sent by Ko Su-Tsung to investigate a case that had already been judged by Li, the prefect, and his Mongol overlord. I shrugged my shoulders.

'I am still not worrying about that. Let's see what's what, and then decide how we can avoid the pit gaping at our feet.'

Lin patted my arm.

'I wish I had your confidence, Nick. But good luck, anyway.' He led me to the door. 'Oh, by the way, I hear that the acting troupe is arriving here tomorrow, and Guan the playwright is with them. At least we will be able to see some entertainment to take our minds off the matter.'

I thought there was a gleam in Lin's eyes at the thought of the players being in Pianfu. Maybe he was imagining the supple charms of Natural Elegance. I certainly wasn't. I went to get Gurbesu, and we started down the road that we were told led to the prison where Jianxu was held.

As we approached it, I could see the prison was a depressing place, as I guess they are supposed to be the world over. It was a long, low building at the end of a dirty, packed-earth road on the furthest edge of town. There were half a dozen doors arranged along the side facing the road, and we could smell the odour of unwashed bodies and human despair as we got close. A grille was set at head height in each door, but the only one that showed evidence of a prisoner in residence was the end one. A pale, round face looked out of the interior gloom, only pulling back when we got close enough to begin to discern its features. Before she had stepped back, I had seen that they were those of a young, attractive woman.

As I knew Jianxu was a woman of only twenty years of age, despite already being a widow, I assumed the pale face had been hers. As we got closer, a short, bandy-legged Chinee appeared from behind the cells, and scurried over. He bowed low, grinning like some tame but fearful monkey. Knowing he would not speak a Latin tongue, or Turkish or even Mongol,

I confined our conversation to the name of the person we were coming to see.

'Jianxu.'

He hissed, and displayed his versatility by bowing and scurrying over to the end door at the same time. He motioned us over and bowed yet again, muttering something in his Chinee tongue. I looked pointedly at the bunch of keys hanging from his belt. In my most communicative way I nodded, and turned my gaze on the cell door. Bandy legs nodded eagerly back and grinned. Obviously my language skills were not working well. Then Gurbesu nudged me in the back and whispered in my ear.

'He wants an emolument, you idiot.'

I frowned, and then enlightenment came.

'Oh, a bribe, you mean.'

I produced a small coin from the purse at my waist, waving it in the air. Amazingly, my ability to communicate suddenly improved. The gaoler grabbed the coin, and inserted a large key in the lock of the cell door. Peering through the grille to make sure the prisoner was not going to rush out, he pushed the door inwards. Before he went in himself, he grabbed a large plank that stood against the outside wall of the cell block. It was split in half, hinged, and had a hole in the middle of it. I realized what it was, having seen petty thieves in Xanadu being punished using it. It was a cangue, which the Chinee called *mu jia*, and was a sort of large, flat collar that prevented the wearer from escaping simply by its bulk. Sometimes, it was used as a means of punishment in itself. The offender wearing it could not reach round to feed himself, and so starved unless others fed him. The gaoler was clearly proposing to put it on Jianxu to prevent her fleeing. I grabbed his arm, and wrenched the device from his grasp.

'You will not put that on her. I am the Investigator of Crimes, appointed by the Great Khan himself, and I will say what happens here.'

I spoke in Mongol, and didn't think he understood a word. But he heard the tone of my voice, and could see the anger and authority in my eyes. Hissing apologies, he backed off, and retreated to a leafless tree that was the only thing that alleviated the drab monotony of the approach to the prison. He sat cross-legged under it and stared back at me. He was not going to desert his post, even if it was Zhong Kui who had chased him off. I tried to outstare him, until a pleasant, light voice spoke from inside the opened cell door.

'Then you are the Investigator of Crimes himself, and not the tame demon of the red robed one.'

I laughed, and looked round. A willowy girl, dressed in a drab shift that did not hide her shapely figure, stood in the doorway of the cell. Her face was pale and drawn, but she faced me boldly, not overawed by my presence. Jianxu was a very attractive young woman indeed.

'Oh, I am both of those things in one body. The Khan's investigator, yes. But also the tame servant of Lin Chu-Tsai, Senior Clerk to the Chief Justice of the Mongol Empire.'

Gurbesu nudged me aside, and spoke to Jianxu herself.

'Oh, he does like to boast. Just like a man.' She gave me a look, and I realized I was probably scaring the girl. Gurbesu carried on smoothly. 'You were right the first time – he's Lin's tame monkey really.'

Jianxu's face remained impassive for a moment, but then she giggled briefly. She was probably amused for the first time since she was accused and judged to be the murderer of Geng Biao. I knew it was time to retreat and leave Gurbesu to do what she did best.

# NINE

*Judge not the horse by his saddle.*

I sat in the shade of the shattered tree next to the gaoler while Gurbesu talked to Jianxu. They had the best of it, sitting comfortably inside the cell. The tree had few branches on it, and fewer leaves, and the bandy-legged Chinee had claimed whatever shadow was cast by them. The ground was hard beneath my arse. When it began to get numb, I tried a few simple Mongol words with the nameless gaoler, and finally he got the idea. He listened with his head cocked to one side like a dog, as I said a word such as 'head' and pointed to the appropriate part of my anatomy. When he had understood what I had said, he told me the Chinee word in return. At first he laughed through broken and blackened teeth when I essayed the pronunciation, but I got it eventually. Then we moved on to another body part. Eventually, I decided I could surprise Lin with my command of his language when we met later that evening. I just hoped the gaoler hadn't taught me obscenities. Lin was a man of refined tastes.

Finally, both women came to the cell door, and my language teacher jumped up, ready to chase Jianxu if she decided to make a run for it. But she didn't. In fact she looked very relaxed for someone whose execution had only been delayed. If I could find no fault with the judgement passed down by Li Wen-Tao, and confirmed by Taitemir, she would still be beheaded. And a beautiful head it was too, with thick, black hair braided and hanging down her back, and a pale face with exquisite almond eyes. She stared at me as Gurbesu crossed the courtyard towards me, and I smiled. And even though her face remained impassive, I suddenly wanted with all my heart for her to be innocent. Gurbesu saw where I was looking, and stood in my line of vision.

'Do you want to know what I learned from Jianxu? Or does it not matter any more?'

I grinned inanely at her.

'Of course. Tell me everything.'

'She says that she doesn't know how the soup that killed Old Geng was poisoned. She admits to making it, but not with the aim of killing Geng. In fact, she says she made the soup for her mother-in-law, Madam Gao.'

'So she intended to kill *her*?'

Gurbesu snorted and shook her head.

'No! Do pay attention, Nick. She made the soup because Madam Gao felt unwell. It was a broth to nourish and revive her spirits, as she hadn't eaten for two days. Old Geng saw her taking it to Madam Gao, and told her to give it to him. He was hungry, he said. She was annoyed, but couldn't show it, and obediently gave Geng the soup. She went back to the kitchen to make some more, and the next thing she knew, the boy . . .'

'Wenbo.'

'Yes, Wenbo came into the kitchen saying his father was dying. That he was complaining of cramps and numbness at the same time, and was vomiting. Wenbo said his father had tried to rise from his bed but his limbs wouldn't move. He begged Jianxu to come and help. When they got to the old man's room, he was lying in a foul pool of his own internal fluids. He was already dead.'

'That ties up with the doctor's report on the body. I saw it in Lin's files on the case. It said that, from the symptoms observed, aconite or wolfsbane must have been added to the soup. If so, it would have been an unpleasant death.'

I could see over Gurbesu's shoulder that Jianxu still stood in the doorway of her cell. She had not moved a muscle as Gurbesu and I had been speaking, and I had the feeling she was a person very much in control of her emotions. In fact, she made me feel uneasy for a moment. Taking Gurbesu's arm, I led her a little way away from the prison. When I no longer felt we were being observed, I looked Gurbesu in the eye.

'If she claims to be innocent, did she say why she signed a confession?'

Gurbesu nodded, her thick, dark hair swirling round her face.

'Yes. She did it to spare Madam Gao being tortured as she, Jianxu, had been by the prefect. Her feet and legs are only just now healing.'

'You see what I mean about torture? It rarely provides you with the truth. So the girl claims not to be the poisoner now. Does she have any idea who might have been? Who could have got in the kitchen to doctor the soup?'

Gurbesu pulled a face.

'She wouldn't say, but I thought she had an opinion. You know what these Chinee women are like. True to the Three Duties of women: obedience to your father before marriage; obedience to your husband after marriage; and obedience to your son after your husband's death. Obedience, obedience, obedience, grrrrrr.'

Gurbesu growled, and if I hadn't been already leaning with my back against the tree trunk, I would have backed off. She was a tiger in this sort of mood. Instead of retreating, I asked her another question.

'Do you believe everything she told you?'

She had to pause and think about that. We watched as the gaoler closed and locked the cell door on Jianxu, leaving her as a pale face outlined by the grille. Finally, she answered me.

'I think so.'

'But you are not sure?'

'Everything she said was so precise and considered. As though she had rehearsed it.'

I shrugged.

'Not surprising. She has been taken through the story many times, and often under duress with her feet tied up and being beaten. She would have ended up telling the prefect anything he wanted to hear. He could even have prompted her. And since being incarcerated to await our arrival, she has had weeks to think about what she would say.' I paused before asking the final question. 'Is she innocent?'

Once again, my favourite Kungurat pondered the question. She pursed her full, red lips.

'Mmmmm. Too early to tell. I am going to reserve judgement.'

That was one split vote, then. And I respected Gurbesu's intuition. But anyway, she was right. It was early days, and we needed to gather a whole lot more information. I took Gurbesu's arm, and we walked away from the prison.

'Let's go back to the house, and see what Lin and Tadeusz have found out.'

The girl watched from behind the door of her cell, which had once again been locked securely. She watched as the red-haired man and the strange woman walked away. She had never experienced such an odd pair. The demon looked as though he would scare anyone into submission, but the dark-skinned woman had brushed him aside as if he didn't matter. He had then sat with her gaoler while the woman spoke to her. The girl had assumed the woman was the demon's wife, though she didn't behave like any Chin wife. They had spoken at first in her native tongue, but mostly they had conversed in the tongue of the Mongols who had conquered her native land many years ago. The true emperor still lived, somewhere in southern Song, but the Mongols were pressing ever southwards. It was inevitable that the barbarian hordes would win, and she had picked up as much of their tongue as she was able. It had now served her well.

The woman had probed for the facts of the death of Old Geng, and she had told her story well, she thought. She felt she had convinced the Kungurat of her innocence. When the woman, who called herself Gurbesu, had asked if she had any idea who had killed the old man, she had hesitated. Just like a good, obedient woman, she had demurred, not accusing anyone directly. But she thought she had convinced Gurbesu that she did suspect someone. So she knew the demon and his wife would be back.

'Li Wen-Tao could tell me nothing that was not in the official records already. I could tell he was toeing the party line. He even had the nerve to refer me to Taitemir, knowing of course that even a Chin official as highly connected as I am could not contradict a Mongol. It was a waste of my time. How about the girl?'

We had met up over a meal in Lin's rooms, which were, as usual, far better organized than any of ours. Mind you, he had a servant, and I would have expected nothing less of Lin. He always surrounded himself with serenity, whereas I thrived on chaos. We complemented each other in that way. Before I answered his question, I looked at Gurbesu. Did she want to voice her opinions directly? She gave a little shake of her head, which left me, as ever, in her debt. She knew I needed to maintain my position as the main investigator, even amongst our little group. So it was I who replied to Lin's question.

'She did no more than confirm what was in the documents we already have. Her story has not changed. So there is nothing new yet. But it is only the beginning. We need to talk to the son and the old lady . . . what's her name?'

'Madam Gao.'

'Yes, we need to speak to her. And maybe I can have a go at the prefect myself.' I grinned wolfishly. 'I can be a mite rougher than you, Chu-Tsai. Besides, I want to appeal to his baser instincts.'

Lin frowned a little, though his face was normally impassive and didn't show too much about his inner workings.

'What have you in mind, Nick?'

'It is better that you don't know. Then you can keep your hands clean.'

Lin settled back on his couch, looking somewhat out of sorts, and I took charge of the meeting. I looked over at Tadeusz, who had been very quiet during my exchanges with Lin.

'What about you, Tadeusz. Did you learn anything in the marketplace?'

Tadeusz Pyka tugged at his beard, and seemed not sure where to begin. Finally he put into words what he had learned by chatting to the tradesmen he had met.

'I wandered around a few of those big squares we came through when we arrived. I reckoned that one of them had to accommodate workshops. I found the one for doctors and astrologers first. They teach reading and writing there too, you know. I saw a local magistrate settling an argument between two doctors who, from what I could tell, were disputing the efficacy of something called *dang gui*.'

Lin nodded his head.

'Yes. It's also called female ginseng, and I believe it's used for all sorts of women's complaints.'

'The argument seemed to be about whether it should be boiled or steeped in wine.'

Gurbesu laughed.

'I would prefer the last method.'

'The magistrate resolved the matter, but by then the client – an older woman – had walked away. So neither doctor gained from arguing. Anyway, the next square I came to was the craft square. They say there were twelve guilds represented, and each workshop employed up to forty men. It was certainly a busy and bustling square, and I could see some men had got quite wealthy from the trade. I went to the silversmiths' quarter – you can always find it by the sound.'

I knew what he meant. The tap-tap of small hammers on silver plates is a distinctive noise, like the sound of tiny bells.

'They were all Chinee, and reluctant to talk at first. But when I spoke about their techniques, and showed them that I was one of their guild, some of them spoke freely. Working in the trade, they knew some Turkish and we got on fine. They wanted to know about Xanadu and Tatu, and what it was like working for the Great Khan. I confess that, as I looked around at all the industry of these men, I was suddenly missing my own workshop and my tools.'

Pyka looked fondly off into the distance, no doubt thinking of a time when he was a silversmith in Breslau and had a wife and children. I had never known him so homesick – it was over twenty-five years since the Mongols had swept through his town like avenging angels. I had thought he was over the tragedy. He suddenly focused on me and looked crestfallen.

'Sorry.'

I patted him on the shoulder encouragingly. I just prayed he wasn't going to cry on mine. I was not good with women and emotions, but of necessity coped – with other men and emotions I was hopeless. He drew a breath, however, and carried on.

'When I got a chance I asked them about Pianfu, and how the Mongols had affected trade. They were a mixed bunch, and some said things had picked up recently, that they were far enough away from the capital not to be bothered too much with the bureaucracy. Others quietly complained that the lord of the region wanted the finest work but didn't want to pay for it. But they wouldn't raise their voices in complaint too loud in case Taitemir got to hear. But one old man said bitterly that local officials collaborated too much with the Mongols. He mentioned the prefect specifically, and the case of Jianxu. There were some mutterings, but I believe everyone thought the case badly handled and the judgement harsh. Apparently Old Geng Biao, the murdered man, did lots of business with Taitemir's people. And it is said they owed him money, leaving Old Geng short of funds.'

My ears pricked up at this revelation.

'Did they owe enough for them to want him dead?'

Tadeusz pulled a face, though only one side responded. The burned left side of his face was tight and expressionless. It gave him a lopsided look, but he was used to the stares of others by now.

'I am not so sure of that. The Mongols don't care whether they pay for the goods they receive or not. Why should they then go out of their way to kill one of the many to whom they owe money?'

In a way I was relieved that Pyka thought that way. I was reluctant to investigate Taitemir and his cronies too closely. But the time might come when we had to. I stored Pyka's nugget of information in my brain, and reached for my cup of wine. Friar Albcroni coughed gently. I had not asked him for a contribution to our debate because I did not think that he had anything to offer. But maybe he had found out something.

'Friar, is there something you wish to add?'

Alberoni studied the ground at his feet closely, and pursed his lips.

'Not exactly. But there is a matter I need to raise with you. I feel I am superfluous to your investigations here.' Before I could protest, he raised a hand. 'It is true. And I have deceived you somewhat concerning my intentions.'

The rest of the people in the room stirred and murmured half-suppressed questions of their own. Alberoni looked around, a pleading look on his face.

'I know what you all think of my quest here in the East . . .'

His pause was enough for me to realize what he was about to say. He had come to Kubilai's empire in order to find Prester John, the supposed Christian monarch from the East, who was to save Western Christianity. As I mentioned before, he had met a man who fitted the bill, only to lose him soon after. Clearly, he was still hoping to find him again. I nodded sagely.

'Prester John.'

'Yes. He is not a myth, as you imagine. We all saw him in Xanadu, a prisoner of Kubilai's family.'

'We saw an old man. That is all.'

I was unconvinced of the man's identity, and looked around at the others for support. Lin's face was impassive, and Gurbesu and Pyka looked away, not wishing to disappoint the friar. Alberoni stared feverishly into my eyes, and I gave up.

'Very well. You think you can still find him. But what made you come with us, then?'

A big smile wreathed the friar's face.

'Two days travel west of here is a grand castle named Caichu, built by a man called the Golden King. He was vassal to Prester John, and once rebelled against him only to be humbled. And I have heard that twenty miles west of the castle is the river Hwang-Ho, that you called Kara-Moran, Niccolò. That river flows from the lands of Prester John.' He held the thumb and forefinger of one hand close together. 'I am that close to finding him again.'

I could not deny the friar his quest. He was going to the castle whatever I would say to him. But I offered him a warning, nevertheless.

'You need protection, Alberoni. You will be close to where Kubilai's forces are fighting those in the south.'

'No. I need no one – I have God's protection.' He touched my arm. 'I shall be back in a week. Two at the most. You will have solved this matter by then, and we will rejoice at our joint good fortunes together.'

I shook his hand, thinking how much I would regret his departure. We were like chalk and cheese, he and I. But he was my last connection with Venice, and Caterina Dolfin. I would miss him. After making his brief farewells with the others, the friar left to pack his bags, and make the preparations for his journey. I drank deep of the Chinee wine.

# TEN

*Better do a good deed near at home than go far away
to burn incense.*

Kubilai has created a magical thing. As a trader, I cannot
believe the audacity of the concept. It is as if he has
mastered the art of alchemy. But it is a sort of reverse
alchemy, because he does not convert base metal into gold.
Instead, he changes gold and silver, pearls and precious stones,
into paper. This paper is made from mulberry bark, which is
crushed and pounded flat. Then it's cut into oblong sheets
which are signed on by high officials of the Khan's court, and
then the impression of the Khan's seal is impressed on the
paper. Different types and sizes of paper are worth different
amounts, and people are happy to exchange the paper as though
it is real gold or silver. The magical part, from my point of
view, is that though the Khan usually exchanges merchants'
precious goods for this paper, he can print as much paper
money as he likes. Of course, if someone else forges the
paper money, he would expect to be executed. Believe me, I
have thought of that fraud myself.

The day after Lin had interrogated Li Wen-Tao, the prefect,
I was on my way to see him. I took a satchel full of paper
money with me – money supplied by Kubilai to fund
our mission. My approach to the prefect this time was somewhat more conciliatory than my first entrance. Then, I had
played the demon come to shake Li up. Now I wanted him to
see me as his friend. Or at least as his compatriot in crime. I
rode to the house by the river and dismounted, letting my
horse be led away by one of Li's servants. I slid the carved doors
open and bowed as I entered the large, open room beyond. Li
Wen-Tao sat as before in the centre of the room on a raised
platform to emphasize his superiority. I had deliberately
dressed in Chinee clothes rather than Mongol ones, and chosen

a modest blue robe to match his own. For the time being I wanted him to see me as an equal, not as a visiting dignitary from the court of the Great Khan. He eyed me with suspicion, his little dark eyes looking like currants pressed into uncooked dough. He was eating from a small bowl with chopsticks made of ivory. Cautiously, not knowing what to expect of me, he indicated a seat beside him. I sat on it, and murmured something deferential with lowered eyes. Still his look was one of uncertainty. I didn't blame him – I could have been leading him into a trap. I fed him a couple of my new Chinee words, and then tried him with the Mongol tongue. If he served Taitemir, he was bound to understand it.

'I believe you convinced my master yesterday that all was in order concerning the case of Jianxu. He said he could find nothing to take you to task with. I congratulate you, Master Li.'

Cautiously optimistic now, Li waved his chopsticks, and wiped his sticky mouth with a napkin.

'I exercised all diligence to come to the right conclusion.'

'Ah yes. I am sure Taitemir was pleased with the outcome.'

At first he wasn't sure how to take my comment. Was I suggesting that he had condemned Jianxu because that was what his overlord wanted? And was I thereby criticizing him, or praising him? I let him hang for a while, before smiling broadly.

'It was just what I would have done.'

Li relaxed, and scooped up some more fish from his bowl, stuffing it in his mouth and chewing noisily. I paused before continuing.

'But tell me, was Old Geng making himself a nuisance with Taitemir? Is that it? I understand he supplied goods to the household, and was always badgering them for money.'

Li laughed throatily, spitting out the remains of his food as he did so. Lin would not have liked such uncouth behaviour.

'The fool believed he should be paid rather than think it a privilege that he supplied items to Taitemir. He was a miser, who was always complaining about having no money. Yet people would go to his house to borrow money, I am told.

Though I must say there was a contrary rumour that had it that, ultimately, he was borrowing money himself. He probably put it around he had nothing as a rumour so that robbers wouldn't come and steal from him.'

I joined in his laughter, while at the same time avoiding the spray of half-eaten food coming from his full, red lips.

'Tell me, do you see many thieves in your court?'

'Often. And I get many complaints from people claiming their neighbour has stolen this or that. I tell them to go away and sort it out for themselves, or to leave some funds at my disposal to ensure my investigations conclude satisfactorily.' He winked at me knowingly. 'I cannot clog the court up with neighbourly disputes, after all.'

'Quite right too. Summary justice is the best form of justice. Next to that sort of justice whose progress is oiled with money.' I let the comment hang in the air for a moment, then went on. 'And the thieves you do see, do they come back regularly?'

Li shook his head regretfully.

'I am afraid there are some who do not respond to a flogging, but come back in front of me time and again. Every time they repent, and claim to have seen the error of their ways as the law demands they do. Confession is an obligatory step in the moral purpose of the courts of law. But I still see some faces too often. Like Ho Shu-heng, for example. He is a thorn in my side – a small-time thief but a thief nevertheless.'

I marvelled at Li's duplicity, casting scorn on the morals of others, when, by his own admission, he had his own snout in the trough taking bribes. I had been sure that was the case, and was about to test it now. I eased the satchel strap off my shoulder and let the flap fall open. Li's eyes opened wide when he spotted the dark sheets of paper money stuffed inside. I feigned not to notice, but continued the conversation.

'I should like to see this Ho person when next he appears in front of you. And how you deal with him. It will all contribute to our report on the way Jianxu's case was handled when we report to the Great Khan. You will be rewarded for your cooperation, of course.'

Li lifted a hand of dismissal in the air, waving away my suggestion of payment.

'My reward will be to have been of service to the Great Khan.'

However, I noticed that his eyes were still on the contents of my satchel. I nodded solemnly, and yet my hand still patted the bulging bag.

'I understand perfectly, Master Li. Now I will take my leave, but I am sure we will speak again very soon.'

I had baited the hook, but wasn't going to act too hastily. I wanted to let Li get his juices flowing and his eagerness to please me to a high pitch. I rose and left the prefect licking his lips. I don't think it was the food this time that had him salivating, though.

When I got back to our temporary quarters, I saw Po Ku, Lin's servant, hurrying towards me. He indicated that his master wanted to see me immediately, and led me to him. Lin was with another tall, handsome man, whom I immediately recognized. It was the writer of plays, Guan Han-Ching, whom we had last seen in T'ai-Yuan-Fu. Both men had serious looks on their faces. On seeing me, Lin came over with uncharacteristic speed. He was not one for hurried actions or thinking, but something perturbed him.

'Nick. Good, you are here. Guan has been telling me about his new play.'

'Oh?'

For the life of me, I couldn't imagine why that would have worried Lin so much. Why would the trifle of a bit of play-acting be a problem? On the other hand, I was glad to see Guan, because it meant the acting troupe was in town also. I wanted to speak to Tien-jan Hsiu, the actress who had played the part of Empress Tu upon my arrival in T'ai-Yuan-Fu, about a matter related to the prefect, and something I could not speak to Lin about. I smiled at Guan, and went to shake his hand. He took my hand briefly in the Chinee way, but did not smile. Lin came up beside me.

'Tell Master Zuliani what you have just told me, Guan.'

Guan nodded, and cleared his throat.

'I was telling Master Lin that I want to write about Jianxu. You know I was personally involved in the petition that brought you here. Well, I want to see justice done, as I told you when we met last time.'

'Yes and that is why *we* are here.'

Guan did not like my interjection, with its pointed reference to the fact that justice would be best served by Lin and me alone. He shook his head.

'You will have to excuse me, but *we* think differently.'

It was his turn to emphasize that little word, and claim the high ground. Not for the first time I wondered why educated men should think themselves so much better than any others at knowing the truth. In my experience truth was something even the lowest had intimate knowledge of. It's just that they didn't have the power to express it. Guan, however, was ploughing on.

'The downtrodden in China think that Mongol justice is no justice whatsoever. And Jianxu's predicament is a shining example of that. I know everything about the case because I spoke to her at length while preparing the petition.'

At last it fitted together. The reason why Jianxu's story had come out so pat when Gurbesu questioned her was now apparent. She had been tutored, even though inadvertently, by this writer of plays. Every word she spoke was akin to a line in a *kung-an* crime play.

'And you will write of her innocence?'

Guan nodded vigorously.

'Naturally. I will present the case next week in the form of a play. I have nearly finished writing it. It only remains to work out an ending.' He looked a little wistful. 'I had expected for the petition to fail and the execution to have taken place already.'

I could see what he was hinting at, and it reached to the true heart of the man. He was not concerned for Jianxu as a person, but as a symbol of injustice as he – a young, and hot-headed youth – saw it. It would have made a more powerful play, and a better ending, if Jianxu had been beheaded. Then the wrong would have been all the greater and her ghost could have called for justice. I smiled coldly.

'What a shame for you that we were despatched to investigate and she was spared.'

Guan did at least have enough shame to blush and look away from my glare. For once, the playwright was lost for words. All he could manage in the end was a defiant stare, and then he turned to leave.

After he had gone, Lin gave me a worried look.

'If we do not sort this matter out before he finishes that play, it will make it almost impossible to be seen to come to an impartial conclusion. If we find Jianxu innocent, Ko will say the play has affected our decision. If we find her guilty, Ko will spread the rumour that we came to that conclusion for political reasons. We can't win.'

'Then we will just have to solve the case within the week.'

I tried to sound confident, but I wasn't. Guan had just made our work that much more difficult. So I told Lin what the prefect had told me. Not about thieves, for that was something I was going to keep from him, but about Geng's apparent lack of money.

'Li told me that Geng claimed to be nearly broke because Taitemir's household had not paid him for goods supplied. Now, I don't think that was the reason he was killed, but it is interesting that Li also told me he was borrowing money from someone.'

'Not lending it? I was told he was a moneylender.'

'Not according to Li, though the prefect passed it off as a tall tale Geng let out to protect him from robbers, who might otherwise think he was rich pickings. But if he was borrowing money, who was it from? And did that have anything to do with his murder?'

Lin began to make notes in that elegant Chinee script of his. I waited patiently, knowing he was not to be hurried. Finally he laid his writing implement down.

'We must dig deeper. This case does not begin and end with Jianxu and Old Geng. We have much to learn from the other members of both families. Tomorrow we will go together and talk to Madam Gao, and the boy, Geng Wenbo. I think we have to go further back into the past.'

'I agree. Oh, by the way, does the presence of Guan mean the travelling players are here also? I should like to see another play, especially if Tien-jan Hsiu is in it. Will you be seeing the boy?'

Lin blushed a little, but retained his composure.

'I am not sure if he wants to see me. But, yes, you are correct. The players are here, and I believe they will be presenting a play in the town square tonight. Shall we go?'

Of course I agreed to go. I was getting a taste for these entertainments, and as so much of it was pantomime and acrobatics, it was easy to follow. Which is why Lin and I, accompanied by Pyka and Gurbesu, found ourselves walking amongst the throng of people making their way to the central square of the town. Banners were draped across buildings along the way, and Lin translated one of them for us.

'On the stage tonight at the Pianfu Theatre, the great actor Yi-shih Hsiu is now performing.'

'Hsiu? Is he related to Natural Elegance?'

Lin smiled at my question.

'Not that you would know from his name, which simply means Fashionable Elegance. But they could be related – most of these travelling troupes are.'

We emerged into a large square, which had a permanent stage set at one end next to a building I knew from its shape to be a temple. I checked that out with Lin, though.

'Is that the Temple of the Earth-Goddess?'

'Yes. And it houses temples and shrines to other gods too.'

'Including the god of lost items?'

Lin looked puzzled at my enquiry, but nodded.

'Yes, that too. You will see opposite the entrance two small statues of young children. That is the form of the god you refer to. There will no doubt be an old priest or priestess who acts as its intermediary. Now, can we get to our seats?'

I raised my hands in submission, but still had time as we passed to cast a quick look into the temple. I could just make out the statues Lin had described, but there was no priest. We made our way to an elevated platform facing the stage, which was obviously intended for important officials such as ourselves. As we ascended the stairs I saw Li Wen-Tao amongst the blue-robed old men already there. We nodded at each other, as Lin explained.

'This is the *shen-lou*. It means god's tower, and I suppose is entirely appropriate seeing those who are seated in it.'

He gave a little grin and we sat down too. The play soon began and developed into what Lin had described as a 'strip-and-fight thriller'. It was an old tale called 'The Three Princes at Tiger Palace', and involved lots of acrobatics from young men who were stripped to the waist. I could see out the corner of my eye that Gurbesu was on the edge of her seat. And I envied the youths their physiques – wine-drinking was not good for my waistline.

As the story progressed I saw that Lin was getting more and more agitated. Eventually, I leaned across and whispered in his ear.

'What's going on, Chu-Tsai?'

He turned his head slightly without taking his eyes off the stage.

'Some of the lines – I have not heard them before in this play. Just now one of the princes said, "When frost fell, men knew how a virtuous woman suffered," and earlier, the same prince said, "The greater the position, the shorter the memory." Often lines are changed in these plays. The words of plays are not set in stone. But . . .'

'It sounds like the lines are meant for us to hear, you think?'

He nodded.

'Let us wait until the end and we will see.'

When the play had finished, we all went backstage to congratulate the troupe. Natural Elegance saw Lin and quickly slipped through the crowd of well-wishers to speak to him. He still had his female make-up on, but close up you could not mistake him for a woman. I wondered how I had been deceived before. Words tumbled out of his mouth as he sought Lin's approval.

'Did you see the technique of my empty exit?'

I looked at Lin questioningly. He explained what the boy meant.

'An empty exit – *hsu-hsia* – is when the actor turns upstage to be out of the action, even though he is still visible to the audience.'

I nodded in understanding, though all this pretence was beyond me.

'Tell him I liked the use of the offstage voices when the

princes were fighting. Even if I didn't quite understand what they were saying.'

The boy laughed, clearly understanding my Mongol.

'There was no one offstage. I can throw my voice.'

I was glad of his confirmation. It was exactly as I had hoped. My plans were beginning to fall into place.

# ELEVEN

*To understand your parents' love you must raise children yourself.*

Lying beside the warm body of Gurbesu that night, I found I could not sleep. It looked as though, with Guan's play due to be performed soon, we needed to dig out the truth of Old Geng's murder more quickly than I had anticipated. Some of the lines from the play that evening were still rattling around in my head. One of them – 'a pinch of arsenic, or an inch of steel' – whispered in my ear by Lin, had particularly struck home. Not that it necessarily had anything to do with Jianxu's case, though it may well have done. No, it reminded me once again of my parents.

I was nine at the time, and the ongoing war between my mother and father was coming to a head. Being the selfish little brat I was then, I assumed it was all about me. Rosamund, my mother, was English and the daughter of a knight who had sojourned in Venice on his way to Outremer. He had stayed overlong because his wife had contracted a fever. It was unusual for a crusader to be travelling with his wife and child, but they had come nevertheless. Now my grandmother was paying the price of her obstinate insistence on travelling. She was bedridden and delirious. In the end, the crusader knight had to depart on one of the ships taking men-at-arms to Cyprus, the launching-off point for Outremer. Two days later, his wife died. He never got to know about it because he was drowned in the Nile when the ship he was on got sunk in a minor skirmish. His chain mail dragged him to the bottom of the river. The dark-haired girl Rosamund – my mother – was only fourteen and suddenly an orphan. But there were already the signs of the startling beauty she was to become, and Agostino Zuliani took her in. He was twenty years her senior, but it didn't stop him marrying her when

she was sixteen. I was the first child to survive any length of
time, and by the time I was nine, I was aware of the feuding
between my parents. Agostino had other children by his first
marriage, but for my mother I was an only child, and therefore
precious. Father accused her of making me soft through not
exposing me to the harsh realities of the world. They were
both hot-tempered, but father was a strong and cruel man,
who used his strength to bully his way to dominance in the
marriage. My mother got her revenge in secretive ways, sometimes spreading rumours about her husband's impotence –
which was not true – and sometimes lacing his food with
mild emetics. I knew this because she delighted in telling me.
It was a secret we shared that united us against the tyrant
who was my father.

At my side, Gurbesu stirred, and gazed sleepily up at me.
I could feel the heat of her body, but I was not excited. The
past bore down on me too heavily. She muttered a query.

'What's the matter, Nick?'

I stroked her thigh.

'Nothing, my sweet. I am just thinking about tomorrow.'

'Do you need some somnifera? I can make it up?'

I knew somnifera, her mixture of opium, hemlock and
mandragora soaked into a sponge. It rendered you happily
unconscious, but left you with a heavy head the following day.
I couldn't afford that, as I needed my mind to be clear.

'No. You go back to sleep. I will be fine.'

She rolled over, pressing her buttocks against my thigh,
and was soon snoring gently. The line from the play came
back to me – 'a pinch of arsenic, or an inch of steel.' You
see, I could not rid my mind of the persistent thought that
my mother had gone one step further than emetics, and actually poisoned my father. Soon after a particularly bad row
concerning how, in Agostino's eyes, Rosamund molly-coddled
me, I had told her that I would willingly stick a dagger into
my father. An inch of steel, you see. She was shocked by my
vehemence, but convinced me it would not be necessary. I
still recall her words to me on that night. She said that evil
acts always result in evil ends. The next day Agostino Zuliani
fell sick. Being poisoned by arsenic resulted in a painful and

slow death. I still believe she killed him first so that I didn't
do it.

The following morning, Lin and I went in search of Madam
Gao and Geng Wenbo. Tadeusz's job was to find out what he
could about the source of the poison – a subject that had not
been pursued yet, if we were to believe the documents related
to the case. It had been surprising that amidst all the piles of
paperwork there had not been one line explaining where the
poison had come from, even though the detailed examination
of the body had been exemplary.

When I had read the report concerning the examination of
Geng's dead body, and seen who had written it, I was not
surprised at its meticulousness. It had been written by Masudi
al-Din. I remembered him well from my time in Xanadu,
picturing again his slight frame and bright, glittering brown
eyes. It had been a coincidence that he had been in Pianfu at
the time of Geng's death, and was due to the fact he was
travelling back to his home in Yazd in Persia. He was a
physician with an interest in how and why people died. I could
see him still, tugging on his straggly beard, and then cutting
open a body with relish, seeking all the clues that led to an
explanation of that strange companion we all must meet –
Death. He was an Arab who used Turkish to communicate
with the Mongol world, so I found following his notes easy.
It read thus:

> Aconite poisoning is verifiable by the symptoms. There is a
> sensation of burning, tingling, and numbness in the mouth,
> and of burning in the abdomen. Death usually supervenes
> before a numbing effect on the intestine can be observed.
> After about an hour, there is severe vomiting. Much motor
> weakness and cutaneous sensations similar to those above
> described soon follow. The pulse and respiration steadily
> fail, death occurring from asphyxia. All these symptoms
> were described to me by the victim's son, Geng Wenbo,
> and by the young woman attending, Jianxu. I cut open
> the stomach and examined the contents, but could find
> no plant material present. I deduced that the cause of

*death was ingestion of aconite extracted from the plant,*
*monkshood. It had not been eaten in its raw state, nor had*
*the plant's sap accidentally found its way onto the victim's*
*skin. Internal tingling would not have resulted from this*
*form of contamination. Whether the ingestion of aconite*
*had been accidental or deliberate, and self-administered*
*or by another party, I leave to the prefect to decide.*

As ever, Masudi al-Din had been concise and objective. It
was not for him to ascribe motive, merely to record cause and
effect. He had also pointed out that aconite was used in very
small doses to good effect by Chinee practitioners as a treatment for Yang deficiency, or coldness, and for a number of
pains. It would, therefore, be in the armoury of every doctor
in Kubilai's empire.

The administering of the poison was to be a subject high
on our list of questions to ask those present in the house at
the death of Old Geng. But our first port of call, out of courtesy,
was the home of Li Wen-Tao. The prefect at first suggested
he call the old lady and the boy to the prison to be interrogated
by Lin and me. But I said that was not a good idea, as they
would both be afraid of being tortured. Li Wen-Tao had looked
astonished, suggesting that is exactly why he made the
proposal.

'Do you not want to frighten and whip the truth out of
them?'

'No, I would rather see them in their own home. They are
not suspects, after all. Simply witnesses at this point.'

The prefect cast a look of appeal at Lin, presumably thinking
his fellow Chinee would understand and countermand my
wishes. Lin merely inclined his head.

'Master Zuliani is the Chief Investigator. I am simply here
to record what we learn.'

Li sighed and gave us directions to the Geng household.

The house was run-down and shabby at first sight. But when
Lin and I stepped through the courtyard doors there were signs
that someone had attempted to keep the place tidy. An old
lady came hobbling over, her tiny feet encased in beautifully
embroidered slippers. I knew from being at Kubilai's court

that only the elite and the rich bound the feet of their children to produce this effect. Madam Gao was not from a poor, peasant family therefore. She approached Lin, and bowed low before him, dressed as he was in his red robe, a symbol of his status. I was once again clad in Mongol jacket and breeches. Even as the old lady deferred to Lin, her eyes flickered over me uncertainly. She couldn't place me in the pecking order, and therefore concentrated on the known quantity that was the official in red. Even so, she would not ignore me, as that in itself could have been a dangerous move on her part.

Lin eased her confusion with some words spoken in Chinee. I was beginning to understand some words now, and knew he was introducing me as the Khan's investigator. She smiled nervously and bowed to me. Indicating that we should follow her, she went inside. A servant was called and a not unpleasant hot brew called tea was served. An awkward three-way conversation then developed, with Lin asking questions of Madam Gao in Chinee, and then translating for me. When I wanted to ask a question, I had to do it through Lin as intermediary. It made for a slow, and for me, frustrating interview. It went something like this, starting with Lin's opening question.

'The broth that your daughter-in-law made was intended for you, I believe.'

Gao pulled a face, the wrinkles on her brow turning into deep furrows.

'Aiii, yes. To think if I had drunk it, I would now be dead. It does not bear thinking about.'

'Then you think the poison was intended for you?'

'I cannot say for certain. But what I am very sure of is that, if it was intended for me, then Jianxu still has to be innocent. Why should she want to kill me? I have looked after her since taking her in as a child. Her father could not afford his studies and her mother had died. He left Jianxu with me, and in return she served me as any proper daughter of my own blood would have. She even married my son.'

She began sniffling at this point, and Lin explained she was upset by having brought up the death of her son, Jianxu's husband. I listened to his explanation of Jianxu's history, and wanted clarification.

'Then she didn't just marry into the Gao family. She was adopted by Madam Gao first. Ask her who she thinks put the poison into the soup, if it wasn't Jianxu.'

On being asked by Lin, the old lady looked cautiously over her shoulder before replying.

'Who else could it have been but that lazy son of Geng's? He didn't want me to marry his father, because then he might lose the money from Old Geng's business. It was him. He tried to kill me, and in his usual ham-fisted way ended up killing his own father.'

After Lin had translated this outburst for me, he asked me if there was anything else I wanted to ask the old woman. I said there wasn't at present, and Lin dismissed her. He told her to send Wenbo to us. She shuffled off, muttering under her breath. I sipped at the bowl of tea, but it had gone cold and didn't taste so good any more. I yearned for a good robust red wine. Just as we thought that the boy wasn't going to turn up, we heard raised voices from another part of the house. Lin smiled.

'That is Madam Gao telling Wenbo to get out of bed and speak to the investigator before she sets the demon on him. I think that's you, Zhong Kui.'

I pulled a face that I imagined resembled the drawings I had seen of the demon in question. And just at that moment a skinny lad entered the room. Seeing me, he whimpered and almost fled. Lin waved his hand imperiously, and coaxed the boy to come and sit. Close up, I could see he was older than I had thought at first. He was twenty at least, though still somewhat gangly and awkward, which contributed to the impression he was much younger. He stared wide-eyed at Lin, hardly daring to look at me. Lin spoke sternly to him.

'You worked for your father?'

The youth nodded.

'If you had dealings with the staff at Taitemir the Mongol's palace, then you can speak their language?'

Another nod. At this rate, I reckoned we didn't need to tax Wenbo's language skills. We would get all we wanted from him with a nod and a shake of the head. But Lin ploughed on.

'Then you will speak directly in that language with the investigator.'

He pointed at me, and Geng Wenbo reluctantly turned his gaze my way. I started with a question designed to unbalance him, and elicit an unconsidered response.

'Did you kill your father deliberately, or was it an accident?'

Wenbo gaped open-mouthed at me.

'Accident? How could it have been an accident?'

'Then you meant to do it.'

The youth's voice went up a pitch.

'Noooo, you are twisting my words. I didn't do it. Nor did Jianxu. You should ask *her* –' he hooked a thumb over his shoulder to indicate the absent Madam Gao, – 'why she let my father eat the broth. I didn't kill him. He was my father.'

'And he was going to marry Madam Gao. Your hold on your father's business would then have been precarious, especially as he thought you were incompetent.'

'Who told you that? That old bitch? Yes, she had designs on my father. But that didn't matter, because I was going to marry Jianxu. Did she tell you that as well?'

# TWELVE

*If you must play, decide on three things at the start: the rules of the game, the stakes, and the quitting time.*

'They're just accusing each other. This is getting us nowhere.'

Lin nodded in agreement at my observations on our morning's work.

'We can't just concentrate on the moment of the murder. We have to delve into the past and find out more about the reason why Geng was murdered.' He sighed. 'We need to go back to the beginning.'

'But where is the beginning?'

I was getting more and more depressed about finishing this before Guan presented his play to the public showing Jianxu in all her innocence.

'Is it when Jianxu was left as a child with the Gao family? How are we going to dig that far back?'

'Jianxu herself can tell you.'

It was Gurbesu who spoke up. She had been sitting in the corner of the room listening to our debate. Tadeusz had not yet put in an appearance, and was presumably still ferreting around finding out what he could about where the aconite might have come from. I challenged Gurbesu's opinion that the girl was the best source to go to for information about the past.

'She was a child when she was left with Gao. Her knowledge of what happened will be clouded by the view of a child. And if she is guilty of murder her testimony will not be the most reliable.'

'It will be a start, and we could check her story with neighbours. As for her fabricating facts to cover up her guilt, you yourself have said often enough that a murderer can be uncovered as much by their lies as by the truth.'

Lin laughed out loud.

'You are caught out by your own words, Nick. Admit it; Gurbesu is right. We should speak to Jianxu again. If only to test Wenbo's statement about him being about to marry her.'

Gurbesu corrected Lin sharply.

'I was saying that I should speak to her, not either of you. It worked the first time, and will work best again if I speak to her alone.'

It was best not to contradict Gurbesu when she had the bit between her teeth. And she was right anyway. Jianxu would talk to her, and Gurbesu would know the truth. If she spun a yarn, Gurbesu would know that too. She was clever that way. We agreed that she would approach Jianxu alone, which suited me as I had business with the prefect that I didn't want her to know about. Lin would have to be kept in the dark too, because it was not exactly above board. Once I had tempted Li Wen-Tao with a bagful of paper money, I had spotted where the business opportunity lay, and couldn't resist taking it. But before I could get away, Tadeusz came rushing in. He had a big smile on his lopsided face that suggested he had made a discovery.

'You won't guess what I found out from one of the silversmiths. He had had some business dealings with Old Geng, and told me that a few months ago the old man had paid off some of his debts. When he asked Geng if he had at last got Taitemir to pay him, Geng pulled a face and said he had not, that he had had to borrow money at an extortionate rate to keep himself going.'

I didn't know why Pyka was so pleased to have been told that. It did not get us any further on. But the little smith had news that did change things.

'This time I had a hint as to who the moneylender was. The silversmith I spoke to was sure it was Madam Gao.'

'The old lady loaned Geng money? Well I suppose she might if they were to be wed.'

Tadeusz sat down at the table and picked up a succulent peach from the porcelain bowl in its centre. He bit deeply, and wiped the juice from his mouth using his sleeve.

'No, you have it wrong. The loan was well before Madam

Gao moved into Geng's house. And it wasn't a loan from one friend to another. Don't forget Geng complained the moneylender's rates were painfully high. It was a purely business transaction at the time. You see, Madam Gao must be a moneylender by trade. She is well known in the town as a hard-headed businesswoman, tougher than her husband was. And the business, which traded in silk material, had many clients. She took over the business when her husband died, and ran it much more successfully than he did. It seems she used her wealth to lend money, extorting punitive rates of return. Everyone was surprised when she moved into Geng's house.'

I looked at everyone around the table.

'This changes matters. Both Gengs had reasons to want Gao dead – one owed her a lot of money, the other didn't want to lose the family business. Do you think the murder of the old man was an attack on Madam Gao that went badly wrong?'

'An attempt by the boy to kill the moneylender who had his father in a stranglehold?'

Tadeusz's question was answered with more from Lin.

'Is the boy so ham-fisted that his poisoning attempt went so drastically wrong? Would he not be totally distraught to have been the cause of his own father's death?'

'Not if he saw the benefits of what happened. He's not that dim.' I got up and straightened my breeches, which were tight around my nether regions. 'Now, I have things to do, and so do you, Gurbesu. Talk to Jianxu today, and try and get to the bottom of this matter. We need to know everything, especially if the boy was going to wed Jianxu. That would change the perspective on him being a suspect. Why kill to keep the Geng business, if he would inherit it anyway? Tadeusz – see if you can discover the names of any of the other people Madam Gao has loaned money to. Without her knowing you want to know.'

'You think someone else might have been trying to kill her?'

'It's a possibility. Though I still think this has more to do with the family than an outsider, but we must not exclude other possibilities.'

Having made sure all the others would be busy that

afternoon, I turned to Lin. I was in no position to order him to do anything, but I did want to ensure he was occupied somehow. He saw my questioning look, and raised his hands, palms outward.

'Don't ask me to do anything. I have much to write up here. If we are to come out of this without falling into Ko's trap, we need accurate records.'

I was relieved. Lin would be busy too.

'I agree. Every step must be meticulously recorded, and every fact substantiated.'

Lin sighed.

'And even then it may do us no good. Ko is a slippery eel of an enemy.'

'I'm afraid he is. By the way, do you know if the actors' troupe are rehearsing Guan's play today?'

Lin shrugged his shoulders.

'I don't know for sure, but I fear they will be. That is another sword dangling over our heads.'

Lin waved for his servant, Po Ku, to bring paper and ink, and I left him to his work and his worries.

At that same moment, Ko Su-Tsung was ensconced in his private room. At the heart of his quarters, the room was deep in shadows, just as he preferred it. Much of his deeds were conceived and controlled from the darkness of this room. Now, he held the second communication from his spy at Pianfu. He smiled his cadaver smile. The letter contained a report on Lin Chu-Tsai's meeting with the prefect, and the fact that Lin found nothing amiss in his behaviour. Ko was satisfied so far with the progress of events, but it was too soon to imagine that his enemy was trapped inexorably. He knew Lin was cleverer than that. And so was that foreign barbarian, Zuliani. Though he felt sure that Zuliani would make some sort of mess by getting involved in a shady deal or some such. It was in the man's nature. In fact, he could make matters worse for Lin by drawing Zuliani into a bad deal that would compromise both men. He lifted his writing implement and began to draft a message to be sent by the great Yam.

\*   \*   \*

I went to Li Wen-Tao's house via the theatre because I had to settle a little business there first. It occurred to me at the time to check on the person who had inserted the lines in the play the previous night – the words that had so concerned Lin. But I didn't have the opportunity as a rehearsal was beginning. I would have to leave it for later, perhaps. For now, the business in hand was with the prefect.

Fat Li was still in the same position as when I had last seen him. In fact he looked fatter, and more food was being conveyed to his mouth with those little chopsticks. He paused long enough though to cast a greedy eye over my satchel. The last time he had seen it, it was stuffed with money. He had to do something for me first before I opened it up again, so I reminded him of our previous conversation.

'Ho – the thief you mentioned. Have you come across him again? Have his light-fingered ways caused him to appear before your court?'

Li grinned, and some rice slid from his lips and down his chin.

'It's odd you should say that. He is awaiting my justice right now, having been found with stolen goods in his possession. A valuable vase and a bead necklace reported stolen from a middle-ranking official. I shall be very brutal with Ho this time.'

I lifted a hand to stay the course of his justice.

'I have another suggestion. Will you let him off with a warning, and have him secrete his ill-gotten gains somewhere where they can be found?'

Li narrowed his eyes, and looked baffled.

'Why would I do that?'

I know I had him hooked, and I began to reel him in.

'I noticed that the Temple of the Earth-Goddess in the square has a shrine to the god of lost possessions. I understand that people who have lost something or have had something stolen go to the priest or priestess and ask them for help with the god who is in residence to have their items restored to them.'

Li was still unclear where I was taking him, but he could sense something profitable at the end of all this, just as I had. I went on.

'It occurred to me that if, say, the old priestess knew where Ho has hidden the items he has stolen, then she could tell the owners, who will be most grateful to the god. They will reward the god through the old woman.'

'They will indeed. But what benefit is that to us?'

I had him for sure. He was looking for the scam already.

'If Ho told you where the goods were, and you told the old woman, then she would feel obliged to share her spoils with you. As for me, I would only want a small amount for suggesting this to you. And by way of sealing our deal, I could . . . deposit some of my paper money with you.'

It put my hand in the satchel, and produced a bundle of black notes with the seals of reputable men. Li's eyes widened. He made to take the money, but I held my hand over the top of it.

'Of course, this is not a one-off deal. If any other thefts should come your way, we could make the same arrangements. As and when they happened.'

Li nodded eagerly, and I lifted my hand off the money. It disappeared as if by magic up his long and voluminous sleeve. My little moneymaking scheme was under way.

Lin seemed preoccupied when I got back to the house we were quartered in, and he called me into the room he had taken over as his private office. Papers lay scattered around in a way I had not seen before. Lin was usually so neat and meticulous. He saw me looking at the mess and apologized.

'I have been busy this afternoon, and haven't had time to get things straight. Let me call Po Ku and he can sort my papers out as we speak.'

He disappeared for a moment and when he returned the rangy Po Ku was following him. With some simple instructions from Lin, the youth began collecting the scattered documents. I was surprised Lin trusted him to understand the order in which they needed to be arranged, but he seemed to be satisfied Po Ku was doing as requested. He turned to me, a grim smile on his soft, oval face.

'After I had finished making notes of our progress so far, I went to the actors' theatre in the square.'

For a moment my heart sank. Had Lin divined the reason for my clandestine visit there? If he had, it would complicate matters no end. But to my relief he made no mention of my having been to see the troupe myself.

'I wanted to speak to whoever had rewritten the words for the play we saw. There seemed to be so many veiled hints in the script, I was sure it had been intended that we heard them and investigated. I tried to speak to Tien-jan Hsiu, but he was rehearsing Guan's play with most of the rest of the acting crew. I did manage to speak with the ticket-seller, but he could only tell me that the manager of the troupe was responsible for the scripts of the older plays. He goes by the stage name of P'ing-Yang Nu – slave from P'ing-Yang – and was playing the part of the executioner in Guan's play. He too was onstage, therefore. I stood and watched for a while, having been told the man I wanted was the one with tattoos all over his arms and legs. He looked my way a couple of times, but wouldn't come offstage. Then, when the rehearsal finished, he must have slipped away behind the *shen-cheng* – the backcloth – because Tien-jan came over to talk to me. And when I looked for Nu he was nowhere to be seen.'

'A guilty conscience?'

'Or fearful of going any further than he has done. Letting the words he wanted us to hear be spoken in public but under-stood only by us was clever. But it suggests he is afraid of being seen to speak directly to us. Never mind, we will find him. And when we do, he will have to tell us what he knows.'

I wasn't so optimistic.

'How can you be sure he knows anything? Could it not be merely coincidence, and you are reading too much into the lines you heard?'

Lin's face hardened in a way I had not seen before. This case and its possible consequences were beginning to tell on him.

'No. I am sure he knows more. You see, I checked some old posters I saw in the street. They had been partially torn down, or new ones had been pasted over them. But I could read enough of the posters to know that the troupe had been performing in Pianfu right at the time of Old Geng's death.'

He looked triumphantly at me. 'It proves they were here when the old man was murdered. Nu could have been seeking a loan – acting troupes are notoriously short of cash and need loans – so, at the very least, he could have seen something. He could have seen who the real murderer was, and not realized it until their return this time round.'

# THIRTEEN

*The palest ink is better than the best memory.*

L in and I kept our information about the theatrical troupe
to ourselves for the time being. Not that there was much
to divulge at the moment. But Gurbesu had returned, and
needed to tell us all she had learned from Jianxu. As soon as
she came through the door, we knew she had much to tell.
Her eyes were bright, and her words flowed out like flood
water down the Hwang-Ho river.

'Jianxu has told me about when she and her mother-in-law
went to live with Old Geng. It is a quite unbelievable story,
except for one thing. I believe every word of what she said.
In fact her whole life story is exceptional. Oh, where to begin.'

I took her arm and made her sit down. Then I gave her a
cup of the local wine to calm her.

'Take a deep draught, then a deep breath, and begin at the
beginning. That is what we said we needed to do with this
case. We have been dodging around picking up titbits here
and there too much. We need the full picture. Start with how
Jianxu came to be in the Gao household in the first place.'

Gurbesu looked from me to Lin and then to Pyka, who had
come in just before the whirlwind that was Gurbesu had taken
over.

'You won't believe me.'

Jianxu had obviously been patiently awaiting Gurbesu's return
for a long time. As she walked towards the prison along the
long approach road, Gurbesu could see the pale face of the girl
set against the darkness inside her cell. It was almost as
though she had been standing there since the last time Gurbesu
had spoken to her. She was staring through the grille in the
cell door, her almond eyes unblinking in the afternoon sun.
The bandy-legged guard scurried out from his post and unlocked

the cell door without being asked by Gurbesu. The afternoon was tolerably warm, with only a hint in the air of how cold the autumn would soon get. Gurbesu drew the girl out of her cell. The gaoler was nervous, and took a step towards them, but Gurbesu's stare froze him in his tracks. She took Jianxu's arm and they sat under the shade of the lone tree opposite the cell door, just as I had done two days previously. Gurbesu called out to the guard to fetch them some water. Grudgingly, he went, and came back with a wooden pail and a ladle. The water in the pail was cool, and both she and Jianxu drank in turn from the ladle in silence. Their thirsts quenched, Gurbesu began her gentle interrogation.

'How did you come to be living with Madam Gao?'

Jianxu stared off into the distance as though she were looking far away into her own past.

'My father was a poor scholar, who had not yet taken his exams when his wife – my mother – died. I was seven years old, and of an age where I could be useful to a household. In order to finish his studies, my father offered me as a servant to Madam Gao. In return, she would give my father an amount of money sufficient to pay for his exams.'

Gurbesu stirred, uncomfortable at the implication.

'In essence he sold you to Madam Gao.'

Jianxu did not flinch from the hard conclusion drawn by her interrogator.

'It was a mutually convenient arrangement. Before he left, he pleaded with Madam Gao to be kind to me, and told me to be obedient. I think both of us kept our bargain. I served Madam Gao well, and she had no cause for complaint concerning my domestic duties. We did not talk much, other than when she gave me instructions, but then Madam did not seek or want a companion. Time seemed to pass with great speed. It was ten years later that Madam Gao's son asked me to marry him, and I was pleased to do so. Once again, it was mutually convenient. Sadly, he was a sickly person and our joining was never consummated. He took ill and died soon after we were married.'

Jianxu paused in her narration, and Gurbesu wondered about her apparent calm. How had she felt when her husband had died so soon after the wedding? Had she mourned for him? What feelings had coursed through her veins? She got an answer of sorts when Jianxu continued her story.

'The Three Duties of a woman are obedience to her father, her husband, and to her son after her husband's death. Sadly we had no son.' Once again she paused, but only briefly this time. 'But one of the Four Virtues says a woman should serve her in-laws. Madam Gao's own husband had died a long time before, so my duty was to serve Madam Gao. This I did, and would still strive to do, if I were not in this prison.'

'She sounds too good to be true.'

Gurbesu smiled sweetly, but insincerely, at my banter. I knew the Three Duties, and the Four Virtues would not play well with her. As a man I might have wanted a woman of such an exemplary nature, but had not yet found one. One can but dream. Gurbesu told us what she thought.

'I don't think she was lying to me. She seemed to want to believe in what she was saying. Whether it represents the actual truth is another matter. I could detect no emotion in her at all.'

It was Lin's turn to make a contribution to the debate.

'In my country, women are assumed to subordinate themselves to men. And there are seven grounds for divorce – disobedience to parents-in-law, barrenness, adultery, jealousy, incurable disease, and theft.'

Gurbesu frowned, counting in her head.

'That is only six.'

Lin smiled sweetly.

'Yes, the seventh is loquacity. Do you think you could be more to the point, dear Gurbesu?'

Gurbesu snorted, and punched Lin playfully on the arm. Lin, however, was making a serious point. Women were subject to the whims of men in Cathay, and it took a particular temperament to overcome that drawback. Madam Gao had achieved it, it would seem, by simply being a determined person whom no one dared cross. But even she had been obliged to consider Geng's marriage proposal. So how difficult was it for a young woman like Jianxu to be in control of her life? Perhaps her situation had required her to suppress her feelings.

'Shall I go on?'

Gurbesu was staring at me with a curious look in her eye. I nodded, not seeing why my inner thoughts should have delayed her.

'Yes, please do. What more is there to tell us, Gurbesu?'

'Quite a lot, actually.'

Jianxu began to explain to the dark-haired woman sitting next to her in the shade of the solitary tree just how things had gone wrong.

'Madam Gao uses the profits from her business to lend money at a rate of interest. The paper money system created by the Mongols has been a boon to her business, and many people come to her to borrow. One of them was Geng Biao. He eventually owed her a lot of money. I think he imagined that by marrying her he could eradicate his debt.'

'But why would Madam Gao even consider his proposal if she was to lose out on a lucrative deal?'

Jianxu shook her head slowly.

'She didn't for a long time. In fact she was becoming quite irritated by his persistent attention. Especially when he suggested his son could marry me. As if this would solve the imagined problem of my being so old and without a husband.'

Jianxu turned her gaze on her interrogator.

'I told Old Geng that I already had a husband. He was sadly dead, and I believed that widows should not remarry. He got very annoyed and stormed out of the house.'

Once again Jianxu returned her gaze to the far distance. There was a long pause before she continued her story.

'Then something happened. I don't know what it was, but it must have shocked my mother-in-law. I thought she had been seeing another client, but suddenly she emerged from her counting house followed by Old Geng. She was clutching her throat, and I thought that Geng had attacked her. But then I saw it was the opposite. Geng was holding her shoulders and comforting her. That night, Madam called for me and told me she was to marry Old Geng, and I was to be wed to his son. She said it was our duty. I cried the whole night, and prayed that my *yun* – my luck – would change overnight. But *yun* moves as slowly as an oxcart's wheel, and the next morning nothing had changed. I was still betrothed to Wenbo, and Madam was set on marrying his father.'

'I did then ask her about the poisoned broth, but her story was the same as when I first interrogated her. She made it for Madam Gao, and Old Geng took it off her before she could give it to her mother-in-law.'

I looked at Gurbesu.

'Did it sound the same story? I mean, exactly the same?'

Gurbesu nodded, and her thick, black hair fell across her eyes. She swept it up with her palm, wedging it behind her ear.

'Yes. It is a considered story, rather than consistent. But it sounds truthful, all the same.'

Lin had been silent for a long time. Now he spoke up, echoing the thought that was in my mind.

'We have to investigate this incident after which Madam Gao completely changed her mind about marrying Geng. What was it, I wonder?'

Tadeusz, who, too, had kept quiet during Gurbesu recital of Jianxu's story, now entered the conversation.

'I may be able to help you there. Among the debtors of Madam Gao was a physician called Sun. He disappeared around the time Gao agreed to marry Geng. By all accounts he was a poor doctor, who sometimes made his patients worse than they were when they went to him.' He paused. 'He would of course have had aconite in his collection of cures.'

This was very interesting news to me. Was this the source of the poison that killed Geng?

'Disappeared, you say? Doesn't anyone know of his whereabouts?'

Tadeusz waved a hand in the air and grimaced.

'I have not so far been able to find anyone who does. But I shall not give up. And there is something else to say about Sun.'

'What's that?'

'They say he dabbled in alchemy too. It has not been proven, but two old men died quite soon after consulting him in their search for greater longevity.'

'Cinnabar.'

It was Lin who offered a theory about this latest matter.

'*Zhusha* – as we call cinnabar – can be roasted to turn it into quicksilver – mercury. It is thought that through ingesting this substance that immortality can be attained. But it is a deadly substance, and if Doctor Sun is as careless with mercury as he is with the herbs he prescribes, then I am not surprised if many have died at his hands. Tadeusz, my friend, you must find him, and bring him to us. He can no doubt tell us to whom he sold the poison. Or if he himself administered it.'

Pyka nodded his agreement to his task, asking just one question.

'Are you then inclined to think that the girl is innocent, after all?'

Lin looked at me inquiringly. He was sticking to his role as recorder of information, leaving me to draw the conclusions from them. I looked back at him, not able to detect in his stare what he might think himself. I was on the spot, and even Gurbesu looked down at the ground when I included her in my stare. I was unsure, but Tadeusz deserved an answer. He had given us a lot of useful information.

'There is a lot more to prove yet. But, if we had begun this investigation from scratch and Jianxu had not already been in prison, then yes, I would be inclined to think her innocent at this stage.'

The girl sat in her cell watching the sun descend over the hills. For a moment, the path to her cell door was imbued with a red glow. It was as though she was witnessing a trail of red blood flowing to her door. She smiled in triumph. The interview with the tall, dark-skinned woman had been very successful. She knew she had convinced the woman of her tragic life to date, and therefore of her probable innocence. Now the path that she once deemed unlucky had become one of lucky red blood – life's blood – that was flowing her way. Her *yun* cycle was in the ascendant, and she knew she would soon be free to do as she wished. Then along the blood path came a dark figure.

She knew it was Wenbo, because he came every day to see

her. He was rather late this time, and she was anxious because she had much to say to him. But when she saw his eager, pinched face at the grille of her cell door, she knew everything would work out. Swiftly she told him what had happened that day, and told him what she would like done. He looked afraid, but determined, when he left soon afterwards. As the sun sank, and the path once again turned to grey, she breathed a great sigh of relief. For the first time, she fell asleep without feeling the sharp blade of the executioner's sword on her neck.

# FOURTEEN

*It is easy to dodge a spear that comes in front of you, but hard to keep out of harm's way from an arrow shot from behind.*

I rose early the next morning because I had much to do. I told Lin that I would follow up the matter of the writer of the words in the play we had seen. Lin was still sure they had hinted at knowledge of the real murderer of Old Geng.

'I keep recalling other lines from the play, but I don't know whether they were in the original or not.'

I was getting more uncertain about this by the day.

'Such as?'

'Well, one character said something like "get your monkshood, and your mountain fennel." Monkshood is aconite by another name – the poison we are looking for. But I'm damned if I can remember if the original play referred to it or another way of killing. You see, just before that line the same character said, "who could have guessed behind the smile a dagger lay?" Why say that if the victim in the play was poisoned?'

'I will go and find this P'ing-Yang Nu and settle your doubts for you. And I will do it right away.'

Lin clutched his chest in a way that suggested staying his beating heart.

'Thank you, my demon. Remember, you are looking for a man with tattooed arms and legs.'

I left him once again seated at his low desk writing notes of all our actions to date. It had always been my intention to go into town this morning, but not to see someone from the players' troupe. I had arranged to meet the prefect, Li Wen-Tao, at the Temple of the Earth-Goddess. It was time for the first return on my investment. As I approached the temple, I noted with satisfaction two well-muscled young men emerging from the crowd and falling in step with me a few paces back. I had no worries about a physical encounter with the prefect, but who knows? If he chose to bring along a couple of heavies in order to foreclose on our deal, I would still be at a disadvantage. If he hadn't thought of it, well, my having arranged for two big bodyguards at my back would keep him in line. Hopefully, I was secure.

I could see that a steady stream of people were entering and leaving through the main doorway of the temple. Ducking through the archway myself, I peered into the gloom of the interior. Incense hung in dense sweet-smelling clouds, and I felt queasy from the cloying odour. Many visitors were going to the main altar, but there was also a long line of people at the altar to the god of lost and stolen items. A stoop-shouldered old woman was very busy, and I watched as she dealt with those at the head of the queue. She first listened to a wealthy looking merchant, who whispered in her ear and pressed an offering into her claw-like hand. She hobbled to the twin statues in the shrine and mumbled her prayers. The merchant was astounded to hear a voice come from the altar, no doubt telling him where to find his lost item. He was so impressed that he took another coin out of his sleeve and pressed it into the priestess's palm. As one happy client left in a hurry to find what was lost, an elderly couple approached the priestess. A similar scenario followed, with the old pair passing money over. The priestess prayed, but there was no voice from the god this time. Returning to her clients, she shook her head. Apparently no response had been forthcoming from the gods, but no doubt she would be advising them to return the next day. Perhaps by then she would have better news – if Li was playing his part. The next supplicant, a woman with a white-painted face, stepped forward. She and the old priestess whispered to each other.

I was aware of a movement behind me, and out of the corner of my eye saw the prefect's large form looming into sight. He saw who the priestess was talking to, and grinned.

'She has good news for the courtesan. Her missing bolts of silk have revealed themselves to the gods. She is telling her where they are.'

As he told me this, I could see the courtesan handing over

a big bundle of paper money. Then she hurried away. Li licked his lips.

'There she goes to dig the bolts up from the embankment by the river, where Ho buried them. Let the old woman deal with the others in her queue first, and then I will take our share of the money.' He grinned broadly. 'What a service we provide.'

We watched from the shadows as the line of supplicants dwindled. Several of them handed over paper money or gold coins as an offering to the gods. Clearly business was brisk, and I asked Li what he thought of the scheme.

'Is it going that well already?'

He laughed at my expression of surprise, his vast belly wobbling under his finely embroidered robe.

'It was a little quiet to begin with. So I decided I couldn't wait for Ho to rob someone, and then come tell me. I gave him a list of wealthy men and women and their property, and told him to get busy. There seems to be quite a crime wave developing in Pianfu now.' He grinned, his dark raisins of eyes disappearing in his fat cheeks. 'But no one is complaining, for they get their goods back, and reward the gods accordingly.'

I told Li that I was full of admiration for his astonishing enterprise.

'Why did I not think of that?'

He sneered and shrugged his shoulders, acknowledging his superiority over the barbarian. The queue had dispersed so we went over and Li extracted his commission from the priestess. She hissed her disapproval and gave me a piercing look. But in return for the money, Li gave her a paper with some more information on it. No doubt the couple who had been told to come back tomorrow would find the gods had answered their prayers. Li turned to me, for the first time aware of the two well-built young men hovering in the background. He gave me a fearful look, perhaps thinking I was going to take all his profits. I smiled reassuringly.

'Just a little insurance policy, Master Li. Say hello to Dao and Yun.'

Li grinned nervously and peeled off some notes, pressing

them in my hand. I secreted them in my purse, and walked
jauntily out of the temple. Looking back I saw that my bodyguards were no longer following. Well, I did not have need
of them now. Turning to my right, I started towards the theatre,
and my hoped-for meeting with P'ing-Yang Nu.

The theatre seemed very quiet – even the entrance arch was
unoccupied. Normally the stentorian-voiced barker sat there
urging people to enter when there was a show to promote, and
then taking the money. Today he was nowhere in sight. I
walked through into the arena, seeking someone who could
tell me where P'ing-Yang Nu was to be found. On the stage,
which in full daylight looked dowdy and worn, a couple of
actors were practising acrobatic moves. One man swung a
punch at the other, and he lurched backwards even though the
fist had not touched him and performed a somersault. He did
it badly, falling on one knee. He clutched his leg, crying out
in pain. The first man called out in derision and the other
stumbled back to his place. They squared up to practise the
move again, ignoring me as I climbed the steps to the platform
on which they were working out their routine. Striding over
to them, I could smell the stale sweat on their bodies. The
blow was flung again, and the recipient performed another
somersault. He landed hard on his backside this time, and the
other one laughed. The one on the floor looked up at me,
acknowledging my presence for the first time. I tried my best
to look stern, though I'm sure he could put on a much more
convincing scowl than I could. Unless his acting was as bad
as his acrobatics, that is.

'P'ing-Yang Nu?'

The actor cocked a thumb over his shoulder in the direction
of the backcloth. The man I sought was obviously backstage
somewhere. I thanked him, and stuck a hand out to help him
get up from his embarrassing position on the tiled floor of the
stage. He refused it, bounding to his feet as though unhurt. I
did notice he walked away with a limp, however. I pulled the
edge of the painted cloth aside and stepped into the gloom
behind it. The smell of men's sweat was even stronger here,
laced with another familiar but elusive smell. I took a step
forward in the dark, and my foot slid on the tiles. They were

wet and sticky. The odour in my nostrils identified itself. It was like the smell of an abattoir. Or a battlefield.

I dragged the backcloth to one side to let more light into this gloomy place. The first thing I saw was a naked leg. It had red and green dragons tattooed all along it. Cautiously taking a step closer, I saw another leg similarly covered in dragon designs. Then the whole body became apparent. It was clad only in a loincloth, and not only were the legs tattooed, the back and arms were covered with dragons too. It was impossible to see if the chest had its adornment also. P'ing-Yang Nu was lying face down in a dark, glistening pool of his own blood.

Together with the prefect, Lin and I examined the body. It now lay on a trestle in a makeshift morgue close to the main square. It would seem that scant attention was paid to the details of a death in Pianfu. It was enough for Li Wen-Tao to know that the man was dead. And that was an obvious deduction from the state of the body. When Nu had been turned over by the funerary attendants, his guts had spilled out. Li, who was in attendance by then, having been fetched by me from the temple complex next door, turned away and vomited his last meal out on the theatre tiles. Now he stood at a good distance from the body, avoiding looking on the mess. Lin and I, on the other hand, were eager to look more closely. I wished Masudi al-Din were here, because I had learned a lot about Geng's death from his meticulous autopsy. Even though I never saw that body, the Arab's written report was quite illuminating. Li had no intention of being so meticulous, especially with a dead travelling actor of no importance. It had been all we could do to get permission to examine the body before the prefect disposed of it.

Lin, his face just a little paler than usual, pointed a long-nailed finger at the dead man's belly.

'See how the cut is from left to right.'

I nodded, following the line of the incision made in Nu's flesh. It cut through the necks of two dragons tattooed on his torso, removing the beasts' heads from their bodies. The man's guts, pushed rudely back into his belly by an attendant, still poked out. It was as though the dragons themselves had been gutted. But I could see what Lin meant.

'Assuming the killer was right-handed, a cut from left to right suggests he did it from behind. He surprised the actor, and killed him without getting too much blood on himself.'

'The alternative is a bold, left-handed murderer . . . now covered in blood and guts.'

Lin's morgue humour was grimly amusing. But I was in no mood to laugh. If I had taken Lin seriously, and gone to the theatre sooner instead of being drawn by the lure of money, P'ing-Yang Nu might not now be dead. And we might have been closer to unmasking a killer. On the other hand, if I had been earlier, I might now be lying on a slab alongside P'ing-Yang Nu. Gutted like a fish. Lin divined my thoughts.

'We could still discover something about what was in Nu's mind.'

'How?'

'We must search for his version of the play script. If he wrote down the amendments he made, we could learn from them. I can only remember a few of the lines we heard on the night.'

Lin was correct, and knew I should have searched for the script as soon as I had arranged for the body to be moved.

'I will go back immediately and see if I can find it.'

Tien-jan was finally at the theatre when I got back, wiping make-up from his face. I asked him if he had been busy, and he said he had had lots to do.

'What do you want now, investigator? To accuse me of the murder of Nu?'

I grinned at the slim youth, who had once fooled me into thinking he was a girl.

'You know I wouldn't do that. No, I am on another mission. Do you know where Nu would have kept any written copies of the plays you perform? I am particularly interested in the one you put on recently.'

'Not Guan's new play?'

I shook my head.

'No. Though I would love to know what slant Guan has

taken on the case of Jianxu. It may affect the outcome of the investigation.'

Natural Elegance put on his best enigmatic look.

'I cannot tell you that. The script is a closely guarded secret. Even those of us in the play only know our own lines, and none of us knows the ending yet. I think it is still unwritten, actually.'

'And the other play? Is the script for that a secret too?'

'Three Princes at Tiger Palace?' Tien-jan laughed a sweet, tinkling laugh. 'It is so old everyone knows the words by heart. Though, now you come to mention it, poor Nu did make some amendments this time.' He paused. 'I sound like an old script myself – "Now you come to mention it . . ." There is so much formulaic dialogue in the old plays. Nu liked to change it a bit, so it was no surprise to us when he issued sheets out to each of us at the rehearsal. Though, as we blocked in the moves, I did think some of the dialogue a little irregular and inconsistent. It didn't fit somehow.'

He was rambling about theatre matters that had me quite confused. Rehearsals? And what was blocking in the moves? I tried to bring him back to the point of my inquiries.

'But Nu would have had a fair copy of the whole piece?'

The boy sighed and nodded.

'Yes, the full script. Follow me, and I will show you where he keeps . . . kept . . . all the scripts.'

He took me to a room backstage that had pigeonholes along one wall. Every slot was stuffed tight with paper documents. Tien-jan began to rummage through them, at first casually, then gradually moving from slot to slot more urgently. It came as no surprise to me when he said that he couldn't find the amended script to 'Three Princes at Tiger Palace' anywhere.

# FIFTEEN

*A closed mind is like a closed book, just a block of wood.*

It was not long before the prefect reacted to the murder in the theatre in the most severe of ways. On the following day, large notices appeared in all public places. They were written in Chinee, of course, but Lin translated for me. We were standing outside the theatre, and the notice had been pasted on one of the columns that formed the entrance archway. The troupe's barker and moneyman was staring disconsolately at the notice. It read:

> *All citizens not engaged in the pursuits proper to them, and who in this city shall practice and sing musical entertainments, or teach and perform tsa-chu dramas, or bring together crowds for the purpose of lewd entertainments*
> SHALL BE PROHIBITED, *and*
> *All animal trainers, snake-charmers, puppeteers, performers of sleight-of-hand, players of cymbals and drums, and those who deceive men and gather crowds for the purpose of practising quack-salving, will be prohibited and those who disobey*
> WILL BE SEVERELY PUNISHED.

The barker turned to us with a glum expression on his face.

'Well, that is a pretty comprehensive coverage. We will not be able to do anything here now. Nu will be turning in his grave. If he was in one, which he isn't yet. But you know what I mean. We have hardly been able to make ends meet for months now. He was always begging and borrowing to keep us going. And this new play of Guan's was our big chance.' He pulled a face worthy of the best actor on the stage behind him. 'We've had it now. Might as well move on.'

He trudged through the archway towards the stage to tell his comrades the bad news. Lin looked at me with a small smile playing on his lips.

'It's an ill wind . . .'

'What do you mean?'

'At least Guan's play won't be performed next week. It gives us some more time to find the truth.'

'That's true. But what about Tien-jan? Won't you miss him?'

Lin's face was stony.

'I don't know what you mean, Nick.'

I let the matter drop. I had my own reasons for keeping young Mister Natural Elegance around for a while longer, but I couldn't tell Lin why. I had hoped he would want to prevent him from leaving so soon himself, but apparently not. We walked away from the square, and towards the Geng household. We had questions to ask.

I took more notice of Geng's house this time, hoping it would give me some clues to what had happened there. It had obviously once stood on the edge of town. The red tile roof with its curved gables gave the impression of a substantial residence belonging to a rich merchant. The aspect of the windows along the frontage spoke of a property that once looked out over open land towards the river. Now all the occupants could see from them were other, smaller buildings. The city had encroached on the house and swallowed it. It was barely possible now to appreciate the symmetry of its frontage. Stepping through the doorway from the road, Lin and I found ourselves in a central courtyard, surrounded by buildings. Once again, I could tell that the house was somewhat down at heel. Wall timbers were splitting and some roof tiles were loose. Two broken red tiles lay on the packed earth of the courtyard, and probably had lain there since they had fallen from above weeks earlier. The whole house was unusually quiet, with not even any smoke coming from the rear of the building where the kitchen stood. I could tell it was the kitchen, because it was built slightly apart from the other ranges. Fire was a constant hazard to timber-framed houses. There was no evidence even of the servant who had been present last time.

A couple of chickens pecked desultorily at the barren earth of the courtyard.

We hovered in the centre of the yard for a moment, before Lin whispered in my ear.

'Do you think they've all fled?'

I grinned.

'No, I don't think so. I just caught a glimpse of a youth peering round the edge of an upstairs window behind you. I will rouse them.'

I pulled my short Tartar sword from its sheath, and took a swing at one of the chickens. There was a squawk from the chicken, which flew up in a blur of feathers. And a responding squawk from a human.

'That is my best layer, I am glad your prowess with a sword is so poor.'

The old lady emerged from the kitchen door, tottering on her tiny feet. I sheathed my sword.

'I aimed to miss, or the bird would have been running around headless by now. Which is not a criticism I can make of you, Madam Gao.'

She narrowed her dark, little eyes, making the wrinkles on the lined face even deeper and more numerous.

'How do you mean?'

Whether she really didn't understand my Western analogy, or was just maintaining her appearance of being a rather stupid, old lady, I wasn't sure. But one thing she had done was give the game away about her ability to understand my Mongol. When we had first interviewed her, I had stumbled through a three-way conversation using Lin as my interpreter. The crafty old bird had used a feigned ignorance of Mongol as a way of avoiding my more searching questions. Now I knew that, I explained my meaning directly.

'You told us you were poor, and needed to marry Geng in order to survive. But the truth is it was you who loaned Old Geng money. Money he desperately needed to keep his business afloat.'

As I spoke, I took a couple of steps towards where she stood. Suddenly, two very large, very hairy men emerged from the kitchen and placed themselves either side of the old lady.

They only had sticks in their fists, but they were such large and hairy fists and such heavy sticks, that I did not think for one moment of drawing my sword again. From behind me Lin piped up in his thin but authoritative voice.

'There is no need for violence here, Madam Gao. We are the defenders of the law, and to threaten us would be a crime carrying a severe penalty.'

The old lady bowed low, her head tilting to one side, until we could see the bald patch atop her head. When she straightened up, she showed a mouth with more gaps than teeth in it.

'I am sorry. My . . . nephews –' she gestured at the two hairy monsters – 'are a little overzealous at times. I asked them to stay with me, as I am fearful for my life.'

She sighed theatrically, in a way I could now recognize as a pantomime *k'o*. Lin would have been pleased that my knowledge of Chinee drama was expanding. Madam Gao continued.

'The times have been so strange of late. What with the poisoning of Geng that could have so nearly been mine. And the attack that I suffered a few weeks ago.'

'Attack?'

Lin was interested now, and pressed her to explain. She sat down wearily on a bamboo chair set in the shade and waved a hand. The two hairy bodyguards disappeared, though I could still feel their presence like a cold wind blowing from the north down the back of my neck. I squatted down on an upturned bucket, but Lin remained standing in that peculiarly still way of his. His question remained hanging in the air, and, once settled, the old lady answered it.

'It was a few weeks before Geng's death. I was still in my own house, living with the girl, of course.'

I decided to interrupt, because I realized the old woman had avoided answering my earlier question about her wealth, and wanted to disconcert her a little.

'Was this before or after your son died?'

The old lady's face hardened, and the lines round her mouth stood out. It was not the reaction I would have imagined a loving mother to have had to my brutal question. She had an answer nevertheless, even though it was brief.

'Afterwards.'

'You see, I have concerns about your son.'

Her eyes were like daggers stabbing into me.

'How so? His death has nothing to do with what happened to me, or to Geng's death. He was a sickly child, and he grew up to be a sickly man. The girl married him at my behest, but he did not live long enough to give her a child. That is all there is to say about the matter.'

I noticed that, finally, a single tear squeezed out of her eye and ran down her wrinkled cheek. I suspected it was manufactured. I held up a hand and signalled for her to go on. She brushed the tear from her face.

'I was explaining about the attack. I suppose, thinking about it, I should have reported the man. It was someone who owed me money, and he said he had come to negotiate a deal. The next thing I knew, quite out of the blue, he leaped at me and tried to strangle me. I was lucky that Old Geng was due to visit me and was a little early. He came into the room and saw what the man was doing. He grabbed him and pulled him off me. There was a scuffle and my attacker fled. Geng was too old to give chase, and anyway, I needed his attention.' She stared Lin in the eye, pointedly avoiding looking at me. 'That was why I agreed to marry him – and that was when my fortunes changed. Geng had saved my life, and I was indebted to him. He said he had been looking for a wife, and now he had found one. It was my fate to obey him, and at his insistence I got rid of my own house and moved in here.' She waved a weary hand at the ramshackle range of buildings. 'I think my *yun* was waning from that point on.'

At last I had the answer to my question about why a rich old woman should marry a poor man who owed her money. I knew a little bit about Chinee belief in fate and luck. So I knew Madam Gao had not been happy to accept Geng's marriage offer, but had felt bound to do so. Her luck had taken a nosedive from that point. She looked tired, but Lin wanted more.

'And was it your idea that Jianxu should marry Wenbo?'

'No, that was Old Geng. He has been looking for a wife for his son for a long time. You can see for yourself how weak the boy is. His father thought my obligation to him would stretch to the girl. And indeed, I saw no reason why she shouldn't have married Wenbo. It was she who objected. She has always been a wayward child, never doing as she was told. You would have thought she owed me nothing the way she behaved.'

As the old lady rambled on, I had noticed that the boy had moved from his window, where I had first seen him, to the edge of the courtyard where we sat. He was hiding behind one of the doorframes to my right. Madam Gao was not able to see him, but he could see her, and hear what she said. His shoulders had slumped when she described him to us, and his fists had clenched. I could see there was no love lost between them, the tough-minded old woman and the skinny youth.

When she had finished her scalding diatribe about both Wenbo and Jianxu, I asked if we could speak with Wenbo now. She contorted her face into some sort of grin.

'Of course you can, Mr Investigator.' She turned her head slightly in the boy's direction, revealing that she had been aware of his presence all along. 'You can come out now, Wenbo. Stop skulking, and show yourself.'

The 'boy', who must have been twenty at least judging by the growth on his chin, shambled over. His head was bowed, and when he did look up, I saw the spark of fear in his eyes. He was scared of us – more than he needed to be, and more than he had been last time we saw him. I wondered why.

'You don't need to be afraid, Wenbo. We are just filling in some of the past in order to be sure of what happened to your father.'

'It wasn't Jianxu that did it.'

Wenbo's face was red and all screwed up. His hands were in tight fists. I stood squarely on to him, facing up his anger.

'Then who was it, Wenbo? Who was it?'

His face returned to its normal colour, and he lowered his gaze again. The rage was momentarily over.

'I don't know.' He stuck an accusing finger out at Gao. 'But she didn't want to go through with the marriage to my father. Ask *her* who did it.'

The old lady was imperturbable.

'He isn't right in the head. He's weak-kneed for the girl, and can't accept she was responsible.'

Wenbo growled, and would have launched himself at his never-to-be mother-in-law had I not grabbed his arm. Lin, who had observed all this silently, coughed quietly.

'I would like you to show me the kitchens where the broth was prepared, Madam Gao.'

The old woman looked puzzled, but eventually shrugged her shoulders, and eased gingerly up from her chair.

'Come this way. You will not see much. The kitchen has been used and cleaned many times over since Geng's death.'

She turned and hobbled towards the kitchen door, the only entrance on that side of the courtyard. I followed, my hand still holding Wenbo's arm firmly. I was curious to know what Lin hoped to learn from examining the kitchen. Whatever it was, the boy would be useful to question also. He was supposed to have been around when the fatal brew was concocted. Inside the kitchen, a large open hearth stood at the back of the room. A fire burned, as it probably did constantly, and a pot of water boiled above it on a hook. The room was very hot. Utensils and cooking pots were lined up on racks, and sacks of provisions lay stacked along one wall. I imagined it was the most normal of kitchens, the only oddity being the presence of the two bodyguards. There was no servant bustling around as there would have been in any other merchant's kitchen. Madam Gao noticed me looking around.

'All the servants are gone. I dismissed the last one yesterday. We cannot afford their wages.' She sighed dramatically. 'I had expected that the girl could carry out their tasks. But now she is in prison, there will have to be some changes made. Especially when . . .'

She paused, but we all knew what she had been going to say. She meant that they would have to replace Jianxu as a general-purpose skivvy after she had been executed. Wenbo looked pale, casting his gaze nervously around. I had let go of his arm, and he looked as though he was seeking a means of escape. But the only doors in the kitchen were ones at either end leading into the two wings, and the one where we had just come in. He would find it hard to get free of me.

Lin asked Gao where she had been on the fateful day.

'I was in my bed through there.'

She pointed to the door at one end of the kitchen.

'The girl and I occupied that wing of the house, and the Gengs the other.'

This time she pointed to the door at the other end of the room.

'The house was built for a large family, and Geng's had been such. But over the last few years, his brothers died, leaving him the sole occupier of the place.' She shivered theatrically. 'It's too big and draughty to my mind. But its size had its uses. Until we were married I insisted on separate quarters.'

Lin nodded his understanding.

'I see. So you were in that wing of the house, and Geng senior in the opposite one on the day of his murder?'

He pointed once again at the two interior doors.

'Yes. He was going through his bills, I believe. You can see his office if you wish.'

Lin, who perhaps had expected Wenbo to object to Gao offering him free run of the side of the house that was his, was surprised when the boy said nothing. He was merely sullen and uncooperative. Lin had his next question for the boy, however.

'And where were you, Wenbo, when Jianxu was in here cooking the broth?'

The boy's mouth opened and closed without a sound issuing as he tried to order his thoughts. Finally, he had a statement to make.

'I was in and out of the kitchen, I suppose. Father was busy with his accounts, and I knew he would spend hours trying to make them balance. But they never would, and he got angry, so I kept out of his way.'

'Did you see Jianxu leave the kitchen at any time?'

I saw where Lin was going with this. He wanted to know if anyone else had had a chance to put the poison into the broth. Wenbo frowned in concentration, and Gao interrupted.

'I saw a beggar. Tell him about the beggar.'

Wenbo seemed to wince at the old lady's prompting, but began to explain slowly.

'Yes. Some beggar came to the street door, and Jianxu wanted to give him some alms. She asked me to keep stirring the broth, but I got bored. There was no one in the kitchen then.'

'And then she came back and carried on with her cooking?'

'Er, yes. I don't know what happened after that because I went to tell father that Jianxu had let a beggar in, and should I kick him out.'

Lin paused, holding his hand in the air to stop Wenbo's story.

'The beggar came in the house?'

'Well, in the kitchen. Jianxu was going to give him something to eat, I think. I said she shouldn't, and I was going to tell my father. She came into the courtyard and told me . . .' He blushed, poking with a toe at the kitchen floor. I prompted him.

'She told you not to be so stupid.'

'Yes, but she didn't mean it. We are going to be married when she is freed.'

Madam Gao sneered, and Wenbo was about to retort, when Lin lifted his hand again. I would give anything to be able to stop an argument like Lin could with his calm and authority. He spoke quietly, but tellingly.

'One more thing, Wenbo. Did you see your father in the kitchen at any time after this?'

Wenbo shook his head.

'No, I told you. He was immersed in his accounts and bills. He didn't emerge from his room until . . . Well, I heard his cries of agony, and I went in to him. I ran off to fetch Jianxu. I didn't know what to do. But by the time we both got back to his office, he was dead.'

# SIXTEEN

*Enjoy yourself, it's later than you think.*

'Did you notice that whenever the old lady talked of Jianxu, she referred to her merely as "the girl?"'

We were walking back through the bustling centre of town, where the streets were full of traders. A cry of warning came from behind us and Lin pulled me to one side. We pressed up against the wall of a food shop whilst a large sedan chair passed us carried by two sweating Chinee slaves. I glimpsed the white, oval face of a pretty girl peering through the side window. I flashed a smile through my red beard and the face disappeared. But not before I saw a look of curiosity pass over the deadpan visage, followed by a smile. Then the sedan was gone. Lin gave me one of his looks.

'Forget her. In such an opulent conveyance, the chances are she is the courtesan of some wealthy man. Besides, she will not be to your taste.'

'How can you say that?'

'Because I know what you have told me about courtesans in your world. How the pleasures of the flesh are all they cater for. In this world, the courtesan is trained in music, painting, calligraphy and poetry. An admirer could expect to pass months in leisurely mutual seduction, when he would not even expect to touch her body. He would shower her with gifts, hold parties and admire her skills at calligraphy while his lust would be brought to such a pitch, he could barely control it. But control it he must until the moment arrived when he was allowed to slake his desires.' He looked disapprovingly at me. 'You would die of boredom before a day was passed in this way.'

I sighed, putting the white-faced vision out of my mind.

'You are right, Chu-Tsai. I have still to come to terms with your people's pace of doing things. It would seem that Chinee lust is to be long drawn out too. And the answer to your original question is, yes, I noticed how Madam Gao spoke of Jianxu as though she was simply a possession – a servant without a name. And strangely enough she spoke of her son in the same terms too. She never gave him a name. It was as though he almost didn't exist.'

'I remember Gurbesu said the same of Jianxu. The son was her husband, yet she never referred to him by his name. It was Cangbi, by the way. It is recorded in the documents attached to the case. Perhaps we are seeing more than there is to see. It may be his illness and death were too much for both women to bear, and that is why they cannot speak his name.'

We had just entered the square where the theatre and temple stood side by side, and we stopped for a moment looking at the scene. I shook my head.

'No. I got the impression that Cangbi was merely a nuisance and yet a means to an end. A nuisance for his mother, who saw him as a heavy weight around her neck. And a means to an end for both women. A way of tying Jianxu closer to here for Gao, and a way of gaining access to the family's wealth for Jianxu herself. He had no other value in himself as a person for them.'

Lin seemed a little shocked by my assessment.

'That would make them both very hard and manipulative people. I can believe that of Madam Gao. But surely Jianxu – at twenty – has more sentiment in her soul.'

I patted Lin's arm.

'You are an incurable romantic, Chu-Tsai. Don't forget Gurbesu was worried that she appeared a little cold and unemotional when she was interviewed. Maybe we should both speak to Jianxu and make our own minds up.'

Lin agreed.

'Yes, there is the matter of the kitchen, and the sequence of events leading up to Geng eating the soup. It doesn't quite all fit together yet.'

I could see he was pondering some small factual detail as he was fond of doing, but I was vexed about the sudden appearance of a new suspect.

'And now there is the matter of the unidentified beggar,

who was perhaps left alone in the kitchen. He could have spiked the soup too.'

'Who do you think he might have been? A business rival of Geng's?'

'Or one of the old lady's debtors. We need to find out who he was.'

'And talking of debtors, we need to find out the whereabouts of the doctor.'

Lin's reference to the elusive Doctor Sun reminded me what Tadeusz had told me that morning. He reckoned he had heard a rumour about the doctor being in one of the villages up in the hills where the Hwang-Ho River came from. He assured me he could track him down if he could borrow my horse. Our party was getting smaller by the day with Alberoni gone – God knew where – and now Pyka seeking to go. I hoped the latter would not be going on such a wild goose chase as the priest and his search for Prester John.

I missed Father Alberoni, and yearned to ask him if he knew what had really happened with my father's death. I had harboured the thought that my mother had killed her husband for so long, it was difficult to discard it. But Lin's talk of Jianxu and emotions had made me think again. My mother – Rosamund – had been a passionate woman, and I could imagine her stabbing Agostino in a rage. But I could not now square the idea of a poisoning with her impetuous nature. Minor tampering with emetics certainly, but not deliberate murder. Poisoning required cold calculation and patience – qualities my mother lacked to any degree. But if my mother hadn't poisoned my father, who had? I suddenly realized Lin had touched my arm. Dragging myself back to the present, I raised a questioning eyebrow. He whispered in my ear.

'Don't look now, but the prefect is coming this way. He was in the Temple of the Earth-Goddess, and as soon as he saw us turned in our direction.'

I could guess why Li Wen-Tao had been in the temple, and imagined that his purse would be all the heavier for speaking with the old priestess there. Our little scam must be proving very lucrative. I leaned down to whisper back to Lin, he being shorter than me.

'Let me speak alone with him.'

Lin nodded.

'Gladly. He makes me feel uneasy every time he looks at me.'

Without a look back across the square, Lin turned and went, leaving me to deal with the prefect. He huffed and puffed towards me, having to catch his breath before he could speak. Casting a meaningful glance at the retreating back of Lin Chu-Tsai, he finally found his voice.

'I am glad to see Master Lin depart – we have some private business to transact, you and I. Besides, there are bad rumours circulating about him in the town.'

I was surprised. Who could know anything about Lin other than that he was a high official at Kubilai's court? That was self-evident from his bearing and his robes.

'What sort of rumours?'

Li pulled a face, expressing disgust at what he was about to say, though I could see he was relishing passing on the rumour.

'It is said he is a sodomite and dallies with one of the actors in the theatrical troupe. Of course I can believe it of their sort. Most actors are nothing more than thieves and prostitutes. But it ill becomes an official of the Khan's court to be so inclined.'

I thought of Tien-jan Hsiu, and what I had seen – or thought I had – in T'ai-Yuan-Fu. The pretty youth had embraced him and stayed in Lin's rooms long after I had left, and the lights had been lowered intimately. But then that had been in another town. No one here could have known of that, except for other actors, and someone in our little group. Who on earth could have spread such a rumour? And why? It sounded like something Ko Su-Tsung would do, but he was hundreds of miles away in Khan-balik. But then maybe he wasn't. He had been likened to a spider in the centre of a web. Did he have an agent here? I would have to speak to Lin, but in the meantime I tried to play down the idea.

'It is impossible that such a thing could have happened. I know Lin Chu-Tsai well, and he is of an unstained character.'

Li grunted, suggesting he was unconvinced. I diverted his thinking by asking about our scam.

'Now, how much have you for me in your purse. You have just been to the temple, have you not?'

Li puffed out his fat cheeks.

'That is the main reason I wanted to talk to you alone. I want to renegotiate our arrangement. It seems to me I do all the work, and you take all the money.'

I smiled coldly.

'Only my fair share. You are paying in instalments for my original idea. However, I am prepared to negotiate. You will find me a generous and accommodating man. Look, meet me in the theatre shortly after dusk tonight. It is empty then, and no one will disturb us.'

Li licked his lips, obviously wondering if he could trust me. But then we were both involved in something illegal, so what could I do that would endanger him? He agreed, and hurried away across the square. I returned to the house, unsure if I would tell Lin about the rumours or not.

As it turned out, I didn't have time.

I was bothered by Wenbo's introduction of the beggar into the story. This person had never appeared in the official documents. I was also mindful of the play we had seen in T'ai-Yuan-Fu – *The Mo-Ho-Lo Doll*. In it, a crucial piece of missing information was the identity of the unknown man who had told the murderer of the victim's illness. This had led to the murderer administering poison, thinking the illness would cover his killing. It was only when the doll-maker had been identified that the truth came out. I was concerned that the unidentified beggar might equally prove the key to this murder case.

Not being able to let matters lie, I hunted out Tadeusz as soon as I got back, catching him before he had disappeared to seek out the doctor. I asked him to put off that search for the time being, and use his connections with the guild members in Pianfu to see if they could identify the beggar. Wenbo had said he was dressed in a distinctive off-white, loose robe that he used to envelop himself in, wrapping the end around his head. Tadeusz said he would try and find out who it might have been.

'Though I am not confident of achieving a result, Nick. On

my wanderings round the city, I am aware there are many beggars in the streets. Some are simply poor and without work, but others have no eyes, or are mutilated in some other way. I have seen beggars without legs, who propel themselves around on little carts. The fact that this is a very prosperous city does not seem to diminish the numbers of the destitute.'

'I would guess, Tadeusz, that the prosperity of the city is the very reason these poor souls have gravitated here. To scrape an existence from the generosity of the rich and well-fed.'

I was reminded again how I, in my own way, lived off the beneficence of Kubilai, picking up scraps from his table almost. These beggars were at the very bottom of that heap. I put my arm over Tadeusz's shoulder, and walked with him across the courtyard.

'Do what you can, and let me know whatever you find out.'

It was early afternoon when I received a curious message from Tadeusz. I had been thinking of the rumour about Lin and how to broach it with him. And I was also planning how I was to deal with the prefect when I met up with him. All that brain work had made me feel tired, and I had resorted to a mind-refreshing doze in the courtyard. I would need to be at my most alert later, after all. I was soon dreaming of white-faced handmaidens singing to me and plying me with grapes, when I felt a tugging at my sleeve. Was it a courtesan, or a nimble and willowy acrobat ready to indulge my every whim?

'My darling,' I murmured, reaching out, only to hear a snort of childish laughter. I opened my eyes, and sat abruptly up. Beside me stood a filthy urchin, wiping the snot from his nose with a grubby sleeve that, from its shininess, I deduced had been long used for the purpose. He had a broad and lascivious grin on his dirty face. I soon wiped that off by grabbing the front of his tattered shirt and pulling him close. I shoved my face into his, putting on my best demonic look.

'What are you doing here, snotface?'

I don't think he understood my words, but he knew their meaning. He gulped, and wriggled out of my grasp. But before I could cuff him, he waved a scrap of paper at me. I went to take it, but he snatched it away, and held out his hand, palm upwards. I growled, but he stood his ground, and only let me take the paper after I had placed a small coin in his sticky hand. The business completed, he bolted for the street door, stopping only to stick his tongue out as a last defiant gesture at the foreign demon. I laughed at his cheek, and unfolded the piece of paper.

It was a message that said simply 'Come to the bathhouse in physicians' square', and was signed 'Pyka'. Though there were few words, I could still sense the urgency of the message. Knowing I had time before my meeting with Li, I left immediately to seek out the place. However, I could not for the life of me think why he had not returned to the house to report to me. I mean to say, what was he doing luxuriating in a bathhouse, if there was something urgent to discuss? It was not somewhere I would like to be seen in all that often for fear of seeming effeminate.

I knew where the square given over to doctors and astrologers was located – we had passed through it when we first arrived. But when I got there, it was not immediately obvious which of the many fine buildings was the place where people came to bathe. I traversed the square once, and finally decided to stop someone and ask. One of the words I had learned from the gaoler, while Gurbesu had been talking to Jianxu, had been the word for washing. I just hoped he hadn't been having a joke with me and had taught me the word for fornication instead. I might get a strange reaction if so. I chose an innocuous-looking elderly man in a *bei-zi* robe, on the assumption that he, rather than a peasant, would use a bathhouse. Striding over to him, I tried my word.

'*Shi-dzaw*?'

He screwed his eyes up, and looked puzzled. At least I had not uttered a profanity, I thought. I tried again.

'*Shi-dzaw*?'

This time he realized what, with my awful accent, I was trying to say. He smiled, and rubbed his hands over his body in a way suggesting he was scrubbing himself clean. I nodded, and he repeated the word back to me. It came out in a much more mellifluous way, and he pointed to a large building at the top of the square. It looked like a palace to me, and I had discounted it as a simple bathhouse. I gave him my thanks, and made my way across the bustling square to my goal. Once inside the building, I could easily tell its purpose. Though the baths were not visible from the entrance hall, the place echoed with conversation and the splashing of water. I made for an archway to my right, only to be shooed away by a female attendant. Glimpsing the unmistakeable shape of bare womanly flesh through the arch, I realized I had chosen the section devoted to females. Thinking that perhaps this communal bathing thing was not such a ridiculous idea, I raised my hand in acknowledgement of the attendant's reprimand, and crossed the hall to the other archway.

At this door into the men's section stood a stocky, hairy and definitely male individual wearing just a loincloth. He sized me up and indicated I should go inside and remove my clothes. I had no way of telling anyone that I was just looking for Tadeusz, so I stripped off and left my clothes in a niche in the wall. Feeling a bit conspicuous with my red hair and height, I strolled past large tubs of what was clearly cold water with naked men vigorously rubbing themselves. Lin had told me once that Chins reckoned cold water was good for the health, and that from childhood they bathed in it regularly. I could only imagine it was conducive to freezing your balls off. As I could not see Pyka in any of the cold tubs, I moved on. At the end of the men's section I could see steam emanating from a separate room. As this looked more promising, and I had not yet found Pyka, I strode towards the room. Inside was a single tub filled with hot water, and in it sat Pyka. He was vigorously scrubbing his skin, and the water splashed over the rim of the tub, causing rivers to run across the floor. As his skin was bright red, it looked to me as if he had been scrubbing for some time. Either that or the hot water had boiled him like a piece of meat. I walked over, and stood before him. He didn't even notice me and continued his frenzied ablutions. I leaned on the rim of the tub, and with the palm of my hand splashed some water at his face. Startled, he stopped his scrubbing and took me in.

'Nick. Thank you for coming. I'm . . . cleansing myself.'

'So I see.'

He still looked agitated, and I gripped the side of the tub. There was room for more than one in it, and perhaps if I joined him, he might relax. Besides, I had not washed for a week or so.

'Oh well.'

Sighing, I hoisted myself up and into the tub. The water splashed over the rim like a waterfall, but it was still warm and felt not at all bad. I lay back with my arms encircling the rim. Tadeusz looked at me for a moment, then started to rub his body again. I reached out and stopped his feverish activity.

'Tadeusz. Tell me what this is all about. Why are you and I here?'

He looked at me, his eyes full of pain.

'It's the beggar.'

# SEVENTEEN

*Life is a dream walking, death is a going home.*

I leaned forward, full of curiosity.

'You have found him already.'

'Well, I don't know. Not really, but . . . let me explain.'

I raised my hand to indicate he should proceed, and returned my arms to the rim of the tub. He took a deep breath, and began.

'When I left you, I went to see my friends in the silversmith guild. I asked them about beggars, and whether they simply begged in the street or went round to houses. They said that most beggars kept to the streets, but sometimes a beggar would try his luck at a rich man's house. They were usually ejected by the servants without any alms, mind you. But sometimes their *yun*, as they call luck, could be in, and they got a scrap of food. When I described the beggar – wrapped all in white with his head covered – they fell silent, so I thought they knew who I meant. But when I pressed them, all they would say was some word that I had not heard before. It sounded like *dafeng*.'

'*Dafeng*? What does it mean? Do you know?'

'If I heard it right, it literally means big wind. But further than that I could not begin to guess. I asked if there was anywhere I would find this beggar, and they said such a beggar would be in the dark alleys, not in the big squares like the others asking for alms. I did not understand why this should be so, but I thanked them and decided it might be worth just looking around in case I came across him. I walked down many of the quieter side alleys leading off the squares, quartering back and forth until I felt quite dizzy. In fact I got lost finally, and thought I would ask someone for directions. Except the area I had come to was silent as the grave. There simply was no one to ask. Then I saw him

– a ghost of a figure in white lurking in the dark just ahead of me.'

Tadeusz shivered, though whether from the recollection of the ghostly sight, or the cooling of the bath water, I was not sure. He moaned a little, but finished his story.

Tadeusz knew the beggar must have seen him because he took a few paces towards him and started to raise his hand from under his white robe. But then something happened to startle him, and he stopped in his tracks. Tadeusz could not see his face as it was hidden by the enveloping white robe, so he could not see his reaction. Perhaps he was scared to be confronted by a barbarian with a burned face. Perhaps he thought, with his disfigurement, Tadeusz was just another beggar and so not worth asking for alms. Whatever it was that disturbed him, the white-clad figure turned and started to run off. Tadeusz called after him in the Chin language.

'Wait. I must speak with you. I mean you no harm.'

The beggar did not stop, and though his gait was ungainly Tadeusz knew that, if he ducked down any of the side alleys, he might lose him. He started to give chase, and soon caught him up. The beggar was hampered by his robe, which enveloped him from head to foot, as well as appearing to be not very nimble himself. Quite the opposite, in fact. Every step he took was a lurch from side to side rather than a fleet progression forward. Tadeusz grabbed the back of his white shroud, and gave him a shove. The beggar stumbled and pitched forward on to the ground, pulling Tadeusz on top of him. His breath came out of him in a great gust, and Tadeusz could feel nothing but bony protuberances under him. He yanked the veil of cloth away that covered the beggar's face.

Tadeusz's eyes were like saucers as he stared at me across the scummy water in the tub.

'Oh, Nick, it was awful. He had no hair on his head, not even on his brows which were like great horny swellings, his nose was eaten away revealing gaping holes in his face. Exhausted by the chase, his breath came in terrible hoarse wheezes. I suddenly realized what the word *dafeng* meant.'

He leaned towards me, and whispered. 'The man was a leper.'

The grim truth of what Tadeusz was describing hit home to me. Leprosy. Some said there was a moral cause to catching the disease, others that the poison of it could be got rid of to a healthy person by sexual congress. The very thought of doing that made me feel cold. Whatever the cause, leprosy was a curse. Tadeusz's description of the white robe that the beggar wore as a shroud was quite appropriate. Many said lepers existed in a place between life and death. Alive but ritually separated from mundane existence. I could see Pyka was scared by his close contact with the man, and he had a fearful addition to his tale.

'Nick, the leper was so worn out by the chase he was gasping for breath, and spittle flew from his mouth and landed on me. Do you think I am infected?'

We were still sitting quite close, and naked, in the tub. It took all my strength not to shrink instinctively away from him at this stage. I had to remind myself of a conversation I had had with the Arab physician, Masudi al-Din. He told me that, despite people's fears of contagion, it was very difficult to catch the disease. I deliberately leaned close to Tadeusz and put a hand on each of his shoulders.

'Tadeusz, you are not infected. You will not get this disease, I promise you.'

Pyka relaxed a little, but still instinctively rubbed his face as he spoke.

'Do you think the beggar could have had anything to do with Geng's murder? I did manage to overcome my disgust at his appearance to ask him if he had ever been to the Geng house. He professed not to know it, even after I had described its location. His tone was guttural, and he was hard to understand, but he still insisted he had never been there. I had to let him go, Nick. How could I hold on to him in his state?'

'You did well. If we want him, I am sure we can find him again. If it was him at the house, he did have a chance to administer the poison. So we can't rule him out. Perhaps it was a random act of evil or revenge on society, who knows?'

I know I would need to keep Pyka busy for the next few days to prevent him brooding.

'What you need to do now is to find Doctor Sun. When we get back, you will take my horse, and seek him in this village you mentioned.'

He nodded his head, glad of the task. I squirmed a little as the wooden slats at the bottom of the tub began to press uncomfortably into my buttocks.

'Now, can we get out of this tub before the attendant thinks we are a couple of sodomites? Besides, the water has gone cold, and my privates are shrivelled to such an extent I would not like a lady to see them until I have had chance to warm them up.'

The girl – she had been called that so much by Madam Gao over the years that she even thought of herself in such terms – was now sure the wheel of fortune had turned in her favour. Wenbo had just shown up at her lonely cell with information about the investigators from Tatu, the capital. The flame-haired one had been suspicious of Madam Gao, he was sure of it.

'And when I told him you were innocent, I think he believed me.'

Jianxu kept silent at this juncture. She could not yet convince herself that what the boy said was the case. He was rambling on, eager to please her.

'Then the red-robe asked to see the kitchen. Why would he do that?'

She was startled by his words. She wasn't sure, but a little bud of doubt began to grow inside her. She wanted to know more.

'Did you tell them about the beggar?'

Wenbo nodded reluctantly.

'Yes, I had to. Madam Gao told them about him. They seemed excited to learn about that. Maybe we should have told the prefect about him before. Then you might not be in this situation.'

He banged his hand continuously against the cell door that separated them, and Jianxu reached through the grille. She stroked his cheek to calm him.

'Never mind that now. What's done is done. They may even find out that the beggar is the guilty party. If so, I will be freed very soon, and it will all be thanks to you.'

Even as she spoke, she could hardly bear to look at his shining face.

I managed to slip away after it got dark. Lin had retired to his own quarters, and for once the wine had got the better of Gurbesu. Mainly because I had plied her with it during the evening. As I left, I could hear her snoring loudly. I hoped it would not disturb Lin too much. The streets were quieter and I got a few curious looks as I made my way to the central square. One woman stopped and rubbed a small charm in the shape of a dragon that hung around her neck. I was clearly an evil spirit to be warded off. Her talisman worked, because I was on my way without a thought for her. She was too old for me anyway.

The theatre was now a dark and gloomy place with scraps of paper drifting across the empty yard. The warning poster put up by Li Wen-Tao had been torn from the entrance door and shredded. The wind grew in strength, and I could hear the structure of the raised platform creaking. One of the pieces of paper lifted up and blew against my legs. I peeled it off, and looked at the Chinee letters. I think it was the last part of the poster – the bit that said 'SEVERELY PUNISHED'. I hoped it wasn't an omen. I screwed the warning up and threw it to one side. The creaking of the platform sounded more than the wind would account for. I guessed the fat prefect was somewhere on the stage waiting for me. So I walked over to the steps that led up to the raised area where the actors performed.

Taking each one carefully, I ended up on the stage and turned and looked out at the expanse of the bare yard. At the back, I could make out the structure of the god's tower, where Lin and I had sat. But no one was present now to observe the little play that was about to be acted out. Once more I heard the creaking of the stage floor. The noise came from behind the backcloth on which was painted a fanciful scene of mountains and frothy rivers. I called out to Li Wen-Tao.

'Master Prefect, it's time to do business. Come out and state your terms.'

Though I didn't turn round to look, the creaking of the timbers told me Li had made his entrance. I made my speech out to the empty yard.

'You will find me very accommodating. If you want a bigger cut, you can have it. But I need my share.'

I could hear his wheezy breath close behind me. Then he spoke out confidently and harshly.

'You will be getting nothing, barbarian monkey. I have been warned about you by a high official of the Khan's.'

I was puzzled by his cryptic comment, but suddenly wondered if somehow Ko was stirring matters from afar. But I did not have long to think on this. I turned round, and saw why the stage had creaked so much. It was not only Li's weight, but that of the two bodyguards I had used when I had first collected my share of the scam from Li. They had, it appeared, changed sides, and I was in for a beating. I tried to escape down the stairs, but one of the muscle-bound young men leaped through the air and stopped me. His fist crunched into my back and I collapsed in a heap. He swung his booted foot at my midriff and all the air was expelled from my lungs. Li watched with joy as the second turncoat joined in, throwing a punch at my unprotected face. Blood spurted from my lips, and I curled up in a ball as the two of them kicked and punched me.

'Enough!'

It was Li who stopped the onslaught, apparently satisfied he had warned me off trying to worm my way back into the scam. Whatever was given to the old priestess would now all be his, apart from the temple's share. I would have nothing. Wiping the blood from my chin, I staggered down the steps and off into the night. Li's triumphant laughter rang in my ears.

# EIGHTEEN

*Never write a letter while you are angry.*

In the morning, Gurbesu touched the bruises gently.

'How did those get there?'

I shrugged my shoulders, putting on an air of masculine hardiness.

'Oh, they are nothing. Just the price of a scheme of mine.'

I could see that she didn't know what I was talking about, but she wasn't going to admit it.

'One that didn't work, by the look of those bruises.'

She leaned across me to reach her bag of cures and salves. I think she deliberately put her full weight on the biggest bruise on my chest. I winced, and she smiled sweetly, unwrapping a pot of something greasy. She began to apply it, and I must say I liked the process. The beating was almost worth it for receiving such compensation. I sniffed the unguent.

'That is nice. What's in it?'

'Marigold mainly. Though I think this also contains some crushed plantain.'

I lay back and allowed her to ease my manly pain. As she massaged the ointment in my wounds, she taxed me on my reply to her question.

'What do you mean by the price of a scheme? What have you been doing? I bet you got mixed up in some underhand deal again like that one you told me about once. The long . . . thing.'

'The long firm.'

I laughed. Once, a long time ago when I was trapped by snow and ice in a hut along with a bunch of warlike Tartars, I had had time to think up this plan. Being a trader, I knew it was possible to obtain goods on credit. Now, if you first bought small quantities of, say, wine, and paid quickly, you would develop a reputation for reliability. The next step would be to place several large orders on credit with different suppliers of wine. Once the big orders arrived, you disappeared and sold the wine under another name elsewhere. Your creditors could go hang. Your reputation could take up to a year to establish, so I called it the long firm scam. I looked at Gurbesu accusingly.

'It was only an idea I once had. How could you think I would ever carry it out? Besides, how could I be doing it now, when we have only been here a week?'

She pinched one of my bruises, and I winced.

'That hurt!'

'Good, it was meant to. I hate it when you keep things a secret from me. I bet you never did it with Kat-erina.'

I corrected her instinctively, as I always did, though it never seemed to have an effect.

'Caterina. I kept plenty of secrets from her, or she would not have liked me as much as she did.' I sighed. 'But then she got her own back by keeping the biggest secret she could have from me.'

'Carrying your baby? All women are afraid to tell their man that secret. We don't know how you will react.'

I could not imagine any man being anything other than joyful at the thought of his lover giving him a child. But I had messed up and left Venice just when Cat had fallen pregnant. Or so I realized only after Gurbesu had explained to me why Cat had been moody and sick just before I had fled Venice to escape charges of wrongdoing. I saw that Gurbesu had swung her legs round and was getting off the bed. She knew what my silence meant. I was thinking about her rival again. But how could there be rivalry between two women who were thousands of *li* apart? They were destined never to meet. In fact, I had no realistic chance of seeing Cat again. Unless I could work my way to making Kubilai so indebted to me that he would release me from his service. So I had need of solving the mystery of Old Geng's death, and pretty soon.

I watched as Gurbesu lifted a white silk shift over her head. It slid down down her dark and alluring skin hiding her rounded arse and falling to her ankles. With her nakedness hidden from me, I too eased my aching hips, where I had been enthusiastically kicked, over the side of the bed. Once dressed, I felt the effects of ointment easing my aches, and I straightened my back and stepped out into the sunlight that bathed the courtyard of our temporary accommodation. Hovering by the street door was a shady-looking figure, who seemed more at ease in the shadows than in bright daylight. He hissed at me and beckoned with a crooked finger. Curious, I strolled casually over to him, though I kept a good grip on my dagger just the same. I stopped a few yards from him, and beckoned in my turn.

'Come forward where I can see you, man.'

I spoke in Mongol, but just in case he didn't understand, I made my gestures clear. He was a skinny Chinee with a dowdy brown cotton robe printed with dull green flowers. It made him blend even more into the background than his dull, grey face, and limp, long black hair did. You could walk past him in the street and never notice him. I had seen many a successful assassin with the same attributes, so I stood my ground. Reluctantly, he stepped into the light and spoke in a voice as dull and nondescript as his physical nature.

'Are you Zhong Kui?'

He gave me my demon name and spoke in Mongol too. I noticed for the first time that his eyes sparkled with intelligence. It was the only bright thing about him.

'Yes, you could call me that.'

'Naturally. Who else could you be with hair like that?'

He was proving a strange character, whose cleverness belied his outward appearance. I was intrigued.

'Now you know who I am. I would like to know who I am addressing.'

He shrugged, as if his name was of no consequence.

'I am Ho.'

He was the burglar, then, who formed part of the little scam I had devised, and that Li had taken over. I was even more curious.

'What have you got that would be of any interest to me?'

He grinned, exposing sound and fine white teeth. They showed he took good care of himself.

'I could tell you many things. But there is one item I hear you are anxious to lay your hands on. A play script.'

He had my complete attention. He must have been referring to the script missing from the players' collection at the theatre. The one that could have information on Geng's death written down by the murdered Nu.

'Yes. I am interested in a particular script.'

'It will cost you.'

I didn't imagine he had brought it out of the kindness of his heart. Not a thief and a robber like Ho.

'If it is the document I want, could you tell me how you came by it?'

He smiled more broadly.

'That information will cost you more.'

I felt like grabbing him and squeezing the information out of him. But I knew he was too canny to have the document on him. I would have to pay for the pleasure of obtaining it, and the name of the person from whom he had stolen it. I had no doubt that was how he had come by it. He just happened to have robbed the one person who would have preferred to have kept his possessions secret. I contained my anger and agreed an outrageous amount of money with him. He once again slid back into the shadows where he looked more at home. But not before he told me how he would let me have both the script and the name I wanted.

'Go to the temple right now, and give the priestess the money. She will be our intermediary. When you return this afternoon she will give you what you want.'

Like a shadow lost in sunlight, he was gone. I hurried back to my rooms and grabbed the satchel that held much of the paper money I had waved under the prefect's nose in order to entice him into the scam that Ho had formed a crucial part of. The return on my investment had proved thin, but there was still plenty to buy what I wanted from the thief. I found it amusing that our go-between was to be the old priestess in the temple. Presumably Ho trusted her enough because of her part in the swindle I had set up.

'What are you laughing at?'

Gurbesu had just finished dressing and was arranging her thick black hair in a Chinee fashion. I caressed her cheek and deliberately annoyed her for my own petty amusement.

'Never you mind your pretty little head about it. I have great plans afoot.'

I dodged out of the room just as her ivory comb flew through the air. It hit the door frame and clattered to the floor, but I was gone. The streets were already busy, and traders were opening their shops for the day's business. I made for the square. My business was with the old woman in the temple. Stepping over the threshold into the incense-filled gloom, I looked around for her. She was in her usual spot, seated on the floor beside the god of lost items. Spotting me she rose more agilely than a woman of her years should have a right to. But then, as other worshippers entered behind me, she adopted her normal stooping gait. She held out her claw of a hand and begged in that grating voice of hers.

'You have an offering for me, red-haired demon?'

I dug my hand around in my satchel and pulled out a bundle of money.

'I do indeed, mistress. Though it is not for you, but for a man who will come today and give you a gift in return for the money. It is a gift intended for me, and not for your shrine, though.'

She grimaced.

'Then why should I do all this, if the god does not benefit?'

I could hear the obvious implication of her question. She didn't care about the god, but about herself, and she played her part well. I added a slimmer bundle on top of the fat one I had already proffered.

'That is to placate the god.'

She felt rather than saw the thickness of the bundle and she grinned.

'Will you then return later today to see if the god is pleased?'

I nodded, playing out the charade.

'Indeed I will. This very afternoon.'

'I hope you will not be disappointed.'

'I hope so too, or someone will be very unhappy.'

I did not say that it would be Ho if he did not come up with what he promised me. If he took my money and fled, he would be a dead man. The old priestess cackled and I left the temple. Waiting for the information I needed was going to be frustrating, so I returned to the house where I thought I could make good use of the time. As it turned out, it was more useful than I had imagined. The rumours being spread about Lin Chu-Tsai were troubling me, and, if they were driven by Ko Su-Tsung, I wanted to know who his agent was in Pianfu.

As I had made up my mind to tell Lin, I went straight to his quarters. Crossing the courtyard, I saw through the window a figure moving in his rooms. It was not Lin; it was a taller person, more awkward in his movements. I slid the door open with a bang, and a shocked Po Ku, his face pale, looked over his shoulder at me. He was sifting through Lin's papers that lay on the low desk in the centre of the room. They were the meticulous notes that Lin had made to date of our whole investigation. The gangly servant was so surprised by my abrupt arrival that he struck one of Lin's brushes with his palm, and set it rolling across the latest set of notes. It left a black scar over the careful Chinee script. He groaned with horror, his eyes boggling out of his head. I shouted at him.

'What do you think you are doing?'

I was immediately convinced I had caught Ko's spy in our camp, and if Po Ku was the spy, then he was also the perpetrator of the rumours. Stories that would ruin Lin, and by connection with him, me also. I grabbed Po Ku's arm and spun him round so I was staring him in the face.

'How much did Ko pay you to betray your master and spread all those evil rumours? Or does Ko have some hold over you that has made you do his bidding, and try to ruin our investigation here?'

Po Ku's mouth flapped open and closed in fear, but no coherent words came out. I would have slapped his stupid, peasant face but a voice rang out behind me.

'Nick, stop it now.'

It was Lin's voice – a little high-pitched, but authoritative nevertheless. I dropped my open palm to my side, but still kept hold of his servant.

'He was rifling through your papers in a way that made me think that he is Ko's spy. You know Ko Su-Tsung will do anything to ruin both you and me, and then he can get closer to Kubilai.'

'Yes, but what makes you think he has infiltrated a spy into our little band of fellows?'

I knew I would have to tell Lin now what evils Po Ku had spread about him in Pianfu.

'I think it because that is just what Ko would do.' I took a deep breath. 'And because this servant of yours, while he was out shopping in the market no doubt, has been spreading rumours about you.'

'What rumours?'

'He has been saying that you had improper relations with that actor.'

Lin's face fell.

'With Tien-jan Hsiu? That I am some sort of . . . sodomite?'

Po Ku wrenched his arm from my grasp and fell on his knees before Lin. He had understood enough of our conversation to know that he stood accused of some bad deed, and babbled a denial in rapid Chinee. Lin lifted him up by his shoulders and calmed Po Ku. He looked over the youth's shoulder at me.

'This boy can hardly be an agent for Ko. Look at him.' He turned the terrified youth to face me. Tears were streaming down his face. 'Besides, how could Ko communicate with him while he is here with us?'

'By letter, of course. You know how fast the Yam postal system is.'

Lin smiled.

'But I also happen to know for a fact that Po Ku cannot read or write. So not only could he not take written orders from Ko, he couldn't send information back about any . . . meetings I might have had with Tien-jan. It would also be pointless for him to examine my notes.'

I was puzzled.

'But you asked him to collect your papers only the other day.'

'Yes, to gather them, but not to arrange them.' Lin stepped close and whispered in my ear. 'It pleases him to imagine that he is my secretary. I often have to tidy the papers up afterwards.'

I realized that Po Ku was another of Lin's lame ducks – people who he strove to help because they reminded him of himself as a poor, peasant youth sold to the Mongol court as a child. I think I had once fallen into that category of lame duck when I had turned up at Kubilai's court. I had wheedled my way into a banquet, and into a position where I had to uncover a murderer, or be accused of the murder myself. Lin had seen me floundering with unfamiliar Mongol ways and helped me.

'But, if it was not Po Ku who spread the rumours, who was it?'

Lin looked a little shamefaced.

'You will not be angry, if I tell you?'

'You mean you know? And you haven't told me before now?'

Lin raised his hands, palms facing me in apology.

'I had to be sure myself. And I only learned it by accident. Ko's messenger was careless, and I saw a letter in Ko's script being brought to this house.'

'Who was it for?'

'Tadeusz.'

# NINETEEN

*If you suspect a man, don't employ him. And if you employ him, don't suspect him.*

'Tadeusz? But he's so loyal? It can't have been him.'

I was astounded at Lin's revelation, but he was very sure of himself. And I knew he never acted precipitately. I looked at his solemn face.

'How long have you suspected?'

'A few days now. That's why I was glad he went on that mission to find the doctor. It has kept him out of the town for a while.' He paused, a blush appearing on his smooth, boy-like face. 'And it allowed me a chance to find this.'

He produced a letter from his stack of documents and handed it over to me. I took it, but it meant nothing as it was written in Chinee. I stared dumbly at the swirling script. Lin explained.

'It is the letter from Ko that I saw in his possession. In it Ko is suggesting that my name be smeared by spreading rumours about my . . . liaison with a certain young actor.' He looked down at his neatly-shod feet. 'I'm surprised you didn't tell me yourself.'

'About the rumours? I wanted to find out the source first, and . . .'

I paused too long, and Lin filled in the gap for me.

'And you thought they were true.'

'Now, look here, old friend, this is none of my business.' I knew I was blustering from embarrassment, but I couldn't stop myself babbling. 'Your life is your own, and if you are so inclined as to—'

'He is my nephew.'

I stopped in my tracks.

'Your nephew? You mean, what I saw in T'ai Yuan Fu wasn't . . .'

It seemed as though I was fated not to get the ending of my sentences out. Lin, a hurt look in his eyes, gazed at me.

'I don't know what you thought you saw, Nick. But it is true, Tien-jen Hsiu's real name is a mundane Lin Jen-pu. He is my brother's boy, and he ran away from the family farm to pursue his dream of being a performer. And though I am his uncle and therefore biased, I think he has found his true calling in life. His father – my brother – is a peasant born and bred. He will never recognize that Jen-pu made the right choice. I do, and saw it was him as soon as he removed his make-up that day at the theatre. I didn't want him to think that every member of his family had cast him out. So that is why he came to my rooms late at night. An actor keeps strange hours, and we talked a lot. Into the early hours, actually.'

I bowed my head in shame at thinking the rumours spread by Tadeusz in the town had been true. Though, even so, I didn't care about a man having yearnings for another man. Stranger things have happened at sea, as they say. I only regretted that Lin was disappointed in me. But then, we had the matters to sort out as a result of all this. Not least how to deal with Tadeusz Pyka.

'You are right by the way.'

Lin looked at me with curiosity.

'About what?'

'Your nephew is a fine actor, and can fool an audience into believing he is anything other than a callow youth. Believe me, I know. But now I have an errand to carry out. We will talk later about this. Tadeusz has got some explaining to do.'

I left Lin to think about what we would say to Pyka, and hurried back towards the town square. I was sure I had left enough time for Ho to have gone to the temple and collected his money in exchange for the information I wanted. When I entered the building, I could see that an elderly couple stood at the shrine of lost objects. The old priestess was hovering beside them, but they seemed unable to decide on the contribution they were going to make to the gods. Impatiently, the priestess left them to their deliberations, and, seeing me, disappeared behind the shrine. Moments later, she returned with a packet in her hands. She hobbled over to me, and passed the packet over. It was a bulky object wrapped in a dirty cloth, and I hefted it to assess whether it had the weight of a book. It felt right. I leaned down and whispered in the ear of the bent old crone.

'And did the gods give you a name to pass on to me?'

The old woman's grey head nodded.

'I am to say to you just one name. Geng.'

She winked broadly at me and turned back to her elderly clients. I raised the book in my hand, and spoke out loud for them to hear.

'I give thanks to the god of lost things. My property is restored.'

The couple looked excited and passed some gold coins over to the priestess. I left them to their further negotiations.

When I got back to the house, Tadeusz was standing in the courtyard talking to Lin. He had returned, but I could see from Lin's eyes that he had not yet plucked up the courage to tell Pyka that we knew of his betrayal. On the contrary, the little silversmith was gesticulating excitedly with both hands. He caught Lin's glance over his shoulder and turned to look at who had just arrived. When he saw me, his face lit up, and he rushed across the dusty yard.

'I have found him. The doctor. He was practising in the village in the hills just as I had been told. But when I eventually got there, he had been called to some remote farm. He is not due back for a couple of days, so I thought I would return. The village is less than a day away, and I reckon it would be better for you to be there when he returns, Nick. If he proved reluctant to talk, I could do nothing. And by the time I came back for you, he might have been scared off. This way, you can be in the village with me before he even returns.'

'How do you know he is our man? Sun is a common name, I believe.'

Tadeusz laughed, and the flame-scorched side of his face turned even redder.

'When I enquired about a doctor, the elders of the village suggested I might like to go and find one elsewhere. They hinted that he was not the best physician in the world, or why would he be hiding away in their poor village. He was all they could afford, but I surely could find better. No, it's our man, I am sure.'

'Good. Then we will set off first thing in the morning.'

I looked enquiringly over at Lin, who inclined his head slightly. It was time to confront Tadeusz.

'But before we do, there is something else you need to tell us about.'

Tadeusz looked ingenuously from me to Lin.

'What is that, Nick?'

Lin whisked the incriminating note from his sleeve, and Pyka's face fell.

'There is no point in asking where you got that, is there?'

Lin looked stern.

'I know it was wrong of me to go through your possessions, Tadeusz. But you have to admit, we deserve an explanation.'

Pyka looked nervously across the courtyard. He didn't want everyone to see his humiliation, least of all Gurbesu whom he worshipped from afar.

'Can we go somewhere more private?'

Lin waved an elegant hand towards his own rooms. Tadeusz went ahead, and we followed, probably as heavy-hearted as he was. Betrayal is bitter, but especially so when it involves one of your closest and trusted friends. Once we were in Lin's room, Po Ku was sent on an errand to get him out of the way. All three of us remained standing, as the tension was palpable. No one seemed ready to speak first, so I took a deep breath.

'Why, Tadeusz?'

He looked a little defiant at first.

'I suppose it's no good denying it.'

In reply, Lin just waved the letter from Ko.

'No, I suppose not.'

Suddenly, it was as if the inflated bladder I had seen Chinee officials kicking about for fun had burst, and Tadeusz's shoulders slumped.

'God, I am sorry, Chu-Tsai. I felt terrible enough reporting to Ko about your meeting with the young actor, but spreading those rumours made me feel worse. Believe me, I did not suggest anything improper took place between you and

Tien-jan Hsiu. I was just under orders to report on anyone you and Nick met. When I got that –' he gestured at the letter still in Lin's accusing hand – 'I was disgusted, but there was nothing I could do but obey Ko.'

'Why?'

It was Lin's turn to ask, and Pyka looked crestfallen.

'Because he has promised me information in return.'

I looked at Lin, who returned my puzzled gaze.

'What information could make you betray your friends?'

The silversmith gulped, and a tear formed in the corner of his eye coursing down his unscarred cheek.

'Information about my family.'

I felt a shock run through my spine. Tadeusz had been captured by the Mongols more than twenty-five years ago, when they devastated his home town of Breslau. He had always told us that his wife and children had died in the attack. Was he now suggesting that Ko Su-Tsung had news of them? It was impossible. Or was it? Ko, as master of the Censorate, a department that spied on all the officials who worked for Kubilai, had unprecedented access to records and files to do with the running of the empire. Could he have found something out? I put an arm on Tadeusz's shoulder.

'Do you really think he knows what happened to them?'

He sighed deeply.

'I don't think so, but I couldn't just ignore it, could I? What if they were still alive?'

My heart went out to this man I had just recently almost written off as a traitor. As a man myself who had lost one he loved in Venice, I could understand his dilemma. I personally thought Ko was playing him, and had no real information to sell, but I would stand by him.

'Tadeusz, you should have come to us as soon as Ko approached you. We are your friends and we would have helped.'

He stared me in the face for the first time since he had been accused.

'I know that now. But I was fearful of losing everything all over again.'

Lin, who was usually embarrassed by shows of affection, touched Tadeusz briefly on the arm.

'You won't lose anything, least of all our friendship. I will help you find this information about your family, if it exists. And in the meantime, you will continue reporting to Ko.'

Tadeusz looked aghast.

'You want me to continue spying on you?'

Lin smiled that little secret smile of his.

'No, but you will send letters back to Ko, misleading him about our investigation to such an extent he will be humiliated on our triumphant return to Tatu.'

I clapped a relieved Tadeusz on the back, and roared with laughter at Lin's clever stratagem.

'Now, let's have some supper together. I have a play script to show you all.'

The meal was a restrained affair, especially as Lin and I had agreed we would say nothing to anyone else about Tadeusz's misdemeanour. Po Ku, who served us, was indifferent to the atmosphere anyway. But I think Gurbesu suspected something was wrong. Tadeusz was more subdued than normal, and only replied tersely to her when she asked for news about the errant doctor. She cast a glance at me, so I shook my head slightly and she got the hint. She stopped pressing him.

Once Po Ku had cleared the remains of our meal, I produced the linen-wrapped parcel. Handing it over to Lin, I invited him to read it.

'This is what we have been looking for. The text of the play with Nu's hints hidden in it.'

Eagerly, Lin unwrapped it, revealing a stained and well-thumbed set of sheets stitched together along the top edge. He began to leaf through the pages, muttering the lines to himself under his breath. Impatient to learn what secrets the play script held, I began to form a question. But before it could emerge from my lips, Lin held up his hand. I quelled my bubbling curiosity, and Tadeusz, Gurbesu and I sat in silence while Lin scanned the script. Only when he had turned the last page did he comment.

'I now can guess what Nu saw, or thought he saw.' He waved the script in the air. 'This is a fair copy of the original text – or as close as any copy ever is – and in it are Nu's amendments.

See, he has scribbled one in on this page and scored the original out.'

I looked closely, and could see where a change had been made, though I did not understand the words.

'What does it say?'

'It should read, "Who could have guessed behind that smile a dagger lay; or that my eyes beheld my own lonely gravesite." But he changed the end of the lines to read, "Or that my eyes beheld the person who sold the poison."'

I leaned forward excitedly.

'Nu did see something at Geng's house. What else did you find?'

'Well, I remembered a line about monkshood, and I thought it was relevant to our case. But it was just coincidence. The line really does read, "Get your monkshood, your mountain fennel." But Nu has drawn a circle round the symbol for monkshood all the same, giving it emphasis. However there can be no doubt about this other textual change.'

Lin flicked through the sheets until he found what he was looking for. He took a deep breath and declaimed the proper lines.

'"Keep the memory safely locked in your head; never hesitate, never wonder am I right?" But now it reads, "Keep the memory safely locked in your head; the boy ensured that he was dead."

For me, that was the final clincher. Ho had told me via the priestess that he had stolen this script from Geng's house. The only person who could have therefore taken it from the storeroom of plays at the theatre in order to suppress the clear hints in the text, and who had therefore probably been at the play to witness the new lines, was Old Geng's son.

Wenbo had to be the killer.

# TWENTY

*If you don't want others to know what you have done,
it's better not to have done it anyway.*

The following morning Tadeusz and I rode out of Pianfu
for the nameless village in the hills where the good
Doctor Sun was skulking. It was barely light, with the
autumn sun just creeping across the sweep of the flat plain to
our right. The air was crisp and cold, presaging a hard winter
to come. Already heavy, dark clouds hung over the mountains
ahead of us. It could mean snow was on the way. I shivered,
eager to finish this mess of a murder case and be gone before
we were trapped by snowdrifts. I had experienced that once
in the land of Rus, where the very breath from your body
would freeze and turn to icicles as it escaped your lips. I did
not want that sort of experience again.

My companion was understandably tense, and maintained a
silence as we rode along. He was no doubt thinking of Lin's
proposal that he should continue to report to Ko, but send him
misleading information. He was still scared about losing his
family for a second time, I could tell. But his course was now
set. As was ours today. We had debated the way ahead last night,
and it had resulted in Tadeusz and me rising early to be on our
way. The decision not to arrest Wenbo first had taken some time.

'Wenbo can be taken tomorrow morning. There is no point
rushing over to the Geng property now. It is very late, and he
and the old lady will be safely in their beds.'

Lin was certain that nothing needed to be done precipitately.
And I agreed, especially as our evidence was flimsy at present.
It was based on the changes in a playscript made by a dead
man. Actors had bad reputations generally, and it would take
nothing at all for Li Wen-Tao to undermine our case in such
circumstances. No actual link had been established between

Old Geng's death, and the murder of P'ing-Yang Nu. Li could argue that internal rivalry might have been the cause of the actor's death. It was only the fact that the playscript had been found at Geng's house that made the link. And the only person who could establish that was the man who had found it there. I voiced my concerns over the thief, Ho.

'It is quite possible that Ho will not even bear witness to the book being at Geng's house. It fell into his hands by theft, after all.'

Lin pulled a face.

'And even if he did speak up, Li could silence him with a threat to imprison him. Li still does not want his original verdict overturned.'

I reassured him on that matter, though.

'Don't worry about Li. I have made . . . erm . . . arrangements which will prevent the prefect from crossing us.'

Lin looked questioningly into my eyes, not sure what I was referring to. I waved a dismissive hand.

'You don't want to know. Let us just say it came at a cost.'

While Lin tried to digest my enigmatic pronunciations, Tadeusz intervened in the debate.

'What about the doctor? Is it possible he could give us the evidence we need? If we can verify that the poison that killed Old Geng came from him, and that he sold it to Wenbo, then we are home and dry.'

'*If* he sold it to the boy. We don't yet know that, and we don't know if this beggar that was present had anything to do with the killing. Let's not forget him.'

Gurbesu, who had been silent throughout the debate, laid out our approach for us.

'Forget about taking Wenbo for the moment. He is going nowhere, because he is infatuated with Jianxu. I could tell that from what she said when I spoke to her. She made a joke of it, because she has no interest in him. She sees him as a boy, though he is the same age as she is. Go and apprehend the doctor, and see what emerges from that.'

That had been our decision.

As we plunged into the rocky defile that was the entrance

to the village where we hoped to find Sun, Tadeusz leaned across in the saddle. He took my arm, a look of deep pain on his ruined face.

'You don't think my wife or children are still alive, do you, Nick?'

I looked him in the eyes, and told him what I thought, not what he wanted to hear. I was no good at platitudes, anyway.

'Truthfully? No. You know more than anyone in the West how savage the Mongols were twenty or thirty years ago. We even called them Tartars, as though they were demons out of Hell. And their reputation was well earned. They would wipe out a whole village, even a whole town to make a point to the rest of us. We learned that resistance was futile, because it only brought bloody revenge. Of course, Kubilai has changed all that, adopting some of the ways of the cultured Chinee that Lin is so proud of. But make no mistake. In their soul, the Mongols are still nomadic warriors, whose only way to grow and progress is by conquest. It is something the Song emperor will find out soon enough.'

I was referring, of course, to the ongoing war Kubilai waged with the remnants of the Chinee empire that he had taken by force in the north. The Song people were stubbornly holding out in the city of Siang-Yang-Fu that sat on the banks of a tributary of the great Yang-tse river. The river was the final barrier between Kubilai and the decadent empire in the south. And the doorway to the Song was the besieged city. It had held out so far. But one day it would fall, and the inhabitants would regret their intransigence. I turned in my saddle to face Tadeusz.

'I am sorry, but I think your family are long dead.'

The silversmith scrubbed his face with his free hand, masking his renewed sense of loss.

'I know you are right. I just wish . . .'

He did not finish what he was about to say because a skinny demon sprung out of the bushes at the roadside, and grabbed the reins of his horse. The nag I was seated on reared up in fear, and I had difficulty controlling it for a moment. I was still better on the deck of a bucking ship than on the back of a plunging horse. Despite all my years away from the sea in

Cathay. When I finally had it settled, I saw that Tadeusz was actually conversing with our attacker. He was twisting round to speak to me.

'The old man is the village elder I spoke to. He says that Doctor Sun has returned. With the body of the farmer he went to heal. It would seem our good doctor's skills have not improved at all. The funeral rites will take place tomorrow, but the dead man's brother is on the rampage. He wants the hide of the doctor and he –' Tadeusz pointed at the village elder – 'is fearful that Sun is about to abscond. If we want him, we had better take him right away.'

I spurred on my horse and followed Tadeusz into the village, leaving the old man to follow in our wake. Tadeusz led me through the village to a grubby shack on the other side. Riding through, I thought it was not the neatest settlement I had ever encountered. But by comparison with the doctor's hovel ahead of us, the other huts were positive palaces. As we dismounted, a lanky man in a blue robe that had seen better days came to the door of the hut. I should have said doorway, because the opening was not graced with any means of shutting out the world other than a piece of sacking. One look at us must have convinced the man that we were either relatives of the man he had just failed to cure, or representatives of a legal system he had spent his life evading. He ducked back behind the sacking with a low moan emanating from his throat. On *terra firma* again, I pushed past Tadeusz, and ripped the sacking away. The doctor, if it was indeed he, was trying to squeeze through a gap in the timbers in the rear of the one-room hut. His robe had snagged on a splinter, though, and he was stuck. He moaned louder, and yanked at the cloth, creating another tear to join the many that afflicted the once opulent blue gown. He began to wriggle through the split in the wall, but it was too late. The satchel over his shoulder had now jammed in the gap, and I grabbed him by his long, plaited hair.

'Doctor Sun, I think you will be safer with me than with the brother of your last patient. Come.'

I dragged him by his hair back through the hole in the wall and out of the hut through the open doorway. Then I slung him across my saddle. Tadeusz and I remounted, just as a

burly, bandy-legged peasant came bowling down the dusty
street towards us. He cried out on seeing the doctor. He must
have been the bereaved brother of Sun's latest victim. But he
was too late to use the large club he held, with which, no
doubt, he had planned to teach the doctor something about
broken bones. We rode off with the doctor unceremoniously
draped over my horse before he could begin his lesson.

Once free of the village and any possible pursuit, the doctor
begged to be allowed to remount my horse in the more usual
fashion.

'My stomach aches from being bounced up and down on
this nag, and my bag is digging into my shoulder,' he moaned.

I reined in the steed, and he slid unceremoniously to the
ground in a heap. Sitting on the packed earth of the roadway,
he began to rifle through the contents of his satchel. One by
one he produced small packets and pots from the pouch and
stood them on the roadside. He muttered their names as he
did so, first finding some twigs and roots.

'Ahhh. It is safe – my *guishi*, *rougui*, *jiang*.'

Then out came some leaves.

'*Renshen*, *dang gui*, *ma-huang*.' He looked up at me. 'I can
treat fifty-two ailments using these and others. My methods
involve the Four Natures of yin and yang – cold, cool, warm
and hot. It is important to have an internal balance, you see.
Then there are the Five Tastes. These are pungent, sweet, sour,
bitter, salty – each with its own functions. Sweet-tasting herbs
help harmonize bodily systems, and drain dampness. Do you
have any ailments that require treatment?'

I quietly cursed letting him off my horse, and indicated he
should remount. But he held up his hand.

'Just a moment. There is one more item.'

He thrust his hand into his satchel, and felt anxiously around.
But his final trawl in the bag was not as successful as before.
He produced a broken clay pot and groaned as he examined
the interior.

'My precious *zhushu* compound! It is almost all gone.'

He clutched his head, and rocked back and forth on the
ground like a lost child. I circled him on my horse, and kicked
his head with my boot.

'Get up now, or I will have you over the horse's back for the whole journey to Pianfu.'

Doctor Sun scrabbled around in the earth for his medicines and crammed them back into his satchel. He then stared fearfully up at me.

'Pianfu? Who are you? Why are you taking me to Pianfu? I don't want to go back there.'

He turned on his heels, and marched off back along the track. Tadeusz made as if to cut him off, but I held up my hand to stop him. Instead, I just called after Sun.

'Go that way if you like. But it will only take you back to the arms of the dead man's brother. And they looked like pretty hefty arms to me.'

Sun stopped in his tracks and cast a furtive glance around him. As we had stopped in the rocky gorge that led to the village, there was no escape route to either side. It was sheer, and the rocks were crumbling. With a deep sigh, the doctor turned and walked reluctantly back to me. He stuck out an arm and I lifted his skinny frame with ease on to the horse's back behind me. We continued our journey with Sun clutching me around the waist and lecturing me on immortality.

'*Waidan*, or outer alchemy, necessitates a belief in natural elements being able to change into others. I can perform it using an elixir made up of substances found outside the body, and the preparation involves observing rules about seclusion and purification. Once prepared, the elixir is ingested and brings about physical changes in the body, separate from the soul. I . . .'

I interrupted him before he drove me mad.

'If you don't keep quiet, I will bring about physical changes in your body that you will not find pleasant.'

The rest of our journey was accomplished in blessed silence.

It was early afternoon before we reached Pianfu again. Riding two-up had slowed us down, and anyway I preferred to enter the city as dusk fell. I did not want anyone associated with the prefect to see us. Doctor Sun was our man, and until I had a chance to question him properly, I did not want Li interfering. So rather than ride through the centre of the city, Tadeusz and I skirted round the edge of the place. That made us even later, and it was almost dark as we dismounted. Po Ku took care of the horses, and I dragged the doctor into the courtyard. Lin and Gurbesu emerged from their respective quarters, having heard our arrival. Sun immediately threw himself on the ground at the feet of his fellow Chinee.

'Master, I beg you to save me from these demons. Look at them. One has only half a face, and the other has fire coming out of his head.'

Lin merely stared down with curiosity at the grovelling supplicant.

'The men you describe are my esteemed companions, and agents of the Great Khan. He would not take kindly to your description of them. And nor do I.' He looked up at me. 'Investigator Zuliani, take this person to my rooms. We will interrogate him there. Bring the bastinado cane.'

Sun had no way of knowing both my and Lin's dislike of torture, and whimpered at the very threat of corporal punishment.

'Please master, don't beat me. I will tell you all you want to know.'

'I know you will. And it will be very painful as you do so.'

I laughed inwardly at Lin's ferocious demeanour, knowing it to be feigned. Playing along, I grabbed Sun by his arm and frogmarched him to Lin's quarters. Tadeusz, meanwhile, plucked from the ground a stick Po Ku used to beat the dust from the matting in Lin's rooms, and waved it menacingly. Gurbesu ambled back to her room, leaving the boys to their silly games.

Inside the gloomy room, lit only by one lamp that cast large and scary shadows on the walls, Sun fell once again to his knees. He clutched his satchel to him, like some child with a favourite doll, and began to tremble uncontrollably. Lin saw how scared he was and I could tell he was about to relent on his hard man act. He would have reassured the man that we had no intention to do him any harm. But that would have lost us our advantage, and so I thrust myself forward, pushing my face into his.

'Tell us about Old Geng. We know he died from aconite poisoning. Was it you who killed him?

Sun gasped, and grasped my wrists in a vice-like grip.

'Please sir, no sir. Yes, I knew Geng Biao. He was one of my patients. But I did not kill him.'

I stared into his eyes, offering him a chance.

'Hmmm. Not deliberately, perhaps. Though I have heard your skills at healing are not the best in the world. Many have died who should have lived because of your feeble efforts. But we are not interested in them and your unfortunate record of medical care. I want to know about the deliberate murder of Geng.'

'Sir. I admit I sometimes fail to help those who come to me. It is unfortunate as you say, but I am often confronted with the hopeless cases of people who should have come to me sooner. Can I help it if they expire before my medicines can take effect? If their lungs have been stricken with influenza, even menthol, which is pungent and cool, may not be sufficient to purge the cold. But Geng's death is another matter altogether. I swear he did not die by my hand. All I did was sell some aconite to be used as a medicine. How can I help it if it was administered in too large a dose?'

'Who did you sell it to?'

Sun looked almost too scared to say. But when he saw Tadeusz swish the heavy stick through the air, he broke down. With a cry, he gave us the truth.

'I sold it to his son, Wenbo. He bought three times what he needed for one dose. I told him it was dangerous. It was he who must have killed his father with it.'

# TWENTY-ONE

*Once on a tiger's back, it is hard to alight.*

There was nothing else for it – we had to arrest Geng Wenbo. The evidence was now piling up against him. The existence of the incriminating play script in the Geng household could have been said to be circumstantial on its own. And the 'testimony' of Nu within it was sketchy to say the least. But put together with Sun's evidence, it all added up to a very sound case against the boy. It was in fact a much stronger set of facts than those which the prefect had lined up against Jianxu. Of course, Li Wen-Tao would be our major stumbling block, and Lin recognized that.

'What are we going to do about Li? He will seek to undermine our case when we present it to Taitemir, the Mongol governor.'

I gave a short, barking laugh.

'Don't you worry about Li. His authority is compromised totally. I have evidence he has been running an illegal scam involving burglary and payment for the return of the stolen goods.'

Lin looked shocked, his face turning pale.

'How do you know this?'

'Because I set up the scam, and then Li took it over. He even used two heavies to beat me up and warn me off.'

Gurbesu gave me a strange look.

'So that's why you came home with bruises all over your body that night. But excuse me for stating the obvious. If you set up the scam – which I can well believe – you can't bring Li down without incriminating yourself. And that smear will stick to Master Lin too. So there's no point in revealing it.'

I had to admit I felt smug at that point. I smiled sweetly at Gurbesu, who scowled, spoiling her pretty looks.

'You'll have to bear with me on this. Just trust me that Li

has been neutralized as a force in this city. We can move forward unhindered. So let's go now and take the boy.'

Lin wasn't so sure, being as ever the cautious one in our partnership.

'It's getting late. Wenbo and Madam Gao may have gone to their beds for the night.'

I rubbed my hands together at the thought.

'All the better for us. He will be so shocked to be arrested, he might break down on the spot. In fact, let's rouse the prefect and take him with us. He may hear a confession with his own ears.'

Lin reminded me that we still had the doctor on our hands. We had locked him in a spare room at the top of the house. But the walls were flimsy, and unless we left a guard behind, he might break out and flee. Tadeusz volunteered for the duty.

'I will redeem myself by keeping an eye on Sun whilst you have the pleasure of taking the real murderer into custody.'

I patted the silversmith on the shoulder.

'You have no redeeming to do, Tadeusz. However, I will take you up on your offer. It would not go well with us to lose our star witness at this stage. He is such a weasel, I can imagine him sneaking away if he thought we had all gone out together. And we can't expect Po Ku to take on such an onerous task. We will be back as soon as we can.'

Leaving Tadeusz on guard, Lin, Gurbesu and I marched across the town towards Li's riverside residence. Flaming torches lit some of the main streets, and pretty, white-faced girls lounged provocatively outside certain establishments. The noise inside, and the girls' presence on the street, suggested that rowdy taverns and brothels were to be found in Cathay just the same as in Venice or Genoa. In any big city in the West, in fact. I might have dallied, but Gurbesu took a firm hold of my arm, and walked me past the alluring girls. I wasn't attracted anyway – the white make-up on most of them clearly hid a ravaged skin, and the teeth I saw when one girl smiled were blackened stumps. We hurried on, but Gurbesu had a question for me.

'What was all that about Tadeusz redeeming himself? He has been behaving very oddly lately. Is there something you are not telling me?'

'So many questions! But seriously, I think you should ask Tadeusz about it. It is his story to tell, and I think you will find him not unwilling to unburden himself to you. He is in love with you after all.'

Gurbesu snorted in derision at this suggestion of mine. But then she gave me a quizzical look.

'Are you being serious?'

I nodded solemnly.

'I will just tell you that Tadeusz was tempted for very good reasons to spy on us all. But he came to Lin and me and told us the truth, and we trust him now as strongly as before.'

I left out the part where we had backed Tadeusz into a corner before he confessed. I would leave it to him to consider the extent of his confession Gurbesu.

Li's house was all quiet when we reached it. The night porter tried to insist his master had retired to bed and could not be disturbed. But I could see a dim light on in his reception rooms, and was not to be put off. I brushed past the porter, and my companions followed, ignoring the servant's protests. Through the open doorway, I could see that Li sat at a low table, a look of pleasure on his face. With her back to us and facing him knelt a richly robed girl. She was pouring tea into a bowl set before the prefect. I stepped forward into the room.

'You will have time for tea later, Master Li. But now, you have an arrest to witness.'

Li's face fell, his mouth an open wound expressing shock. His cheeks turned bright red and I thought he might explode. The girl, also surprised by our bursting in, turned to look behind her. She had the white-painted face of a lady of pleasure, but beneath it her looks were finer than those of the street whores. I knew from stories told by Lin, that a Chinee's preferred sexual encounter began with a song and the serving of tea. Unfortunately, Li would not now be able to consummate his drawn out dalliance. I picked up the strange-looking stringed instrument lying at the girl's feet. It made a noise like a strangled chicken when I thrust it at the girl.

'I hope he has paid you, miss. Because your services are no longer required.'

She looked me in the eye for a moment, then, seeing I was

in earnest, stood and gathered up the hem of her long robe.
She left the room quietly on dainty steps. Li, meanwhile, had
boiled over. He waved at the harassed servant who had scurried
in on our heels, and the man helped Li to his feet. Once he
had regained his dignity, Li was all bluster.

'How dare you enter my house unannounced and order
my servants around. The girl is a perfectly respectable entertainer and will be shocked at your innuendo. I shall have to
pay her more to placate her now. So leave before I call in
my bodyguard.'

I grinned in what I hoped was a wolfish manner.

'Oh, please do. If they are the two youths who gave me a
few bruises the other day, I want them present to hear what I
have to say.'

Li looked at me suspiciously, but sent his servant off to
fetch the two bodyguards. Lin, meanwhile, intervened in an
attempt to calm the situation down. He cast a quizzical glance
at me and then stepped forward.

'Forgive our abrupt entrance, Master Li, but we have urgent
business with you that cannot wait. We have discovered the
real murderer of Geng Biao, and perhaps of the actor P'ing-
Yang Nu also.'

Li's little piggy eyes narrowed.

'I hope you are not going to cast doubt on my judgement,
Lin. I care nothing about the death of the actor, which was
probably the result of an argument over drink or money. As for
the murderer of Geng, she is in jail awaiting execution. It is
only the formality of your . . . investigation that has delayed
the matter. I had expected you to confirm my decision.' He
turned his gaze on to me, while still talking to Lin. 'If not, some
unpleasant information about your man, here, may come out.'

I think Li felt very comfortable about accusing me of the
confidence trick involving Ho's thefts and the return of stolen
goods by the agency of the priestess in the Temple of the Earth
Goddess. He thought my accusing him of being involved would
not be believed in the circumstances. And if the situation had
been as he imagined, I would have agreed with him. I would
sound like a trickster trying to shift the blame. But he was
unaware of one thing.

A con is nothing more than a play. Everyone knows it is a play except the victim, until he is stung. But sometimes the con is more convoluted, and involves the victim thinking he has seen the trick. At this point the victim is dragged into joining in the con. This is where the real con starts. Li had willingly joined the stolen goods scam, and had missed the real con. He didn't know it, but he was still playing a part in my play, even though we were not in a theatre. I addressed those present.

'Master Li is going to accuse me of having been involved in a confidence trick concerning burglary, and the return of stolen goods for money. I think he is the one who planned the scam, however.'

Li looked at me angrily.

'Very well, if you wish to force my hand, I will unmask you. Lin, you can ask my men what they witnessed in the theatre the other night, when your man tried to bribe me with money obtained by his trickery.'

At this point, the two bodyguards appeared in the doorway – the same two guards I had trusted, and who had then turned on me. Lin looked at the two bodyguards, a truculent smile on his face. He asked them what they had seen happen in theatre. One of them looked at Li questioningly.

'You really want us to say, Master Li?'

The prefect lifted a hand, giving his man permission to speak.

'Tell him what you saw.'

The two men grinned at each other, and the taller one spoke up.

'Master Li, we saw you trying to bribe this man –' he pointed at me – 'who said he knew about your scam. You offered him the money the priestess gave you as her pay-off for the scam. When he refused to be bribed, you told us to beat him up, so we did. That was all right, wasn't it?'

Li was speechless, gasping for breath as though someone had punched him in his not inconsiderable stomach. I told the bodyguards to leave, and pushed my face in Li's.

'Now, don't imagine for one moment that you will try to impede our search for justice in the case of Jianxu and Old

Geng. Just come with us, and watch us take the real killer. Then you can release the girl.'

Jianxu sat up on her cot where she had been lying. The sun had just set, turning the blood red colour on the wall of her cell to grey. She listened for a while, thinking she had heard the cry of a wild beast as she lay half asleep. Whatever had roused her, the sound did not come again. The countryside beyond the walls of her grim cell was silent. Not even the chirp of a bird or the call of a wild creature stirred the darkness. But as she sat, now alert to the turning of the world around her, she knew her time had come. As long as Wenbo stuck to what they had agreed, she would be free soon. She recalled the dream she had been having in which the boy had been stumbling through the woods of the place where she had been born. He was scared and didn't know that hunters used the woods to catch game. He was lost and afraid, stomping carelessly through the long grass. Somewhere behind him, the cries of the hunters could be heard. She knew the dream's interpretation. It meant that Wenbo had been found out. And that she would soon be freed. The sound that woke her had been the scream of the boy as the trap snapped viciously closed, trapping his leg.

Li was reluctant to come with us to that part of Pianfu where the Geng house stood. It had once been a prosperous district, but now the encroaching houses told their own story. Geng lived amidst poor people, their shanties leaning against his walls for support. It was not a place where the prefect wished to be after dark. But come with us he did, as he now had no choice. As we marched grimly through the town, Gurbesu came to my side.

'Now I see what you were up to. I recognized those two bodyguards as actors from the play we saw. I would know those manly torsos anywhere.'

I grinned at her recollection of the half-naked acrobats she had ogled that night when we watched 'The Three Princes at Tiger Palace'.

'I thought you might. They were out of work, so were glad

to play a part for me. They were my bodyguards until Li thought he had turned them against me with money. But that was all part of the plan too. Mind you, they did get a bit carried away with the fake beating.' I touched my bruised body and winced. 'But the clincher as far as Li was concerned was when they kicked my teeth in, and drew blood from my mouth.'

Gurbesu was horrified.

'They hit you hard enough to draw blood?'

I laughed.

'No. Before we started our little charade, they gave me a bladder with chicken's blood in it. At the right moment, I slipped it in my mouth and bit down on it. Lots of blood to spit out, and a pleasant sight for Li.' I shuddered. 'Mind you, the chicken's blood was so awful, I had to drink two goblets of wine before the taste was washed away. Li was completely taken in by greed, as you always hope a mark will be. He didn't see the inconsistencies in my scam, which I had to put together very quickly.'

I looked back at the prefect to make sure he was still behind us, and had not sneaked away. His cheeks wobbled, and his face was red with the exertion, but he was still there glaring at me as he strove to keep up with our fast pace. Finally, we stood in front of Geng's house in all its run-down glory. A light burned dimly in the courtyard, but no servants were in evidence. I knew they had all gone, as there was no one in a position to pay them any more. I strode towards the range of rooms that I knew was where Old Geng had lived. Wenbo was bound to be in there somewhere. I slid the outer door open and began searching the rooms leading off the long corridor. The others would have followed, but Lin raised a hand to stop them.

'Let Zhong Kui do his job. He is good at winkling out little devils.'

He was right, in the second room that I looked in, I found Wenbo huddled in a tangle of blankets. He was barely awake, having only just been roused by the noise I had made upon entry to his quarters. He scratched his head, and yawned.

'What . . .?'

I grabbed him by his grubby shirt and hauled him to his feet.

'You are coming with me, Geng Wenbo.'

He turned a ghastly shade of green, perhaps thinking he was having a nightmare. After all, he didn't seem truly awake yet. He rubbed his eyes, but the demon didn't go away. Flame-haired and big-nosed, Zhong Kui, as Lin was fond of calling me, had come for the boy.

'You are brought to account for the murder of your father. And for the death of the actor too, I have no doubt.'

The boy's legs gave away, and he fell to the floor, vomiting his stomach's contents between his knees.

# TWENTY-TWO

*Rotten wood cannot be carved.*

Matters progressed swiftly once we had arrested Geng Wenbo. The only hitch came when I dragged him out into the courtyard to face the prefect. A voice screeched out from the other side of the yard, wanting to know what was happening. We had forgotten Madam Gao, and she flew out of her quarters like a harpie, her outer robe pulled roughly around her night attire for modesty's sake.

'Who are you? What right do you have coming into the house of law-abiding citizens, and making such a bother?'

Her eyesight was poor or she would have recognized Lin and me straight away. It was Li who stepped in and quietened her down.

'Madam, calm yourself. It is I, the prefect, who stand before you. We met before under trying circumstances, you may recall.'

I thought that they were very trying for the old lady. Li had been on the verge of torturing her by beating the soles of her feet with a cane in order to extract information about Geng's death. Well, we had solved the case without such unnecessary violence. Thank the Lord that Jianxu had risked her own life to stop the bastinado being imposed on Gao.

The old lady stalked up to Li and peered closely at him. Finally realizing who he was, she tidied her dishevelled grey hair and pulled her robe closer around her skinny frame. I almost saw her simper at the sight of such authority. Perhaps I was mistaken though, because suddenly her gaze was fixed on the boy. She pointed a claw-like finger at him.

'What has the boy done now? It must be something serious to bring the prefect and this foreign demon out in the middle of the night.'

Li gazed uncertainly at Lin and me, unsure whether he was in control here or not. Finally, he spoke up.

'Madam, this boy has been accused by these people of the murder of Geng Biao. It remains to be proven if this is the case. But he must be taken in for investigation.'

Wenbo howled at the thought of the torture that awaited him. But the old lady's eyes simply gleamed with pleasure. She cared nothing for the person who could have been her son-in-law in other circumstances. Another thought occurred to her, though.

'Does that mean the girl will be released?'

Li was about to speak, but I did not give him a chance to prevaricate.

'She will be freed this very night. As soon as we can deliver Geng Wenbo to the same jail.'

I could see that Li wanted to disagree, but he knew the consequences if he did not now cooperate with us. He merely growled, and stalked off across the courtyard. We all followed, with Wenbo firmly held in my grip. The old lady called after us.

'Good. Send the girl back as soon as you can. I have need of her services around the house. There is much tidying up to do.'

As we marched up the road that led to the jail, Gurbesu shook her head in astonishment.

'Did you hear what that old witch said? Jianxu, who protected her from Li's bastinado by falsely confessing, and who was near to being executed, is to be freed. And all she can think about is, good, my slave and chattel is coming back.'

'Yes, those are old-fashioned values for you. Always thinking about duty.'

Gurbesu snorted.

'Of the woman, not the man.'

'I am not so sure, though I know what you are getting at. Look at Wenbo, on the other hand.'

The boy was walking along ahead of us now and at the heels of Lin and the prefect. I had released him from my grip, and fallen back to talk to Gurbesu. With all his hopes of escape gone, he should have been subdued. But he almost seemed exultant, as though with all the subterfuge shed away, he had achieved his goal.

'He should be afraid, and he was when I grabbed him. But now he looks as though he is the happiest person in the world.'

'Of course he's happy. He has secured Jianxu's freedom.'

'At the cost of his own life.'

'I am not sure he realizes that yet. He is naive enough to think that if Jianxu can escape the executioner, then so can he.'

'Hmmm.' I was still puzzled. 'Maybe he did what he did to win her over in the first place, thinking he was doing what she wanted.'

Gurbesu put a hand on my arm.

'You are not going to let Li torture him, are you? If we can get a full confession, there is no need to do the poor boy any more harm, is there?'

'That poor boy poisoned his father's soup and murdered P'ing-Yang Nu in cold blood in order to hide his guilt. But no, we don't need to hurt him any further. Just so long as he confesses.'

By now, we had almost reached the cell block where the girl had been incarcerated for so long. Unable to contain himself, Wenbo rushed ahead of us all, shouting for Jianxu to come and see.

'Jianxu, look! I have saved you. They have arrested me for the murder of my father, and you will be freed.'

He fell to his knees before her cell, his arms outstretched. It was as if he was welcoming his fate. A pale face appeared at the grille in the door. There was a calm smile on Jianxu's face, and I got the impression she had expected this turn of events all along. The gaoler came scurrying out of his back room, caught unawares by the lateness of our arrival. It was almost pitch dark, and he quickly lit a lamp with a burning taper. When he saw the prefect, he bowed low and jabbered in his coarse dialect. Even Lin had difficulty understanding him, but Li was more used to his toothless gabble. He pointed at the girl's cell and ordered the gaoler to open the door.

'Let the girl go. The ruling of the court has been overturned.'

I could see that the words stuck in Li's throat, but there was nothing he could do. The little man hurried to carry out his master's command, whilst shaking his head in disbelief.

He unlocked the door and pulled it open. For a moment, Jianxu hesitated on the threshold, as if unsure of herself at this last moment of her confinement. Then, more confidently, she took a step out of her cell, then another and another until she was free. Gurbesu took her in her arms, but Jianxu, not knowing how to respond, I suppose, stiffened with her arms held down by her side. Gurbesu gently released her, and spoke words of encouragement.

'It will take some time to appreciate it fully. But you are free now.'

A faint smile crossed Jianxu's lips, and, encouraged, Gurbesu led her away. Meanwhile, at Li's command, the gaoler bundled Wenbo into the cell he had so often peered into from the outside. He was now to be its occupant, changing places with the girl he had so frequently visited. I warned Li to take good care of our prisoner.

'He is not to be tortured. I will be back tomorrow morning and I expect him to be fit and well enough to make a full confession of his crimes.'

The prefect gave me a mocking bow.

'I am as ever at your command, Investigator of Crimes.'

I did not like the evil look in his eye, but Lin indicated that we had done all we could. We followed Gurbesu and Jianxu back down the track towards town, leaving Li to pass on our commands to the gaoler.

Our triumphant return to our temporary quarters was witnessed by Tadeusz, who had kept the doctor securely locked away. Sun's pale face poked out from the barred upper window of a storage room we had had no use for. Gurbesu had brought Jianxu here because she thought it a better place than the Geng house for the time being. Sun stared hard at the girl as she crossed the courtyard and passed inside the communal room we all used. Tadeusz congratulated us.

'So, it is done then? The girl is freed?'

Lin was more cautious than I was.

'For the time being. But we must get a confession out of Wenbo, or the prefect may try to change the verdict again. And we must get Sun's evidence on paper.'

He glanced up at where the doctor's sad face had been. But he was no longer at the window. Lin touched Tadeusz's arm.

'Bring him to us and we will get it all down tonight, before he has reason to think again, or deny what he has already told us.'

Tadeusz nodded and hurried away to fetch the doctor from his cell. Meanwhile, we followed Gurbesu and Jianxu inside. The girl looked a little bewildered by the course of events, and was seated in a corner hugging her knees to her chest. Her eyes were dull and appeared to be staring far off. Gurbesu came bustling back into the room with a ladle of water. She offered it to Jianxu, who drank greedily. But when she had finished drinking, she resumed her original motionless position. Gurbesu looked at us and shook her head slightly. She whispered in my ear so as not to be overheard by the girl.

'She will take some time to recover, I suppose. She has been no more than a slave to Madam Gao for so long. And then under threat of execution'

Jianxu must have heard the sound of her mother-in-law's name in the Mongol that Gurbesu spoke to me. Her eyes flickered, and she spoke finally.

'When am I to return to Madam Gao? She will have need of me.'

Gurbesu went to pat her on the shoulder, but thought better of it. Any intimacy had seemed to cause Jianxu to flinch. Instead she just reassured her verbally.

'All in good time, Jianxu. Madam Gao has managed without you for a while now; a few more days won't matter.'

She looked at Lin and me, and indicated that we should leave. We nodded, and crossed the courtyard to intercept Tadeusz's arrival with the doctor. We were in time to stop them entering the room where Jianxu was closeted and manoeuvred Sun into Lin's own suite of rooms. He had been bound by Tadeusz in such a way that his ankles and wrists were tied, while still allowing him to hobble. He squatted awkwardly on the floor, with Tadeusz standing over him holding a large stick. Lin sat cross-legged at his low desk, and Po Ku provided him with writing materials and paper. We began to take down Sun's story.

I started by asking him the reason for his being at the Geng house on the day in question.

'The day I sold the aconite to the boy?'

'Yes. Did he ask you to go there?'

I wanted to know whether it was a deliberate plan of Wenbo's, or a more spur of the moment decision. Sun frowned, looking at each of his captors in turn. There was something he didn't want to tell us. I pressed him, and Tadeusz tapped his stick on his palm ominously. The weak-willed doctor broke down.

'You must understand that I was not . . . popular in the Geng house. But Wenbo insisted that I went there, so I turned up in disguise.'

'Disguise?'

'Yes. I dressed as a . . . mendicant.'

Something came together in my mind, and I was firm with him.

'A mendicant? Were you not dressed as a beggar? Like a leper, in fact, who was well known in the city.'

He nodded glumly, his subterfuge having been uncovered.

'Yes. I thought if I looked like the leper, no one would come near me. And I would not be identified. I particularly did not want Old Geng to see me.'

I should have questioned him more on his reluctance to be seen by Old Geng, but I was in a hurry, and raced on.

'But Wenbo told us that he tried to get rid of the beggar. Why would he be doing that when he had asked you to come in the first place?'

'There was someone else there. A man with tattooed arms. He saw me giving the aconite to the boy and taking money from him. I suppose Wenbo wanted to keep our transaction a secret. When he saw we had been spotted, he treated me like the beggar I appeared to be. Besides, he was glad to be rid of me as soon as he had got what he wanted.'

I looked at Lin.

'So that was what Nu saw, that later sealed his fate. Now, doctor, did you tell Wenbo what a fatal dose would be?'

Sun's face went green, and he began to gasp in deep breaths that stopped him speaking for a while. I put my hand on his shoulder, and squeezed hard.

'Come now. It is too late to escape your fate. You must tell me everything.'

A squeal emerged from his throat, and then he began to nod vigorously. When he spoke his voice was high pitched, and false.

'Yes. He insisted on knowing how much was fatal. And I told him. But I had to do it you see. I had to.'

There he faltered and would say no more. It was curious as to why he felt he had to do what the boy had said, but it was no matter now. We had our evidence. Lin began packing away his writing materials, and Tadeusz yanked Sun up from the ground by the rope attached to his wrists.

'I will take him to the jail right now.'

'But it's dark, Tadeusz.'

The little silversmith grinned evilly by the light of the lantern he bore.

'I don't think the doctor will try and escape. But if he does, I shall be pleased, for then I can beat him insensible.'

I hoped Tadeusz didn't mean what he said. But recently he had shown a side to his character that I had not encountered before, and I was no longer certain of his intentions. His fall from grace over spying for Ko had hardened him. I watched as he poked Sun across the courtyard with his stick, causing him to almost stumble due to his hobbled legs. I resolved to reassure Tadeusz when he got back that he didn't have to go too far in the opposite direction to prove his loyalty to me.

Deep in the night, she sat up, alert to any sound that took place. But the house was as quiet as her cell had been. Located as it was on the edge of town, there were none of the noises that characterized Geng's old house. No sound of creaking timbers or of scurrying rats disturbed the calm of the night. No sound of neighbours coughing or shuffling feet as old men with weak bladders made for the slop bucket. She crossed her arms over her knees and contemplated her future. She could tell the red-haired Westerner viewed her with some suspicion, not understanding her deeply-ingrained sense of obedience. And the wild, dark-faced native girl also had expected a more emotional reaction to her release. She resolved to give them what they expected in future. That way she would not be closely watched, and she would be free. Yes, she would learn to shed a tear, as she had done when her husband had died. She rose quietly, and walked out into the silent courtyard.

# TWENTY-THREE

*Of all the stratagems, to know when to quit is the best.*

The following morning the sky was bright blue, and Lin and I were optimistic. Today we would obtain Wenbo's confession – without beating his bare feet to a pulp – and our case would be complete. I was ready quickly, and soon got irritated by Lin's slow progress. He was fussing around with his papers and castigating Po Ku for not having his writing equipment ready. The poor servant got even more flustered by his master's badgering, and dropped a brush in the dust of the courtyard. Lin groaned, and told Po Ku to go and wash the brush.

'It will be no use with grit in it.'

Po Ku ran back indoors to carry out his task, whilst Lin continued to fiddle with his satchel of papers. He was digging through it, obviously trying to find a particular document. I walked over to him.

'Chu-Tsai what on earth is going on? Why are you so worked up about this? We will have the boy's confession soon, and everything will be cut and dried.'

Lin sighed deeply.

'I know. It is all so straightforward from now on, isn't it? It's just that I have a small niggle about the detail of that fatal day.'

I knew Lin's predilection for the fine detail of cases. I thought he got bogged down too often in irrelevant detail and missed the bigger picture. I wanted to tell him so, but suspected that, if I told him to forget it, he would persist even more in his hunt for the worm that was wriggling through his brain. And to be frank, now that he had raised the matter, I recalled there had been something that puzzled me to.

'We will piece it all together when we interrogate Wenbo. It will come back to you.'

Just then, Po Ku reappeared with the cleaned brush, which he gave to Lin, and we set off for the jail. Tadeusz was left with the task of drafting another report for Ko that would mislead him but still leave him thinking the silversmith was in his pocket.

The message Ko received two days later was read with deep satisfaction. Tadeusz reported that Lin and I had gone out on a limb, pronouncing the girl, known as Jianxu, innocent. This was contrary to the ruling made by the local prefect, Li Wen-Tao, which had been confirmed by Taitemir, the Mongol governor of the district. Ko's cadaverous face split into what passed for a smile. His plan had worked. When he had seen the petition written by the playwright, Guan Han-Ching, and read the accompanying documents, he could see that the ruling of Li's court was flawed. So many possibilities had been ignored in the face of the confession wrung out of the girl by the use of the bastinado. Normally, Ko would not have cared. One more innocent girl's execution would not bring Kubilai's empire tumbling down. And for him, as the Master of the Censorate, to have a hold over a local official concerning a bad judgement, was invaluable for the future. It was a means of controlling this prefect, Li, should he ever need to. At first he was minded to tear the petition up and consign it to the flames.

But the possibility of destroying Lin Chu-Tsai's career, along with that of the damned barbarian, had proved too tempting. He had decided to use the petition as a trap to snare them both, knowing they would seek out the truth rather than confirm the original judgement. They couldn't help themselves as they were too honest for their own good. But if his suspicion that the girl was innocent proved wrong, and his enemies confirmed the judgement after all, Ko had a strategy for that possibility too. Now, it looked as though he would not need it. His enemies had walked straight into the trap he had set according to his tame spy, Tadeusz Pyka. He would destroy Lin and Zuliani, and then that man too, when he no longer had any need of him.

Ko eased out of his hard, upright chair, and called for his servant.

'I need to make an appointment with the Great Khan.'

*　　*　　*

Tadeusz's faked report to Ko Su-Tsung, whilst it did what was required of it, was overtaken by events. Even before it was in his hands – in fact on the very day it was despatched – matters took a strange and unexpected turn. As Tadeusz was writing the message, Lin and I were on our way to obtain Wenbo's confession. It all now seemed easy, with only the muddy waters of Ko's possible entrapment to avoid. But I reckoned my corrupting of the prefect would prevent any complaints from the local administration about our overturning his verdict. Li would endorse our conclusions; he would even applaud our uncovering of the truth. A grave miscarriage of justice would be overturned. And Mongol justice – in the safe hands of Lin Chu-Tsai – would be seen to be upheld. Unfortunately, it was not as easy as I had imagined.

The first strange and perturbing thing was a summons from Taitemir, the Mongol governor of the region. It came in the form of a uniformed Mongol on our threshold. He was dressed as a light cavalryman with a quilted blue tunic called a *kalat*, underneath which he wore grey breeches and thick, laced-up leather boots. A short, but razor-sharp sword was belted at his waist. There was no objecting to his master's command – the messenger's stiff and uncompromising presence in the doorway of our house determined that. Lin and I would be seeing Taitemir. The Mongol cavalryman had arrived on horseback, and Lin and I hurried to make two horses ready. Gurbesu watched anxiously on as we left, but did not forget to offer us some advice.

'Remember. He still may have been one of those guilty of the murder of Old Geng. Ask him about it.'

I knew by 'him' she meant Taitemir, and was reminding me that she had said from the beginning that we should question him. It was easy for her to say, though. We might as well have put the Great Khan on the spot for the murder. Besides, hadn't we solved the case?

The journey took us out of the city towards the river. We knew that Taitemir's residence was south of Pianfu, somewhere on the banks of the river. What we did not know until we got there was that it was not a house but a Mongol encampment of *gers* – the black felt tents of his race – set in a compound of grazing horses, marching soldiers, and perpetual clouds of dust.

The largest tent stood right in the centre of the compound, like a big black spider in the heart of its web. Our Mongol envoy rode us right up to the entrance and we all dismounted. Three boys scurried over to take the horses and lead them away, while the envoy indicated we should wait. He went inside the tent to announce us. The tent flap – a brightly decorated carpet – fell closed behind him, and Lin and I stood and waited. And waited. The dust began to get in Lin's throat, and he coughed into his hand. I was less genteel, so I hawked and spat my phlegm on to the ground. Finally, the envoy emerged from the tent and waved us over. He stood stiffly to attention, holding the tent flap open, as we bent down and stepped into Taitemir's *ger*. I was experienced enough by now about Mongol ways not to step on to the threshold board. To do so was a great insult, and could result in a beating. At the very least. I stepped over it, and turned to the left. That side of the tent was the men's area, whereas the right was reserved for the women. In our early days in the Mongol empire, Friar Alberoni had persisted in demeaning himself in Tartar eyes by going to stand in the women's side of the tent. I could never teach him the proper protocol.

Several lamps burned inside the tent, and there was no difficulty in seeing the stocky and imposing figure of the governor, Taitemir. Just as we had seen him at the play in T'ai-Yuan-Fu weeks earlier, he was dressed in the long armoured coat of a heavy cavalryman. Short strips of boiled leather were laid in row upon row, covering the coat from the shoulder to the bottom hem at calf height. Leather boots poked out from under this armoured exterior. He stood at a small table surrounded by several *bahadurs*, that we in the West would call knights. As we approached the group, not knowing what our reception would be like, he turned to stare at us. That piercing gaze was all too familiar from the evening of the play. I wondered if we were to be taken to task for counter-manding his ruling concerning Jianxu. Had we fallen into Ko's trap already, and would we find ourselves despatched back to Khan-balik in disgrace? Or treated even worse?

The moment it took for Taitemir to recognize us, and remember why we had been summoned, seemed an age. By now the knights were staring at us too, as though we were something to be pitied. Then Taitemir strode over, and with a grunt took each of us by the arm and led us outside his tent. Back in the light of day he squinted at the brightness and looked around at the bustle that was his camp. He sighed deeply, and when he spoke it was in quite sad tones.

'I know the fashion of the court is now to adopt all things Chin. To live in big houses and have servants waiting upon you hand and foot. And I do have a governor's palace in T'ai-Yuan-Fu. But at heart I am old-fashioned, and I like being here.' He waved a hand at the encircling tented encampment. 'Besides, we shall soon be on the move. You see me preparing for war.'

Lin understood what he meant.

'The siege of Siang-Yang-Fu?'

He was referring to what everyone had been speculating about for months. Kubilai's attempts to conquer the southern Song had stalled around the city that Lin mentioned. It was on the banks of the Han river, and without it Kubilai's efforts would fail. It was said that a young general called Aju was planning to take charge of the siege. It looked like Taitemir was going to be involved too. He scanned the preparations for war again, as though reluctant to tear his mind away from war to discuss the matter he must have brought us here for. But after a long pause, which involved him sucking the ends of his straggly moustache, he got to the point.

'I believe you have overruled Li Wen-Tao and released this Chin girl.'

Despite my reservations about mixing it with the Mongol, I was prepared to wade in and defend us. But Lin surreptitiously tapped my arm, and spoke instead.

'My humble apologies for being so crude as to countermand one of your officials, but there did seem to be . . . inconsistencies in his case.'

Taitemir looked hard at Lin.

'But his decision is effectively my decision. So you are not merely going against the prefect's ruling, but mine also. And now the Great Khan himself is interested, I understand.'

The atmosphere was getting tense, but I suddenly realized that Taitemir was trying to find a way out of a dirty business that had, like the gunpowder-filled bamboo explosives the Chinee loved, backfired on him. Lin saw it too.

'What if you were to discover, by your own efforts, that Li Wen-Tao was a corrupt official? Then you could, with a clear conscience, change your ruling.'

'Is he corrupt?'

Taitemir examined Lin's face closely, and I held my breath. Lin said nothing, but his face spoke a thousand words. Taitemir's face broke into a grim smile.

'Yes, you are right Master . . . er . . . Lin, I *have* uncovered evidence of the prefect's corruption. So his judgement on the girl is clearly flawed. I have suspended the death penalty accordingly until fresh evidence is produced.'

Our relief must have been audible, and Taitemir nodded, also glad to be out of a possible bind himself. He had a couple of points to mention though.

'You have found the probable murderer in this case, then? You need investigate no further?'

Lin eagerly nodded.

'Yes, my lord.'

'Oh, and you can furnish me with the written documentation concerning the corruption I discovered as soon as you like.'

I thought with admiration what a crafty manipulator he was. Our evidence against Li had become his. But it had served its purpose, and we had avoided Ko's trap, it seemed. With the business out of the way, Taitemir was more relaxed, and he seemed keen to show us the extent of his preparations. He led us over to a curious device of wood and rope. Set on wheels, it was a large frame on which pivoted a long pole. The pole was set off-centre with ropes attached to a T-bar on the short end. The longer end had a sling attached. I recognized it as a siege engine called a trebuchet in the West. Taitemir patted it proprietorially.

'Of course it can hurl rocks great distances, but we also now use projectiles made of gunpowder packed in a bamboo tube along with broken porcelain. When it explodes the results are devastating.' He grinned evilly. 'But even that is not enough.

My Chin experts have created a device we call the excrement bomb.'

Lin grimaced in distaste at such an uncouth weapon. But I was interested.

'What goes into it?'

'The main ingredient is powdered human shit, croton oil – that blisters the skin on contact – white arsenic, and a sort of beetle that causes blistering. Oh, and aconite. We have heaps of aconite root here.'

# TWENTY-FOUR

*An ant may well destroy a whole dam.*

As Lin and I rode along the grey, stony track that led to the low building that was Pianfu's prison, we discussed the interview with Taitemir. It had left me with an uneasy feeling.

'Did you get the impression the governor was relieved we had found a culprit for the murder of Geng?'

Lin tried to be noncommittal, but he knew what I was intimating.

'You think we should still consider him a possible suspect because of his reaction to our identifying Wenbo as the killer? Are you backing away from that position?'

'No, no. Wenbo did kill his father. But think what Taitemir said about that dirty bomb. It is to be loaded with aconite. He has mountains of the very poison that killed Geng lying around outside his tent. The agent of the killing could still be Wenbo. The prime mover might have been Taitemir.'

'Because he owed Geng money? He didn't care about being indebted to him, Nick. It is a normal state for a Mongol governor to use his position to obtain goods for free.'

I groaned in frustration.

'You are right. But you know how Kubilai is cracking down on corruption and building up his bureaucracy. Even the governor in a remote region such as Taitemir might feel he has to clean out his stables before more government officials arrive. Especially with Kubilai's war-machine shedding light on the governor's activities. The quiet disposal of a nuisance might have been a better option than the summary one of a slit throat.'

Lin remained unconvinced, but I was prepared to store my misgivings away for another day. Besides, as we approached the prison, I could see signs of unusual behaviour. It was still early morning, but the bulky figure of the prefect, dressed in his blue silk robe, was in evidence already. He was stomping around the compound in front of the cell block, waving an elegant bamboo cane at the cowering gaoler. The door to Wenbo's cell stood half open, the interior dark and ominous. I murmured to the already shaken Lin Chu-Tsai.

'I will go ahead and see what has happened. If they have let Wenbo slip through their hands, either deliberately or accidentally, then heads will roll.'

The mood I was in, I meant what I said quite literally. The executioner's blade had been denied Jianxu – it could be slaked on Li's blood for all I cared. I spurred my horse up the track towards the two men, who were still squabbling and had not seen my approach. I dismounted and called out.

'What is going on here?'

Both Li and the gaoler turned to face me, startled by my sudden appearance. The gaoler cowered before the demon, and even Li looked crushed. He could not look me in the eye, and poked at the ground with his silver-topped cane.

'There is a problem, Master Investigator.'

I was angry, and prodded the prefect in his soft breasts.

'I hope Wenbo has not escaped, or worse still been deliberately released by you. I have to see him today.'

Li's face was ashen.

'Geng Wenbo is still in his cell, and you can see him. But it is going to be impossible to get a confession out of him.'

By this time, Lin, at his horse's more sedate pace, had caught me up.

'And why is that, Master Li? Are you denying us access to our suspect? The Great Khan himself will hear of this.'

Li blustered as Lin got off his mount.

'No, you don't understand me.' He sighed, his whole fat face collapsing over the stiff collar of his gown. He waved his cane at the gaoler.

'Show them what you found this morning.'

We followed the bandy-legged gaoler into Wenbo's cell, and at first I thought it was empty. I could see no sign of the boy. I called out to Li.

'Is this some sort of trick?'

In a quavering voice, he replied.

'Look behind the door.'

Both Lin and I peered into the darkness immediately behind the half-open cell door. We gasped simultaneously. Wenbo was pinioned halfway up the door his legs folded under him. His head stuck out at an awkward angle and his face was red and bloated. My immediate reaction was that somehow Geng Wenbo had hanged himself from the bars of the cell door grille. Looking more closely, my suspicion was confirmed. I could see a thin cord embedded in his neck, which must have originally been used as a belt around his waist. From his neck, a loop of it went around one of the bars in the grille. Lin spoke in wonderment, and with not a little suspicion.

'Is it really possible to kill yourself by hanging when your feet can still touch the ground? He is practically kneeling.'

I nodded my head.

'I have heard that it is so. If you are determined to die and can tie a noose that will not slacken when you black out, then it is perfectly feasible. What we need to ask ourselves is whether this boy had that determination. He would only need enough desire to do it to carry him off into unconsciousness. After that, his own weight would ensure there was no return.'

Lin suddenly tipped his head to one side.

'Listen. Can you hear something?'

I cocked my head, and concentrated on the sounds coming from the cell block. Li made as if to speak, but I held my hand up. There was no sound of birds in this desolate spot, but then I heard it. A soft mewling sound like the faint squeak of newborn kittens, followed by a scratching. I stepped out of the cell, trying to follow the sound. I realized it came from the cell next to Wenbo's. As I stepped up to the door, the sound ceased, as though the kitten was aware of danger and was holding its breath. Silently, I tipped my thumb at the door, and raised an eyebrow, questioning what might be in there. Li hissed under his breath.

'It's the doctor. I had forgotten about him.'

Lin emerged from the death cell and offered a suggestion.

'Then I propose that you open the door and see if he is alive or dead too.'

At the wave of Li's pudgy hand, the gaoler rushed forward and thrust a key in the lock of the door. As he turned it, we all heard a scuttling sound like rats skittering through old straw to find a dark corner to hide in. The gaoler swung the door inwards, and poked his lamp into the darkness. A creature cowering in the farthest corner held up a claw of a hand over his face against the unwelcome intrusion.

'Aiii, don't kill me, demon.'

Something had terrified Doctor Sun out of his wits.

Gurbesu had risen early that morning, aroused by the fuss caused by the arrival of Taitemir's messenger. She knew Lin and I would go straight to our interrogation of Geng Wenbo afterwards, and was glad of the time alone that our tasks gave her. She wanted to talk some more to Jianxu about her life, having the, in my opinion, forlorn hope that she could bring the young woman out of herself. It irritated Gurbesu more than a little that Jianxu had been no more than a slave all her life. First her father had sold her into slavery, and then she bowed down to her husband, and then when he died to her mother-in-law. I thought she was mad to try and change one girl who merely stood as an example of the fate of most women in Cathay. It would be like trying to push back the *acqua alta* in Venice with a broom. Raging high tides came and inundated the city whether we Venetians liked it or not. It was a force of nature. And so were the Three Duties and the Four Virtues in Cathay.

Gurbesu had dressed and sat combing her shiny black locks, while pondering how she would approach her task. Finally, she could put it off no longer. She got up and walked out into the central courtyard of their lodgings. Predictably, Jianxu was already awake and dressed. But, surprisingly, she wasn't bustling about carrying out tasks as Gurbesu had imagined she might. The young woman sat on a stone bench in the middle of the yard, apparently contemplating the outside world as it passed the open doors of the house. A fruit-seller hurried by with a bucket full of prickly oval fruit clutched in each

hand. Then a sedan chair went by, its two bearers transporting
a pretty white-faced woman somewhere. Gurbesu could see a
look of strain and tiredness on the woman's face as she glanced
into the courtyard. She was probably returning to her lodgings
after a night entertaining a rich Chinee client. Gurbesu heard
a sigh, only after a moment realizing it was not the white-faced
entertainer, but Jianxu who had made the sound. Jianxu
turned to her, and spoke sadly.

'We are all slaves to men, are we not?'

Her attractive oval face and almond eyes had for the first time
some animation in them. Gurbesu even thought she saw a small
tear running down her peach-like cheek. She smiled in relief.
Perhaps the girl was not as cowed as she had imagined.

Sun refused to come out of the corner of his cell where he
had first cowered when I entered. So I sat on the floor next
to him. Lin circumspectly retired from the cell, so as not to
cause the doctor any more anxiety. He hustled the prefect
away, too. For a long time, Sun and I sat side by side in
silence, staring out of the open door. Finally he plucked up
the courage to speak.

'Will you close the door, demon? I will feel safer.'

I rose and pushed the door closed, glancing through the
grille at a quizzical Lin, who stood patiently outside. I shook
my head gently and he nodded in understanding. Lin was
the most patient man I had ever encountered. He would wait
all day if necessary to see what troubled Doctor Sun. As the
sun reached the highest point in the sky, a few rays filtered
through the grille of the door, chasing away some of the
gloom of the cell. This is what Jianxu would have experienced every day for weeks, perhaps imagining that that
particular day's sun would be the last she would see. The
doctor began to weep.

'I heard the Devil last night. It took Wenbo, and I was afraid
it would come for me next. And I have sins on my soul.'

I did not tell him that Wenbo had killed himself. I was far
more interested in his sins. Without Wenbo's own confession,
I would need a statement from Sun, if Lin and I were to
overturn the verdict on Jianxu.

'Tell me the sins that burden you.'

A random ray of sunlight cut across his face, illuminating his fearful, staring eyes.

'I planned with Old Geng to murder Madam Gao. And I would have done it, too.'

His words jolted through me as if I had been standing on the deck of a ship struck by lightning. I recalled the old woman saying she had been rescued by Geng from an attacker. Was this the incident that Sun was referring to? But if it was, why did he say that Geng was in on the plot?

'You mean you planned it, and Geng stopped you?'

Sun suddenly became agitated, beating the packed earth floor of the cell. I saw Lin's face appear briefly at the grille then disappear once he assured himself I was safe. Sun was adamant.

'No, no, no. Old Geng and I both owed Gao a great deal of money. It was his suggestion that we sneak round to her house together. He said we were going to catch her on her own, and do away with the old bitch. But just as we were about to rush into her office, Geng said he had heard the girl – Jianxu – and he would check on her first. I entered Gao's inner office on my own and grabbed her by the neck. She was screeching like some old cat but I just kept squeezing. The next thing I knew, Geng was in the room acting like some avenging angel. He pulled me off her and hit me in the stomach. I realized I had been betrayed – that Geng had planned it this way from the start – and I ran out of her house. After that, I knew I couldn't show my face in Pianfu again and began to practice in the hill villages.'

All the facts were beginning to fit together nicely now, but I still needed something more.

'But you did come back. You sold Old Geng's son aconite in order that he might kill his father.'

Sun nodded.

'The boy knew what I had tried to do to Madam Gao. The old bitch must have told him or the girl, I am not sure. One day, in the village where you found me, I got a message. It simply said, "I know about you and Gao. If you would like to revenge yourself, come to the Geng household in disguise.

Bring poison. If you don't come, remember that I know how to find you.'"

He stared at me with horror in his eyes.

'Save me from the Devil. Don't leave me in the dark on my own.'

# TWENTY-FIVE

*A man who waits for a roast duck to fly into his mouth will wait a very long time.*

'He told me he had heard the Devil scratching at his door.'

We were all back together in the house allocated to us. Lin, Gurbesu, Tadeusz and I sat in a circle around the low table piled high with documents about this case. Jianxu was sitting in the late afternoon sunshine, revelling in its warmth, no doubt. I could hear her singing a lilting song in quiet tones. Tadeusz questioned my statement.

'It must have been a rat or a mouse. Those prison cells have straw on the floor that has not been cleaned for weeks.'

I tilted my head, not quite so sure of his rational explanation. Normally, I would have agreed, but I knew what Sun had said next.

'He said himself that he thought it was a rat at first, and told it to go away. When it heard his voice, it stopped scratching at his door. But then the noise began at the next cell door. The cell occupied by Wenbo. Sun claims he heard the murmur of voices.' I looked at Tadeusz. 'Do you know of a rat that can talk?'

The silversmith was still not convinced.

'He probably heard Wenbo talking to himself, trying to talk himself into self-murder. Or maybe Wenbo imagined he was hearing voices, and was talking to thin air. Either way, the boy killed himself.'

'I am not so sure.'

Lin was concerned about my story now.

'You are not sure that Wenbo killed himself?'

'No, I'm not. Though I don't have a lot of evidence to back up my fears. Only the words of a half-demented doctor scared of his own shadow.'

Tadeusz indicated with a snort that he reckoned that was an accurate summary of Sun's state of mind, and therefore he was not to be trusted. Lin, however, was still open-minded.

'Tell us exactly what he said.'

I paused, recalling the terror in Sun's eyes, and what he said next.

'Then the whispering stopped, and for a moment there was silence. I heard a strange low moan. It was a man's voice saying "no" over and over again. More and more insistent, as if whoever it was had been forced to do something against his will, and now he had changed his mind.'

Sun stopped speaking and stared down at the straw and packed earth that we both sat on. I could hear his breath coming faster and faster. I had to make him go on before he collapsed.

'And then?'

'And then the sound of the voice was cut off, as though a hand or a cord had been squeezed round the man's neck, cutting off his air. I heard a wheezy gasp, then a drumming sound on the door like he was kicking it with his heels, or hitting it with his fists. It went on so long. I pressed my own fists over my ears but the sound just went on and on. Then I heard a gurgle, a sort of . . . death rattle, and all was still.'

The doctor looked me in the eye and asked a question.

'Was it Geng Wenbo in the next cell?'

I nodded, grimacing. Sun groaned in despair.

'Don't leave me. The Devil will come for me next.'

'Of course, I had to leave him, though I persuaded the gaoler to leave a light in his cell. Let's just hope he doesn't knock it over and burn himself to death.'

Gurbesu had been frowning during my retelling of Sun's story.

'It sounds as if he heard Wenbo being strangled against his will, rather than a self-murder. But then how would someone get into his cell to do that?'

'No human could get inside without a key, so maybe it really was the Devil.'

She laughed at my suggestion, but it was a nervous laugh. Looking round, I felt we were all a little unsure about Sun's evidence. In the courtyard, Jianxu's spellbinding song, that had wound itself quietly through my recounting of Sun story, suddenly ceased. It was as if, though she couldn't hear us, she too was perturbed by the story, and had lost the sense of happiness she had so recently found. I asked the obvious question.

'If someone killed Wenbo, are we still sure we have found the real killer of Old Geng?'

A grim silence descended on us, which was only broken by a familiar voice.

'What are all the gloomy looks for? Have you not solved the case?'

I sprang to my feet.

'Alberoni, you are back.'

In the doorway stood the long, lanky figure of the friar, his shabby, patched black robe speckled with dirt. He had a broad smile on his face. I patted his shoulder and urged him into the centre of the room, where we all crowded around him. I could not wait for his news. Sure that his hunt for Prester John was a wild goose chase, I had been prepared for him to return more disconsolate than before. But he seemed to be happy enough, and he took my arm.

'I can see, Niccolò, that you imagine my search was wasted.'

I held up my hands to signify a truce between us on the matter. But he had good news, from his point of view.

'True, I did not find Prester John, but I learned much more about him. At the castle of Caichu I was told an intriguing story about Ung Khan.'

This was a name we had encountered before, which some thought synonymous with Prester John. Ung Khan had been the name ascribed to the old man who had given us the slip in Xanadu. Alberoni's excitement communicated itself to us, and while Gurbesu went to fetch some food, we all sat down. The vexed matter of Wenbo's death was momentarily forgotten. When Gurbesu returned with food, she put it before Alberoni, and he continued his story.

'The castle was formerly owned by a man called the Golden

King, who, it is said, had damsels not horses to pull him around in a chariot.'

Gurbesu laughed at such a fantasy, but I quieted her with a finger to my lips, and the friar spoke on.

'This king was subject to Ung Khan, but there was a war between them because of the Golden King's arrogance. Seven men of Ung Khan's court said they could overpower the Golden King in return for great rewards. Prester John said he would be glad if they could accomplish this. So the seven men went to the Golden King and presented themselves as men from a faraway country who had come to serve him. He willingly took them in and they served him well for two whole years.' The friar looked at me and smiled. 'When I heard this, I was put in mind of you, Niccolò, and your clandestine dealings that rely so much on trust.'

I knew he meant how I cheated people using underhand trickery. But I was so glad to see him again, I allowed him his small reprimand. Gurbesu caught my look, and mouthed a phrase silently. I understood it straight away. A long firm. My name for a particularly long-winded scam. The seven men of Ung Khan's court were building up trust, before making use of it for their profit. Alberoni finished his tale.

'One day, when the Golden King and his seven courtiers were out for his sport, they seized him and took him to Ung Khan. Prester John enslaved the king for a time, but then released him and reinstated him to his former glory. Having convinced the Golden King he could always be taken, he returned him to his kingdom a wiser man.'

'And did this get you closer to Prester John?'

It was Lin's question.

'I think I know a little more about him, Master Lin. And, reassured of his existence, I feel I am hot on his heels. I will not now give up my search, as I was going to do in Khanbalik. Prester John's land is said to be west of the Golden King's.'

Gurbesu busied herself pouring some wine for everyone, and even the friar indulged. As we relaxed and chatted, I was briefly aware of Jianxu appearing in the doorway with a strained smile on her face. But before I could say anything, she slipped away, having assumed, I supposed, that she did not fit in to our reunion. And as the drink went down, I forgot about her, I regret to admit. It was much later in the night, when everyone else had retired, leaving Alberoni and me alone, that I fell to thinking about Venice. I must have been silent for some time because suddenly the friar stirred from where he had been happily slumped and tapped my arm.

'Are you thinking of Venice again?'

Am I so obvious a soul that both Alberoni and Gurbesu can see right through me? She always knew when sweet Cat was on my mind, and now here was the friar reading me like some illuminated manuscript. I sighed deeply, because he was correct.

'This case we are investigating and all the tales of murder, attempted murder and poisoning, has brought back the death of Agostino to me.'

'Your father.'

Alberoni always corrected me in the same way when I spoke thus. I could never bring myself to call him my father, only referring to him by his given name. It made me tetchy every time the friar corrected me.

'Yes, yes. You know who I mean.'

'And what is it about his death that still bothers you?'

I took a deep breath.

'I cannot convince myself that my mother didn't kill him. And I think that she did it for my sake, before I went and got myself in trouble by killing him myself.'

Alberoni gasped, then began to chuckle. I turned on him angrily, my face ablaze.

'What are you laughing at?'

The friar managed to control himself, with difficulty putting on the solemn look that served him well in the confessional.

'You think that Rosamund poisoned your father?'

'Yes. Or at least I fear so. And that she did it because I would have killed him otherwise for all his violent acts against her. That's why I feel guilt about his death even now.'

Alberoni patted my arm comfortingly.

'Then set your mind at rest. You were a child when Agostino died, and you saw the world through childish eyes, if I may

speak plainly. And despite their stormy relationship, your
mother always loved your father. And he loved her in return.'

I did not like what I was hearing from Alberoni. I had long
convinced myself that my father was a brute and deserved to
die violently. But I was aware that the friar had been the
confessor to the Zulianis for many years. When I was a child,
he had seemed a very old man, and yet now he looked no
older than fifty. I realized he must have been quite young back
then.

'Then who did kill him? And why?'

'As ever in these matters, it was over money. Do you recall
Guido Sarpi? He was a cousin of yours.'

I frowned, trying to remember those long-ago times.

'I remember a tall man with a trim beard, who used to play
rough games with me.'

'That is the man. I think he had been a suitor of Rosamund's
before your father stole her away. He visited Agostino more
often than his family relationship warranted, probably because
he was not able to give up his interest in her. Then one day
he formed a *colleganza* with your father.'

Alberoni used the familiar word describing the sort of business partnership that many Venetian merchants entered into
with each other. I myself had pulled together many a *colleganza*
to fund my enterprises. Often they worked, and the partners
walked away with the spoils. Sometimes they failed, and were
the cause of acrimony and argument over what had been lost.

'Sarpi and my father lost money?'

'Yes. And Guido accused Agostino of cheating, making a
profit and stealing the proceeds all for himself. The argument
got quite heated, and Sarpi stormed out threatening vengeance.
I thought he had cooled off because it was weeks before . . .
Agostino's death.'

'But I recall my mother and father arguing on the day before
his death. That is what convinced me it was all to do with her.'

'Yes, I think your mother, typically, was trying to pour oil
on the troubled waters of his dispute with his cousin. But
Agostino would have none of it.' He sighed. 'You know how
pig-headed your father was. After all, you have inherited that
trait of his.'

In other circumstances I would have berated the friar for suggesting I had inherited anything from my father. Least of all an unwelcome character trait. But tonight I wanted to learn the truth.

'You think Sarpi poisoned my father?'

'I know so. An anonymous denunciation was made against him. He was arrested a few days later, tortured and confessed in the Doge's prison. He was executed for his deed.'

Once again, torture and confession reared their ugly heads.

'Why did I never learn of this?'

'I suppose your mother did not want you – a child – to be tainted with the sordid nature of the matter. Family killing family over money and possessions. She did it for the best of reasons, I am sure. It is a shame that it left you for all these years with a false picture of your father. And your mother. Now I must say goodnight. I am dog-tired after a long journey to get back here.'

I waved a hand, and watched the friar drag his exhausted limbs across the courtyard and into the room that had been set aside for him. Slowly my wine-befuddled mind began to turn over everything that had been said that evening. Of family disputes over money, and of Prester John's knights, who had planned a long-term strategy to achieve what they wanted. Gradually, a picture began to emerge out of the threads we had left hanging when Alberoni burst into our conversation earlier concerning Old Geng's death, and that of his son. I knew what I had to do, and realized I would have a busy night ahead of me. There would be no time for sleep.

# TWENTY-SIX

*Have a mouth as sharp as a dagger, but a heart as soft as tofu.*

I must have fallen asleep at some point, because Lin woke me in the morning. He looked perturbed, in so far as he was able in that reserved way of his. His eyes shone at least, even if his face showed calm. I shrugged his hand off my arm and tried to turn over and reach for Gurbesu. But the other side of the bed was empty, so I assumed it was later than I thought. Gurbesu was an early riser usually. Lin was insistent, however.

'Nick, you must get up. Doctor Sun has escaped.'

This got my attention and I groaned, levering myself upright. I dragged open a bleary eye.

'Escaped, you say? How is that possible?'

'The gaoler is drunk and must have forgotten to lock the cell door properly after he took Sun his food in the evening.'

By now I was fully alert.

'What were you doing at the prison so early?'

Lin looked a little rueful.

'I found some aspects of his story that you retold last night too fanciful for my liking.'

He meant, in his own polite way, that he hadn't believed me. Or at least my interpretation of Sun's story. I was not offended – it was a strange tale.

'Go on.'

'I thought that if I could speak to him in the cold light of day I might get closer to the truth. There are aspects of the day of Old Geng's death that still worry me. Things that don't fit together.'

I was going to ask him what he meant, but he hurried on with his recounting of the events of that morning.

'When I got to the prison, I could see that one of the doors was ajar. I just assumed at first that it was Wenbo's cell that had been left open after his body had been removed. As I had been with you when we found him dead, I should have remembered which cell it was, and which was the doctor's. Under the mistaken impression that the doctor would be tucked up safely in his cell, I looked in each of the other ones. But they were all empty, save for the last one in the row. And that housed a fat, young man who stunk of rice wine and was snoring. He was clearly sleeping off a drunken rampage that had resulted in him being thrown into the cell. Anyway, it was not Doctor Sun. I went back to the open cell and saw a lamp still burning on an upturned log. I remembered about your kindness over Sun's fear of the dark, and realized this was his cell. So I went in search of the gaoler, only to find him in a stupor with a jug of wine beside his bed. His keys had been discarded on the floor.'

Lin was unusually angry at the turn of events, and I could understand why. If Sun had absconded, our last witness had gone, and our case lay in tatters again. But I still had other plans to bring the matter to a satisfactory conclusion. In the meantime it would do no harm for Lin to occupy himself with hunting down the doctor.

'Go to Li Wen-Tao, Chu-Tsai. Throw your weight about, and get him to allocate some of his resources to finding the doctor. Ultimately, it was his responsibility for ensuring the safe imprisonment of Sun. He will suffer if the man is not found again.'

Lin stopped his pacing of my room and calmed a little.

'You are right. It will be the end of his lacklustre career if he can't find him. I will do what you suggest right away.'

He left my bedroom to go and harass the prefect, giving me the chance to get dressed. And select a sharp dagger to stick in the belt of my Mongol coat. I was sure I was going to need it as matters came to a head. I next went in search of Gurbesu, who had undertaken to look after Jianxu. Finding her wasn't difficult as she was sitting snoozing in the courtyard catching the rays of the weak autumn sun. As I approached, she opened one eye and squinted at me. She couldn't help but notice my dagger and gave it a pointed look.

'Are you expecting trouble, Nick?'

'Sun has escaped. The gaoler was drunk.'

She stood up abruptly, knowing what the loss of our only witness meant to me.

'That is a disaster. But you can't expect any trouble from his quarter, can you? He will be halfway to the south by now, if he has any sense.'

I nodded in agreement.

'I suppose so, but there is no harm in being cautious.' I looked around. 'Is Jianxu safe?'

Gurbesu indicated with a thumb pointed over her shoulder that Jianxu was safely closeted in the small room at the rear of the house.

'Yes. Should Sun have any reason to seek her out, he will have to come past me. But why worry about him? You don't think he is the killer, do you? I mean, if it was the same person who killed both Old Geng and Wenbo, then it couldn't be him. He was locked in the next cell when the boy was killed. And, according to his testimony that you retold to us last night, he was in fear of his own life.'

'You're right. It's not him I am really worried about. It's . . .'

I thought I saw a movement from the direction of Jianxu's room, and moved Gurbesu away a little.

'It's Madam Gao.'

Maybe I said it too loud, I couldn't be sure, but the slim figure I assumed was Jianxu slipped back into the shadows as I said the name. Gurbesu was surprised, but not extremely so.

'After we talked with the friar last night, I fell to thinking about what you had said.'

'What about?'

'The Devil being the only one who could have killed Wenbo, as no human agency could have gained entry to the cell. I kept wondering if someone could have done it from outside, but couldn't see how. Now you tell me that Sun escaped because the gaoler was drunk, the whole business seems a lot easier to explain. Doors left open and keys discarded. Madam Gao may be an old lady, but she is a very determined one, and Wenbo lived in fear of her. Do we know where she is now?'

'I would assume she is still at the Geng household. That's where I would look.'

'Do you want me to go and see if she is there?'

'No.' I stopped Gurbesu from getting up with a restraining hand on her arm. 'I can do that later. Anyway, you look tired, you should rest.'

She sighed, and fell back into her chair.

'I am tired. I stayed awake thinking about the case and waiting for you to come to bed. Where were you, anyway? And when did you get to bed? I must have fallen asleep before you returned.'

I waved a hand desultorily in the air.

'Ohhh, I spoke to Alberoni for a long time about my family and Venice. We talked until the early hours. You get some rest and I will deal with the case. I have a feeling it will all resolve itself today.'

She closed her eyes and I tiptoed away.

When I returned to our temporary quarters, Lin was there too. Seeing me walk in the courtyard, he hurried over.

'Li's men are scouring the countryside for Sun. Let us hope they will turn him up before long.'

'Indeed.'

'But there is something more important I want to talk to you about.'

'And what is that?'

'I have worked out what has been bothering me for almost a week now. It's about the day of Old Geng's murder. I had it fixed in my mind when we interrogated Madam Gao in the kitchen that day. Then we got sidetracked by the sudden appearance of the beggar.'

I remembered the conversation. It had been my obsession with the beggar that had overridden a clue Lin had winkled out, and then made him forget it. I felt guilty about it.

'And what have you uncovered?'

'I have been going over the sequence of events as we now know it. Jianxu was cooking a broth for Madam Gao in the kitchen. The old lady herself was in the eastern range of rooms feeling unwell. Old Geng was closeted in the western range trying to make his accounts add up, and we presume his son, Wenbo, was also close by. But Doctor Sun had been summoned by an anonymous letter that threatened to expose him for attacking the old lady. We can assume that it was sent by Wenbo, because when Sun arrived dressed as a beggar, he was met by the boy. He gave or sold him the aconite, and when Nu saw them together, Wenbo pretended to kick the beggar out. Do you agree with me so far?'

I think I knew where Lin was going with this, because the same inconsistency had come back to me. But I did not want to spoil his triumph. I merely nodded.

'Go on.'

'Then we come to the difficult part. At some point, Jianxu left the kitchen. We know that because Wenbo admitted as much. At that point, anyone could have laced the broth with poison. Wenbo, Madam Gao, or Sun in the guise of a beggar, could all have done it. I exclude Old Geng because he ended up eating the broth, which he would not have done if he had poisoned it intending to kill Madam Gao. Whatever his motive might have been for that.'

I could hold back no longer and worked out where this led Lin to.

'So you think either Madam Gao was the target, which means Sun or Wenbo put the poison in the broth in order to kill her. Madam Gao is excluded here as she would not have poisoned her own soup. Or one of the three – Gao, Sun or Wenbo – poisoned the broth and arranged for it to be fed to Geng. Madam Gao is not excluded by that possibility, of course.'

'But there is a stumbling block.' Lin had seen it, just as I had at last. 'How did the soup get taken to Old Geng instead of Madam Gao?'

I pointed out what Jianxu had told Gurbesu.

'Jianxu said Old Geng took it from her. An act of greed that had fatal consequences.'

Lin would not leave it there, however. He was like a dog shaking a rat until it was dead.

'But the boy said his father did not leave his office. He was quite sure of that. So how could Geng have taken the soup?

Now, what if Jianxu was lying? To protect Madam Gao, as she had done when she confessed in order to save the old lady from being tortured? If she thought Madam Gao had poisoned the soup, and then told her to feed it to Geng, her sense of duty might have been enough to cause her to lie to protect her.'

I had another theory, but agreed Lin's could be right. Before I could say anything about my own ideas however, Lin turned and walked to the door.

'There is only one way to check the truth or otherwise of all this. Where is Jianxu now?'

I confessed I didn't know.

'The last time I saw her was when the friar came back last night. We were all so engrossed in his story, I am afraid we must have left Jianxu out a little. I saw her look in on us and then retire. I presumed she went back to her room. I will go and ask Gurbesu.'

When I found Gurbesu, and asked her about the girl, she went to the small room at the back of the house that she had selected for Jianxu. Its location meant she could keep an eye on her, like a big sister. But Jianxu wasn't there – she had gone.

# TWENTY-SEVEN

*Clear conscience never fears midnight knocking.*

O nce we had searched the rest of the house to be sure Jianxu was not elsewhere, Lin began to get concerned.
'What if she has gone back to Madam Gao? If what I suspect is true, and the old lady is at the heart of all this, Jianxu's life may be in danger.'

I tried to calm him down.

'Don't worry so much, Chu-Tsai. I think I can prevent that from happening. You can leave it to me.'

He didn't look convinced, but I insisted he stayed at the house.

'You too, Gurbesu.'

She was about to protest, but I put up both my hands, palms out, to stop her.

'I can deal with this. You should both be here if Jianxu returns.'

Gurbesu looked at me with those dark, penetrating eyes of hers.

'This is like your scheme to incriminate the prefect in an illegal scam, isn't it? I thought you were doing it on the side to make money for yourself at first. But it was all about sucking Li into something that you could use against him later. You've known for some time who the killer is, and you've set another scheme up to trap her.'

I gazed modestly at the ground, though I was in fact very pleased with myself. But I knew it was hard to hide things from Gurbesu.

'Well, I wouldn't say I've known for some time, but you are right, I do intend to catch her.'

I left them both uncertain and worried and crossed the courtyard, easing loose the dagger I had stuffed in my belt when I had got up that morning. I needed some reassurance, in case my plans went wrong. Jianxu's disappearance had accelerated the situation, and I had to hurry. The conclusion of this vexed case was in sight, but the threads were unravelling faster than I might have wished.

I strode through the back alleys of Pianfu in my desire to avoid the bustle of horses and sedan chairs on the main highways. The delicate twanging of tuning forks signalled the presence of travelling barbers ready to serve their customers. As I passed one side street, I heard the clatter of copper bowls and knew that a water seller was close by. I found that noise and the cries of street vendors a comforting and familiar sound after well nigh five years in Cathay. Was I settling down here? Would I stay, and live my life out amongst the Chinee and Mongols? I liked my life, but Venice and Caterina Dolfin always came back to haunt me. And the boy who was my son. It was strange, but thinking of him brought me back to Madam Gao, Jianxu and the task in hand. I suppose I was reminded because the girl had lost her father, and lived her life under the watchful and heartless eye of Madam Gao. My son had no father to bring him up, either. Would it affect him as it seemed to have done Jianxu? I hoped not.

The Geng household was now just ahead of me. I approached it cautiously, peering through the gate at the apparently deserted courtyard. Where was Madam Gao? And had Jianxu come here after all?

She had crept into the house keeping to the shadows cast by the afternoon sun on the far side of the courtyard. It had proved easy to slip away from the supervision of the Kungurat woman. After all, she had long experience of sneaking away from the old lady now and then. And she had been much more watchful than Gurbesu. She felt no sorrow about leaving them. Despite all their shows of friendship towards her, when that black crow of a Christian priest had arrived, she had dropped completely out of their minds. When she had looked in on their revelry, only the red-haired man had noticed her presence. And he had only engaged her look for a moment before returning to the conversation with the priest. And his fondling of Gurbesu's thigh. The dark-skinned Kungurat had ignored her completely, revealing how false her concern for Jianxu had really been. In a way, she couldn't blame them. From a child she had been brought up to be silent unless spoken to, and subservient to all men in her family, and that of her husband. Madam Gao was a tyrant, and she did her every bidding. So why would the rowdy and undisciplined foreigners even notice her? She was to them no more than the pile of documents that represented her case to them.

Now she stood in the shadows, shivering slightly, in the morning chill. She had returned to the only person whom she knew and understood. She had come back to be under the scrutiny of Madam Gao and she was fearful of what might happen to her. But there was now no going back.

I thought I saw a shape in the shadows on the far side of Geng's courtyard. I moved that way, but it must have been my imagination. A weed blowing in the wind, perhaps. But then I saw the marks of a woman's pattens on the packed earth. However small, they were not as tiny as Madam Gao's bound feet, and there were no servants in the house to have made them. Jianxu must have come here. They led towards the kitchen.

She quietly made her way to her old domain – the kitchen of Geng's house. At the door, she took off her wooden pattens and carefully placed them side by side on the threshold. She stepped inside. The kitchen was cold with no fire burning in the hearth. If she had been here in the past and had let the fire go out, Madam Gao would have given her a tongue-lashing. Even the servants got treated better than her. She picked up a metal poker and prodded the ashes. They drifted up into the air, and a cold wind whistling through the kitchen blew them across the floor. She could not see even a dim red glow left in the embers.

She pricked her ears, thinking she heard a sound. If so, it could only be her mother-in-law. There was no one left in the house. In fact, she had not been sure that the old lady would be here. But then she would not have returned to her old house as it was empty, and all her possessions moved to Geng's. No, Madam Gao had to be here, and the creaking of timbers above suggested she was awake and moving around. Gripping the heavy poker more tightly in her hand to defend herself, Jianxu crept towards her mother-in-law's upper room.

The old lady sat upright in the darkened room of the empty house. She had always been taught never to slouch, and though her back troubled her more and more often, she still did not give in to its niggling pain. There was time enough to lie down when you were dead. Her thoughts drifted over the last few years that had been such difficult ones for her. It had started when that penniless scholar had brought his girl child to her. She had needed a servant, and gave the man the money he wanted to complete his studies. She had assumed he would come back to claim his daughter, but he never did. The old lady had no complaints about that – she had got a compliant servant at a very cheap price. The first real piece of bad luck had been Cangbi being so sickly. He had always been a weak child, but she had assumed he would grow out of it as he became a man. He didn't, and was reliant on her for most of his needs. It had been a surprise and a relief when her son had begged her to let him marry the girl. She was even more surprised when the girl agreed. She had always ignored her son, only doing for him what the old lady told her to do. It had been a great tragedy when he had died, despite the ministrations of the doctor.

Things then had gone from bad to worse in a way that suggested her great *yun* cycle was on the wane. Old Geng saving her life had seemed like a boon, until she saw what an obligation it had created. The only way out of his clutches that she could see was if he died. She paused in her reverie. Her feet were hurting, and she bent down to squeeze and pummel them. It was the only relief she could find for the aches. If only Jianxu had been here, she could have massaged them for her.

Where was the girl anyway? She had been released, had she not? Why had she not returned where she belonged? The old lady sat up, thinking she heard the floor boards creaking outside the room where she sat. But when she listened hard, she could not detect another sound. She bent down again to manipulate on her feet. One thing she was sure of. When the girl did turn up, she would kill her.

I saw the pattens on the threshold of the kitchen. They had been placed with such exact precision that it had to have been Jianxu's work. I looked cautiously round the door, but couldn't see her. The kitchen was cold and silent, the pots left dirty, and several utensils were scattered over the table. It would not have been so when Jianxu was working there. I saw a smear of cold, grey ash had drifted across the floor. In it were the imprints of a woman's feet clad in socks. I followed the grey marks on the floor towards Madam Gao's quarters.

She sneaked up the staircase, keeping to the edge to prevent any step creaking and giving her away. If she alerted the old woman to her presence, she feared for her safety. But she had the poker and the element of surprise. She saw that the door to Gao's bedroom had been slid open, but the room was still in darkness. Gao must have risen, but had not yet opened the shutters to let the daylight in. As she got closer, Jianxu could see strips of sunlight cutting across the room. The shutters were old and warped, and didn't fit tightly any more. A huddled figure in a blue silk gown sat on a low stool, her head bowed. Her grey hair hung over her face and she seemed oblivious to the intruder. It appeared Madam Gao was examining her bent, bound feet that often still gave her pain in the mornings. Jianxu knew she could hardly bear to put her weight on them until she had rubbed and pummelled them into some sort of feeling.

Jianxu couldn't believe how easy it was to get right up behind her without Gao knowing. The old lady was even muttering to herself, unaware of someone else being in her room. Jianxu had feared this woman all her life and had been afraid Gao might kill her. Now she gripped the poker firmly, and swung it up into the air. But before she brought it down in its murderous arc, Jianxu could not resist a cry of triumph.

'I killed them all one by one. Now only you stand in my way, you bitch.'

As she brought the heavy iron poker down towards Madam Gao's delicate skull, Jianxu was astonished to see the old lady rise into the air, and fly across the room, landing with her legs akimbo on feet that were no longer painful and tiny but a man's firm feet. A burst of applause came from the doorway behind her. She spun round the see the red-haired barbarian filling the opening. He was clapping his big, coarse hands like he was watching a play.

I applauded the actor's skill that had saved his life.

'Well done, Natural Elegance. Your role as Empress Tu prepared you well for the part as Madam Gao. The somersault was a little flashy, though, don't you think?'

The young and limber actor Tien-jan Hsiu, nephew of Lin Chu-Tsai, executed a bow, and pulled the grey wig off his head. He grinned youthfully at me through the heavy make-up.

'Forgive my little theatrical flourish. But you didn't tell me that I was to be brained with a poker when I agreed to substitute myself for the old lady.'

'Yes, well, I had planned to be here sooner, but Jianxu slipped away without my being aware.'

I turned to look at the still stunned young girl.

'What was that you were saying about killing them all? Can I take that as a confession?'

Jianxu's otherwise pretty face twisted into a snarling mask in a transformation that Tien-jan would have envied. She took a step towards me, and raised the poker above her head. I put my arm up to protect myself from the blow, but it never came. Tien-jan had stepped smartly up behind her, and grabbed the weapon at the top of its arc. Yanking it backwards, he pulled Jianxu off her feet and on to her behind, removing the poker from her grip in the process. He looked astonished at his own skill.

'Heavens! I thought that only worked as a move onstage.'

'I am glad you can perform your part so well, young man.'

I bent down to lift Jianxu back to her feet. But she shook off my grip and got up by herself. By the time she was standing, her face had once again shaped itself into an impassive mask. And her eyes were dead orbs in the middle of an oval void. She had retreated into herself once again.

\*     \*     \*

Tadeusz, who, under my instruction, had taken Madam Gao back to her own house for safety's sake, was nearly bowled over by the old lady. She either imagined he was a burglar – forgetting why she had been removed from the Geng household in the middle of the night by him – or that he was Jianxu come home. The old lady was ignorant of the girl's misdeeds and probably wanted to chastise her for not returning to the fold immediately she was released. If so, it was the first time Tadeusz had been taken for a twenty-year-old woman. He managed to save the tray of tea he had brought her and calm her down. He even agreed to massage her mutilated feet for her.

Jianxu remained impassive and acquiescent even when she was returned to the cell she had, until recently, occupied for so long. The same cell through the grille of which she had seduced Wenbo into putting a cord round his neck, and then had pulled it hard until she had strangled him. She sat impassively on her pallet while I extracted a confession from her as required by Chinee law. There was no need for the bastinado this time.

# TWENTY-EIGHT

*The confession of Jianxu*

I killed Old Geng by poisoning him with aconite. I knew Geng Wenbo was infatuated with me, and I convinced him that I had to get rid of Madam Gao because she had treated me cruelly. He thought he was buying the poison from Doctor Sun for that purpose. But while he was distracted, I took the broth with the aconite in it to Old Geng instead. The boy was distraught and wanted to confess, but I couldn't let him or he would implicate me too. I promised him the comforts of my body if he kept our secret. He was too distracted by the thought of what I promised to do anything other than what I told him to do. When the red-hair arrived, I thought I would be freed, as my yun cycle had changed. And I believed that I had convinced the barbarian of my innocence. When his interfering ways seemed to be getting close to the truth, I seduced Wenbo into doing what he originally intended; to confessing to the murder of Old Geng. He actually believed that, if I were freed, I would save him as he appeared to have saved me.

I confess to the murder of Geng Wenbo. It was too much of a risk to let him live. I came to the prison in the night, and convinced him that he must seem to have tried to kill himself. When he took his belt cord and put it round his neck, I reached through the bars and strangled him. I had the idea of stealing the prison keys and unlocking the doctor's cell that night. If I had done so, then Sun would have been seen as the murderer of Wenbo. But the gaoler must have heard Wenbo's death throes and woken up. I had to leave quickly. However, I came back the next night and unlocked the door of Sun's cell. His disappearance would then have been linked with the murder of Madam Gao that I planned to carry out the same night. But the fool was too scared to leave his cell, muttering about the Devil being abroad. So I had to take a stick and beat him *to death in his cell, and drag the body down the unlucky road to where I could bury it. You will find it close to the bare tree. He deserved to die, as he had also helped me kill my husband Cangbi with cinnabar under the pretext of curing him and conferring immortality upon him.*

# TWENTY-NINE

*Behind an able man there are always other able men.*

'She killed her husband too?'

Gurbesu was genuinely shocked when I read out Jianxu's confession to my companions. It had surprised me too, until I had begun to analyse her behaviour. She had always seemed so unemotional, so controlled, and we had put it down to her upbringing in Gao's household. And her acceptance of the role of a woman in Chinee society. It now appeared there had been some more sinister worm inhabiting her heart. I hesitate to use the word, but all I saw in her actions was pure, cold evil. I answered Gurbesu's question.

'It would appear so. Though whether Sun did it deliberately at her instigation, or was seduced into administering his "cure" to ensure immortality a little too eagerly we shall never know.'

Lin spoke up.

'By the way, the prefect's men found Sun's body, barely covered, exactly where she said it was. The fact that the doctor was missing from his cell will go badly for Li Wen-Tao. I imagine his career, as stalled as it was already, will go backwards now. And he deserves it to do so.'

Gurbesu looked at me, pain showing deeply in her dark, brown eyes. She was hurting at having so misjudged Jianxu.

'When I asked how long you had known who the murderer was, and you said not long but you knew it was her, I really thought you meant Madam Gao.'

Lin chipped in too.

'And so did I. But you must have been sure it was Jianxu by then, because you hid Madam Gao away in her old home and substituted my nephew for her. I can forgive you for letting me think I had solved the case by landing on Madam Gao, but I may not forgive you for placing Tien-jan in danger. He could have been killed by Jianxu.'

'Yes, I am sorry about that. I had it all planned so well. But Jianxu sneaked off before I knew. I took my chance to speak to you in her hearing, Gurbesu. Do you remember?'

'I wondered why you moved me away from her room, but then bellowed something out loud about seeking Madam Gao, who you made clear was still at Geng's. I should have guessed it was one of your scams.'

I grimaced at the thought of my crude efforts.

'I didn't do it very well, because I had not yet arranged for Tien-jan Hsiu to play the role of the old lady. I had spent the night convincing Madam Gao to leave the Geng house, and arranging for Tadeusz to stand guard over her.'

Tadeusz laughed.

'Yes, and I almost got brained by her when I brought her some tea. She leapt at me calling me a lazy child and hitting me round the head. She cannot see so well, and I suppose she thought I was Jianxu. Ironic really.'

I continued my story.

'So, that took so long that I had to leave it to the daytime to get Tien-jan to stand in for her. A part, I may say, he performed almost as well as the role of the priestess in my scam to trap the prefect.'

Lin gasped in astonishment.

'The priestess in the temple was my nephew? I gave her – him – some coins and didn't even guess.'

'As you yourself said, he is a good actor. I went straight from talking to you, Gurbesu, to get him to agree to the role as the old lady. Unfortunately, Jianxu chose that moment to slip away. My original plan was to lay in waiting for her and follow her more closely.'

It was Lin who asked the obvious and most pertinent question.

'How did you figure out it was Jianxu, when all the evidence pointed to Madam Gao.'

I looked at the friar, who had been quiet through our whole conversation.

'Alberoni put me on to her.'

The friar looked astonished.

'Me? How could I have helped you? I knew nothing about the case.'

'But you told me something about my own past that showed me the way to the truth in this case. About families falling out over money with tragic consequences. And your own quest for Prester John and the tale of the Golden King made everything slot into place. You spoke of men who spent two years of their lives planning an outcome that would enrich them.'

Alberoni was still puzzled.

'How did all that guide you to Jianxu?'

'No one else had such a compelling motive to murder as she had. Oh yes, Madam Gao had a reason to do away with Old Geng. She had money, and didn't need a penniless old man as a husband forced on her. She wanted rid of him, but it didn't make sense for her to have Wenbo as an accomplice. She knew the boy was stupid. Sun, I discounted as a possible killer quite early on. He did try to strangle the old lady once, but he didn't plan properly then, and couldn't have done so now. No, Jianxu had a clear motive, and was working to a long-term plan. She knew how wealthy Madam Gao was and arranged to marry her son. She probably seduced him into asking his mother, so it didn't seem as though she was the prime mover. Once she had married into the family, she got rid of Cangbi with the help of Doctor Sun. The next step would have been to wait for the old lady to die, or maybe to help her along if she appeared to be living too long. But then Old Geng came into the picture and spoiled all her plans.'

Gurbesu smacked her hands together.

'If the old lady married Geng then she would lose everything she had worked for. She could have married Wenbo, and waited again. But who's to say Geng wouldn't have squandered all Gao's money before she could get it?'

'Exactly. Jianxu dragged Wenbo into an imaginary plot to kill Gao, and he got the poison for her from Sun. When Geng – the real target of her plan – died, she pretended to Wenbo that it had gone badly wrong. She persuaded him he would have to keep quiet, and he did. When the family were being interrogated, she was afraid that Wenbo would break down, and confessed.'

'And made it seem as though she had done it to spare Madam Gao.'

Gurbesu was right. Jianxu had been calculating all the time under torture. Just as she had been all her life.

'Yes. She confessed, knowing full well that she could manipulate Wenbo later. Then, once *he* had confessed, he was no longer useful, so she killed him to ensure his silence. And the same applied to Sun.'

It was Tadeusz's turn to speak. There was some guilt in his voice.

'If we had not found the doctor, he might still be alive. It would not have been necessary for Jianxu to kill him.'

I laughed grimly.

'If we had not found him he would have been beaten to death by one of his patients' relatives. He was incompetent and a conspirator in murder, so don't blame yourself for his death.'

The facts I had laid out were sobering, and we all were silent for a while as we contemplated the turnings of fate. It was Gurbesu who finally spoke out.

'Do you think that her confession covers all Jianxu's deeds? I mean to say, in her confession, she tosses off her murder of Sun and her husband as though they were nothing to her.'

I knew what she was implying.

'You mean to say did she kill others? Maybe her mother too?'

Gurbesu nodded.

'We will never know, I imagine. That may be buried too deep in Jianxu's mind. And the executioner will soon put an end to her life and any hopes of discovering the truth.'

Tadeusz could not believe what Gurbesu and I had suggested.

'You cannot mean what you say! The girl was . . . what . . . seven when her mother died? What reason could she have for killing her? I mean, we can guess why she killed the others and tried to do away with Madam Gao. It was a pursuit of the money the old lady possessed, sure. Geng stood in her way, and the deaths of Wenbo and Sun were merely to keep her deeds secret. She said herself that she planned to have Sun accused of the murder of Madam Gao. If she had succeeded in that, she would then have her money free and clear.'

I agreed with Tadeusz.

'But she did all this with a coldness and precision that transcends mere greed. And the ease with which she killed people who stood in the way of her wishes may have begun earlier in her life. Maybe that is why her father so readily farmed her out to Madam Gao for money and never returned. Perhaps he feared her without knowing quite why. And whether he knew it or not, his action probably saved his life.'

A sad silence descended on the room. Outside an unseasonal flurry of snow began to fall.